Its all in t[illegible] of Wi[illegible] and that makes you fortunate—anyone else might go clear out of his skull.

For here you have everything from a cruel little comment on family training for the bomb shelter to smart but decadent snails who come down from Betelgeuse to con Earth.

Everything from reality to wildly improbable hilarity. (Not to mention the magnificent "Masculinist Revolt" which we can't bear not to not mention again.)

And as if to point the moral for his wide-ranging thesis, Mr. Tenn also gives you an average world, a world of no extremes, a world that specializes in mediocrity. It's horrifying but, logically, it averages out. Because at least dog lovers the world over will love this story.

But behind the verbal jibes, needles, barbs, harpoons, and humor there is a mind with something real to say.

It's really almost unfair that anything which is so much fun should also leave one thinking. On the other hand, it doesn't have to. As we said,

Its all in the mind. . . .

Books by William Tenn:

OF MEN AND MONSTERS

THE SQUARE ROOT OF MAN

THE WOODEN STAR

THE SEVEN SEXES

THE HUMAN ANGLE

OF ALL POSSIBLE WORLDS

THE WOODEN STAR

William Tenn

BALLANTINE BOOKS • NEW YORK

First Printing: June, 1968

Printed in the United States of America

BALLANTINE BOOKS, INC.
101 Fifth Avenue, New York, N.Y. 10003

To Morris and Bess Breecher
with much, much affection

CONTENTS

AUTHOR'S NOTE:

Most of these stories are social satires, thinly disguised as science fiction. They have generally encountered what satire deserves: trouble—occasionally they have effected what satire attempts: change.

"Generation of Noah" was rejected across the board by the general-fiction magazines in 1949 ("a shade too fantastic"). Eight years later it was rejected by a movie producer who was interested in filming some of my work ("far too prosaic for today's audiences").

"The Dark Star" was published just as the Space Age was about to enter formal history. It has had, I have been told, a peculiar effect upon Projects Mercury and Gemini, the announcements of which came years later, of course. Publicity for both projects emphasizes that all the astronauts are fathers. I wonder: would this be an example of a self-*un*fulfilling prophecy?

My own two favorite stories are "Null-P" and "The Masculinist Revolt." For a long time there seemed to be only three people in the world who thought "Null-P" a good story: myself, Damon Knight who purchased it for his fine, short-lived magazine *Worlds Beyond* in 1950, and August Derleth who used it in an anthology. Everybody else ignored it. Then, a decade after its first publication, "Null-P" was applauded by Kingsley Amis in his critical study, *New Maps of Hell*. Anthology requests began coming in from everywhere and references to it now appear in the most unexpected places. All right—maybe it isn't that good, but certainly it couldn't have been that bad either for ten long years. Joyce Cary, in *A Fearful Joy*, has himself a long bitter chuckle at the power fashion holds over intellectuals.

The same applies to "The Masculinist Revolt," except

that the happy ending is not yet in. I have lost one agent and several friends over this story. A woman I had up to then respected told me, "This castration-nightmare is for a psychiatrist, not an editor"; and a male friend of many years put the story down with tears in his eyes, saying, "You've written the manifesto. The statement of principles for all the guys in the world." My intention was neither castration-nightmare nor ringing manifesto: it was satiric, very gently but encompassingly satiric. I may have failed.

1961, the year in which the story was written, was well before the hippies created a blur between the sexes on matters of clothing and hair styles. The first few editors who saw the piece felt that 1990 was a bit too early for such major changes as I described. My own feeling now is that I was subliminally aware of rapidly shifting attitudes toward sexual differentiation in our society, but that what I noticed as an anticipatory tremor was actually the first rock-slide of the total cataclysm.

—State College, Pennsylvania
March, 1968

GENERATION OF NOAH

THAT WAS the day Plunkett heard his wife screaming guardedly to their youngest boy.

He let the door of the laying house slam behind him, forgetful of the nervously feeding hens. She had, he realized, cupped her hands over her mouth so that only the boy would hear.

"Saul! You, *Saul!* Come back, come right back this instant. Do you want your father to catch you out there on the road? Saul!"

The last shriek was higher and clearer, as if she had despaired of attracting the boy's attention without at the same time warning the man.

Poor Ann!

Gently, rapidly, Plunkett *shh'd* his way through the bustling and hungry hens to the side door. He came out facing the brooder run and broke into a heavy, unathletic trot.

He heard the other children clatter out of the feed house. Good! They have the responsibility after Ann and me, Plunkett told himself. Let them watch and learn again.

"Saul!" his wife's voice shrilled uphappily. "Saul, your father's coming!"

Ann came out of the front door and paused. "Elliot," she called at his back as he leaped over the flush well-cover. "Please, I don't feel well."

A difficult pregnancy, of course, and in her sixth

month. But that had nothing to do with Saul. Saul knew better.

At the last frozen furrow of the truck garden Plunkett gave himself a moment to gather the necessary air for his lungs. Years ago, when Von Rundstedt's Tigers roared through the Bulge, he would have been able to dig a foxhole after such a run. Now, he was badly winded. Just showed you: such a short distance from the far end of the middle chicken house to the far end of the vegetable garden—merely crossing four acres—and he was winded. And consider the practice he'd had.

He could just about see the boy idly lifting a stick to throw for the dog's pleasure. Saul was in the further ditch, well past the white line his father had painted across the road.

"Elliot," his wife began again. "He's only six years old. He—"

Plunkett drew his jaws apart and let breath out in a bellyful of sound. "Saul! Saul Plunkett!" he bellowed. "Start running!"

He knew his voice had carried. He clicked the button on his stopwatch and threw his right arm up, pumping his clenched fist.

The boy *had* heard the yell. He turned, and, at the sight of the moving arm that meant the stopwatch had started, he dropped the stick. But, for the fearful moment, he was too startled to move.

Eight seconds. He lifted his lids slightly. Saul had begun to run. But he hadn't picked up speed, and Rusty skipping playfully between his legs threw him off his stride.

Ann had crossed the garden laboriously and stood at his side, alternately staring over his jutting elbow at the watch and smiling hesitantly sidewise at his face. She shouldn't have come out in her thin house-dress in

November. But it was good for Ann. Plunkett kept his eyes stolidly on the unemotional second hand.

One minute forty.

He could hear the dog's joyful barks coming closer, but as yet there was no echo of sneakers slapping the highway. Two minutes. He wouldn't make it.

The old bitter thoughts came crowding back to Plunkett. A father timing his six-year-old son's speed with the best watch he could afford. This, then, was the scientific way to raise children in Earth's most enlightened era. Well, it was scientific . . . in keeping with the latest discoveries. . . .

Two and a half minutes. Rusty's barks didn't sound so very far off. Plunkett could hear the desperate pad-pad-pad of the boy's feet. He might make it at that. If only he could!

"Hurry, Saul," his mother breathed. "You can make it."

Plunkett looked up in time to see his son pound past, his jeans already darkened with perspiration. "Why doesn't he breathe like I told him?" he muttered. "He'll be out of breath in no time."

Halfway to the house, a furrow caught at Saul's toes. As he sprawled, Ann gasped. "You can't count that, Elliot. He tripped."

"Of course he tripped. He should count on tripping."

"Get up, Saulie," Herbie, his older brother, screamed from the garage where he stood with Louise Dawkins, one pail of eggs between them. "Get up and run! This corner here! You can make it!"

The boy heaved to his feet, and threw his body forward again. Plunkett could hear him sobbing. He reached the cellar steps—and literally plunged down.

Plunkett pressed the stopwatch and the second hand halted. Three minutes thirteen seconds.

He held the watch up for his wife to see. "Thirteen seconds, Ann."

Her face wrinkled.

He walked to the house. Saul crawled back up the steps, fragments of unrecovered breath rattling in his chest. He kept his eyes on his father.

"Come here, Saul. Come right here. Look at the watch. Now, what do you see?"

The boy stared intently at the watch. His lips began twisting; startled tears writhed down his stained face. "More—more than three m-minutes, poppa?"

"More than three minutes, Saul. Now, Saul—don't cry, son; it isn't any use—Saul, what would have happened when you got to the steps?"

A small voice, pitifully trying to cover its cracks: "The big doors would be shut."

"The big doors would be shut. You would be locked outside. Then what would have happened to you? Stop crying. Answer me!"

"Then, when the bombs fell, I'd—I'd have no place to hide. I'd burn like the head of a match. An'—an' the only thing left of me would be a dark spot on the ground, shaped like my shadow. An'—an'—"

"And the radioactive dust," his father helped with the catechism.

"Elliot—" Ann sobbed behind him. "I don't—"

"Please, Ann! And the radioactive dust, son?"

"An' if it was ra-di-o-ac-tive dust 'stead of atom bombs, my skin would come right off my body, an' my lungs would burn up inside me—please, poppa, I won't do it again!"

"And your eyes? What would happen to your eyes?"

A chubby brown fist dug into one of the eyes. "An' my eyes would fall out, an' my teeth would fall out, and I'd feel such terrible terrible pain—"

"All over and inside you. That's what would happen if

you got to the cellar too late when the alarm went off, if you got locked out. At the end of three minutes, we pull the levers, and no matter who's outside—*no matter who*—all four corner doors swing shut and the cellar will be sealed. You understand that, Saul?"

The two Dawkins children were listening with white faces and dry lips. Their parents had brought them from the city and begged Elliot Plunkett, as he remembered old friends, to give their children the same protection as his. Well, they were getting it. This was the way to get it.

"Yes, I understand it, poppa. I won't ever do it again. Never again."

"I hope you won't. Now start for the barn, Saul. Go ahead." Plunkett slid his heavy leather belt from its loops.

"Elliot! Don't you think he understands the horrible thing? A beating won't make it any clearer."

He paused behind the weeping boy trudging to the barn. "It won't make it any clearer, but it will teach him the lesson another way. All seven of us are going to be in that cellar three minutes after the alarm, if I have to wear this strap clear down to the buckle!"

When Plunkett later clumped into the kitchen with his heavy farm boots, he stopped and sighed.

Ann was feeding Dinah. With her eyes on the baby, she asked, "No supper for him, Elliot?"

"No supper." He sighed again. "It does take it out of a man."

"Especially you. Not many men would become a farmer at thirty-five. Not many men would sink every last penny into an underground fort and powerhouse, just for insurance. But you're right."

"I only wish," he said restlessly, "that I could work out some way of getting Nancy's heifer into the cellar. And if eggs stay high one more month I can build the tunnel to the generator. Then, there's the well. Only one well, even if it's enclosed—"

"And when we came out here seven years ago—" She rose to him at last and rubbed her lips gently against his thick blue shirt. "We only had a piece of ground. Now, we have three chicken houses, a thousand broilers, and I can't keep track of how many layers and breeders."

She stopped as his body tightened and he gripped her shoulders.

"Ann, *Ann!* If you think like that, you'll act like that! How can I expect the children to—Ann, what we have—all we have—is a five-room cellar, concrete-lined, which we can seal in a few seconds, an enclosed well from a fairly deep underground stream, a windmill generator for power and a sunken oil-burner-driven generator for emergencies. We have supplies to carry us through, Geiger counters to detect radiation and lead-lined suits to move about in—afterwards. I've told you again and again that these things are our lifeboat, and the farm is just a sinking ship."

"Of course, darling." Plunkett's teeth ground together, then parted helplessly as his wife went back to feeding the baby.

"You're perfectly right. Swallow, now, Dinah. Why, that last bulletin from the Survivors Club would make *anybody* think."

He had been quoting from the October *Survivor* and Ann had recognized it. Well? At least they were *doing* something—seeking out nooks and feverishly building crannies—pooling their various ingenuities in an attempt to haul themselves and their families through the military years of the Atomic Age.

The familiar green cover of the mimeographed magazine was very noticeable on the kitchen table. He flipped the sheets to the thumb-smudged article on page five and shook his head.

"Imagine!" he said loudly. "The poor fools agreeing with the government again on the safety factor. Six minutes! How can they—an organization like the Survivors Club making that their official opinion! Why freeze, *freeze* alone . . ."

"They're ridiculous," Ann murmured, scraping the bottom of the bowl.

"All right, we have automatic detectors. But human beings still have to look at the radar scope, or we'd be diving underground every time there's a meteor shower."

He strode along a huge table, beating a fist rhythmically into one hand. "They won't be so sure, at first. Who wants to risk his rank by giving the nationwide signal that makes everyone in the country pull ground over his head, that makes our own projectile sites set to buzz? Finally, they are certain: they freeze for a moment. Meanwhile, the rockets are zooming down—how fast, we don't know. The men unfreeze, they trip each other up, they tangle frantically. *Then* they press the button, *then* the nationwide signal starts our radio alarms."

Plunkett turned to his wife, spread earnest, quivering arms. "And then, Ann, *we* freeze when we hear it! At last, we start for the cellar. Who knows, who can dare to say, how much has been cut off the margin of safety by that time? No, if they claim that six minutes is the safety factor, we'll give half of it to the alarm system. Three minutes for us."

"One more spoonful," Ann urged Dinah. "Just one more. *Down* it goes!"

Josephine Dawkins and Herbie were cleaning the feed trolley in the shed at the near end of the chicken house.

"All done, pop," the boy grinned at his father. "And the eggs taken care of. When does Mr. Whiting pick 'em up?"

"Nine o'clock. Did you finish feeding the hens in the last house?"

"I said all done, didn't I?" Herbie asked with adolescent impatience. "When I say a thing, I mean it."

"Good. You kids better get at your books. Hey, stop that! Education will be very important, afterwards. You never know what will be useful. And maybe only your mother and I to teach you."

"Gee," Herbie nodded at Josephine. "Think of that."

She pulled at her jumper where it was very tight over newly swelling breasts and patted her blonde braided hair. "What about *my* mother and father, Mr. Plunkett? Won't they be—be—"

"Naw!" Herbie laughed the loud, country laugh he'd been practicing lately. "They're dead-enders. They won't pull through. They live in the city, don't they? They'll just be some—"

"Herbie!"

"—some foam on a mushroom-shaped cloud," he finished, utterly entranced by the image. "Gosh, I'm sorry," he said, as he looked from his angry father to the quivering girl. He went on in a studiously reasonable voice. "But it's the truth, anyway. That's why they sent you and Lester here. I guess I'll marry you—afterwards. And you ought to get in the habit of calling *him* pop. Because that's the way it'll be."

Josephine squeezed her eyes shut, kicked the shed door open, and ran out. "I hate you, Herbie Plunkett," she wept. "You're a beast!"

Herbie grimaced at his father—*women, women, women!*—and ran after her. "Hey, Jo! Listen!"

The trouble was, Plunkett thought worriedly as he carried the emergency bulbs for the hydroponic garden into the cellar—the trouble was that Herbie had learned through constant reiteration the one thing: survival came before all else, and amenities were merely amenities.

Strength and self-sufficiency—Plunkett had worked out the virtues his children needed years ago, sitting in air-conditioned offices and totting corporation balances with one eye always on the calendar.

"Still," Plunkett muttered, "still—Herbie shouldn't—" He shook his head.

He inspected the incubators near the long steaming tables of the hydroponic garden. A tray about ready to hatch. They'd have to start assembling eggs to replace it in the morning. He paused in the third room, filled a gap in the bookshelves.

"Hope Josephine steadies the boy in his schoolwork. If he fails that next exam, they'll make me send him to town regularly. Now *there's* an aspect of survival I can hit Herbie with."

He realized he'd been talking to himself, a habit he'd been combating futilely for more than a month. Stuffy talk, too. He was becoming like those people who left tracts on trolley cars.

"Have to start watching myself," he commented. "Dammit, again!"

The telephone clattered upstairs. He heard Ann walk across to it, that serene, unhurried walk all pregnant women seem to have.

"Elliot! Nat Medarie."

"Tell him I'm coming, Ann." He swung the vault-like door carefully shut behind him, looked at it for a moment, and started up the high stone steps.

"Hello, Nat. What's new?"

"Hi, Plunk. Just got a postcard from Fitzgerald. Remember him? The abandoned silver mine in Montana? Yeah. He says we've got to go on the basis that lithium bombs will be used."

Plunkett leaned against the wall with his elbow. He cradled the receiver on his right shoulder so he could light a cigarette. "Fitzgerald can be wrong sometimes."

"Uhm. I don't know. But you know what a lithium bomb means, don't you?"

"It means," Plunkett said, staring through the wall of the house and into a boiling Earth, "that a chain reaction may be set off in the atmosphere if enough of them are used. Maybe if only one—"

"Oh, can it," Medarie interrupted. "That gets us nowhere. That way nobody gets through, and we might as well start shuttling from church to bar-room like my brother-in-law in Chicago is doing right now. Fred, I used to say to him— No, listen Plunk: it means I was right. You didn't dig deep enough."

"*Deep* enough! I'm as far down as I want to go. If I don't have enough layers of lead and concrete to shield me—well, if they can crack *my* shell, then you won't be able to walk on the surface before you die of thirst, Nat. No—I sunk my dough in power supply. Once that fails, you'll find yourself putting the used air back into your empty oxygen tanks by hand!"

The other man chuckled. "All right. I *hope* I see you around."

"And I hope *I* see . . ." Plunkett twisted around to face the front window as an old station wagon bumped over the ruts in his driveway. "Say, Nat, what do you know? Charlie Whiting just drove up. Isn't this Sunday?"

"Yeah. He hit my place early, too. Some sort of political meeting in town and he wants to make it. It's not enough that the diplomats and generals are practically glaring into each other's eyebrows this time. A couple of local philosophers are impatient with the slow pace at which their extinction is approaching, and they're getting together to see if they can't hurry it up some."

"Don't be bitter," Plunkett smiled.

"Here's praying at you. Regards to Ann, Plunk."

Plunkett cradled the receiver and ambled downstairs. Outside, he watched Charlie Whiting pull the door of the station wagon open on its one desperate hinge.

"Eggs stowed, Mr. Plunkett," Charlie said. "Receipt signed. Here. You'll get a check Wednesday."

"Thanks, Charlie. Hey, you kids get back to your books. Go on, Herbie. You're having an English quiz tonight. Eggs still going up, Charlie?"

"Up she goes." The old man slid onto the crackled leather seat and pulled the door shut deftly. He bent his arm on the open window. "Heh. And every time she does I make a little more off you survivor fellas who are too scairt to carry 'em into town yourself."

"Well, you're entitled to it," Plunkett said, uncomfortably. "What about this meeting in town?"

"Bunch of folks goin' to discuss the conference. I say we pull out. I say we walk right out of the dern thing. This country never won a conference yet. A million conferences the last few years and everyone knows what's gonna happen sooner or later. Heh. They're just wastin' time. Hit 'em first, I say."

"Maybe we will. Maybe *they* will. Or—maybe, Charlie, a couple of different nations will get what looks like a good idea at the same time."

Charlie Whiting shoved his foot down and ground the starter. "You don't make sense. If we hit 'em first how can they do the same to us? Hit 'em first—hard enough—and they'll never recover in time to hit us back. That's what *I* say. But you survivor fellas—" He shook his white head angrily as the car shot away.

"Hey!" he yelled, turning into the road. "Hey, look!"

Plunkett looked over his shoulder. Charlie Whiting was gesturing at him with his left hand, the forefinger pointing out and the thumb up straight.

"Look, Mr. Plunkett," the old man called. "Boom! Boom! Boom!" He cackled hysterically and writhed over the steering wheel.

Rusty scuttled around the side of the house, and after him, yipping frantically in ancient canine tradition.

Plunkett watched the receding car until it swept around the curve two miles away. He stared at the small dog returning proudly.

Poor Whiting. Poor everybody, for that matter, who had a normal distrust of crackpots.

How could you permit a greedy old codger like Whiting to buy your produce, just so you and your family wouldn't have to risk trips into town?

Well, it was a matter of having decided years ago that the world was too full of people who were convinced that they were faster on the draw than anyone else—and the other fellow was bluffing anyway. People who believed that two small boys could pile up snowballs across the street from each other and go home without having used them, people who discussed the merits of concrete fences as opposed to wire guardrails while their automobiles skidded over the cliff. People who were righteous. People who were apathetic.

It was the last group, Plunkett remembered, who had made him stop buttonholing his fellows at last. You got tired of standing around in a hair shirt and pointing ominously at the heavens. You got to the point where you wished the human race well, but you wanted to pull you and yours out of the way of its tantrums. Survival for the individual and his family, you thought—

Clang-ng-ng-ng-ng!

Plunkett pressed the stud on his stopwatch. Funny. There was no practice alarm scheduled for today. All the kids were out of the house, except Saul—and he wouldn't dare to leave his room, let alone tamper with the alarm. Unless, perhaps, Ann—

He walked inside the kitchen. Ann was running toward the door, carrying Dinah. Her face was oddly unfamiliar. "Saulie!" she screamed. "Saulie! Hurry *up,* Saulie!"

"I'm coming, momma," the boy yelled as he clattered

down the stairs. "I'm coming as fast as I can! I'll make it!"

Plunkett understood. He put a heavy hand on the wall, under the dinner-plate clock.

He watched his wife struggle down the steps into the cellar. Saul ran past him and out of the door, arms flailing. "I'll make it, poppa! I'll make it!"

Plunkett felt his stomach move. He swallowed with great care. "Don't hurry, son," he whispered. "It's only judgment day."

He straightened out and looked at his watch, noticing that his hand on the wall had left its moist outline behind. One minute, twelve seconds. Not bad. Not bad at all. He'd figured on three.

Clang-ng-ng-ng-ng!

He started to shake himself and began a shudder that he couldn't control. What was the matter? He knew what he had to do. He had to unpack the portable lathe that was still in the barn.

"Elliot!" his wife called.

He found himself sliding down the steps on feet that somehow wouldn't lift when he wanted them to. He stumbled through the open cellar door. Frightened faces dotted the room in an unrecognizable jumble.

"We all here?" he croaked.

"All here, poppa," Saul said from his position near the aeration machinery. "Lester and Herbie are in the far room, by the other switch. Why is Josephine crying? Lester isn't crying. I'm not crying, either."

Plunkett nodded vaguely at the slim, sobbing girl and put his hand on the lever protruding from the concrete wall. He glanced at his watch again. Two minutes, ten seconds. Not bad.

"Mr. Plunkett!" Lester Dawkins sped in from the corridor. "Mr. Plunkett! Herbie ran out of the other door to get Rusty. I told him—"

Two minutes, twenty seconds, Plunkett realized as he leaped to the top of the steps. Herbie was running across the vegetable garden, snapping his fingers behind him to lure Rusty on. When he saw his father, his mouth stiffened with shock. He broke stride for a moment, and the dog charged joyously between his legs. Herbie fell.

Plunkett stepped forward. *Two minutes, forty seconds.* Herbie jerked himself to his feet, put his head down—and ran.

Was that dim thump a distant explosion? There—another one! Like a giant belching. Who had started it? And did it matter—now?

Three minutes. Rusty scampered down the cellar steps, his head back, his tail flickering from side to side. Herbie panted up. Plunkett grabbed him by the collar and jumped.

And as he jumped he saw—far to the south—the umbrellas opening their agony upon the land. Rows upon swirling rows of them. . . .

He tossed the boy ahead when he landed. *Three minutes, five seconds.* He threw the switch, and, without waiting for the door to close and seal, darted into the corridor. That took care of two doors; the other switch controlled the remaining entrances. He reached it. He pulled it. He looked at his watch. *Three minutes, twenty seconds.* "The bombs," blubbered Josephine. "The bombs!"

Ann was scrabbling Herbie to her in the main room, feeling his arms, caressing his hair, pulling him in for a wild hug and crying out yet again. "Herbie! Herbie! Herbie!"

"I know you're gonna lick me, pop. I—I just want you to know that I think you ought to."

"I'm not going to lick you, son."

"You're not? But gee, I deserve a licking. I deserve the worst—"

"You may," Plunkett said, gasping at the wall of clicking geigers. *"You may deserve a beating,"* he yelled, so loudly that they all whirled to face him, "but I won't punish you, not only for now, but forever! And as I with you," he screamed, "so you with yours! Understand?"

"Yes," they replied in a weeping, ragged chorus. "We understand!"

"Swear! Swear that you and your children and your children's children will never punish another human being—*no matter what the provocation."*

"We swear!" they bawled at him. "We swear!"

Then they all sat down.

To wait.

BROOKLYN PROJECT

THE GLEAMING bowls of light set in the creamy ceiling dulled when the huge, circular door at the back of the booth opened. They returned to white brilliance as the chubby man in the severe black jumper swung the door shut behind him and dogged it down again.

Twelve reporters of both sexes exhaled very loudly as he sauntered to the front of the booth and turned his back to the semi-opaque screen stretching across it. Then they all rose in deference to the cheerful custom of standing whenever a security official of the government was in the room.

He smiled pleasantly, waved at them and scratched his nose with a wad of mimeographed papers. His nose was large and it seemed to give added presence to his person. "Sit down, ladies and gentlemen, do sit down. We have no official fol-de-rol in the Brooklyn Project. I am your guide, as you might say, for the duration of this experiment—the acting secretary to the executive assistant on press relations. My name is not important. Please pass these among you."

They each took one of the mimeographed sheets and passed the rest on. Leaning back in the metal bucket-seats, they tried to make themselves comfortable. Their host squinted through the heavy screen and up at the wall clock, which had one slowly revolving hand. He patted his black garment jovially where it was tight around the middle.

"To business. In a few moments, man's first large-scale excursion into time will begin. Not by humans, but with the aid of a photographic and recording device which will bring us incalculably rich data on the past. With this experiment, the Brooklyn Project justifies ten billion dollars and over eight years of scientific development; it shows the validity not merely of a new method of investigation, but of a weapon which will make our glorious country even more secure, a weapon which our enemies may justifiably dread.

"Let me caution you, first, not to attempt the taking of notes even if you have been able to smuggle pens and pencils through Security. Your stories will be written entirely from memory. You all have a copy of the Security Code with the latest additions as well as a pamphlet referring specifically to Brooklyn Project regulations. The sheets you have just received provide you with the required lead for your story; they also contain suggestions as to treatment and coloring. Beyond that—so long as you stay within the framework of the documents mentioned—you are entirely free to write your stories in your own variously original ways. The press, ladies and gentlemen, must remain untouched and uncontaminated by government control. Now, any questions?"

The twelve reporters looked at the floor. Five of them began reading from their sheets. The paper rustled noisily.

"What, no questions? Surely there must be more interest than this in a project which has broken the last possible frontier—the fourth dimension, time. Come now, you are the representatives of the nation's curiosity—you must have questions. Bradley, you look doubtful. What's bothering you? I assure you, Bradley, that I don't bite."

They all laughed and grinned at each other.

Bradley half-rose and pointed at the screen. "Why does it have to be so thick? I'm not the slightest bit interested in finding out how chronar works, but all we can see from here is a grayed and blurry picture of men dragging apparatus around on the floor. And why does the clock only have one hand?"

"A good question," the acting secretary said. His large nose seemed to glow. "A very good question. First, the clock has but one hand, because, after all, Bradley, this is an experiment in time, and Security feels that the time of the experiment itself may, through some unfortunate combination of information leakage and foreign correlation—in short, a clue might be needlessly exposed. It is sufficient to know that when the hand points to the red dot, the experiment will begin. The screen is translucent and the scene below somewhat blurry for the same reason—camouflage of detail and adjustment. I *am* empowered to inform you that the details of the apparatus are—uh, very significant. Any other questions? Culpepper? Culpepper of Consolidated, isn't it?"

"Yes, sir. Consolidated News Service. Our readers are very curious about that incident of the Federation of Chronar Scientists. Of course, they have no respect or pity for them—the way they acted and all—but just what did they mean by saying that this experiment was dangerous because of insufficient data? And that fellow, Dr. Shayson, their president, do you know if he'll be shot?"

The man in black pulled at his nose and paraded before them thoughtfully. "I must confess that I find the views of the Federation of Chronar Scientists—or the federation of chronic *sighers,* as we at Pike's Peak prefer to call them—are a trifle too exotic for my tastes; I rarely bother with weighing the opinions of a traitor in any case. Shayson himself may or may not have incurred the death penalty for revealing the nature of the work with which he was entrusted. On the other hand, he—uh, *may not* or *may* have. That is all I can say about him for reasons of security."

Reasons of security. At the mention of the dread phrase, every reporter straightened against the hard back of his chair. Culpepper's face lost its pinkness in favor of a glossy white. They can't consider the part about Shayson a leading question, he thought desperately. But I shouldn't have cracked about that damned federation!

Culpepper lowered his eyes and tried to look as ashamed of the vicious idiots as he possibly could. He hoped the acting secretary to the executive assistant on press relations would notice his horror.

The clock began ticking very loudly. Its hand was now only one-fourth of an arc from the red dot at the top. Down on the floor of the immense laboratory, activity had stopped. All of the seemingly tiny men were clustered around two great spheres of shining metal resting against each other. Most of them were watching dials and switchboards intently; a few, their tasks completed, chatted with the circle of black-jumpered Security guards.

"We are almost ready to begin Operation Periscope. Operation Periscope, of course, because we are, in a sense, extending a periscope into the past—a periscope which will take pictures and record events of various periods ranging from fifteen thousand years to four billion years ago. We felt that in view of the various critical circumstances attending this experiment—international, scientific—a more fitting title would be Operation Crossroads. Unfortunately, that title has been—uh, preempted."

Everyone tried to look as innocent of the nature of that other experiment as years of staring at locked library shelves would permit.

"No matter. I will now give you a brief background in chronar practice as cleared by Brooklyn Project Security. Yes, Bradley?"

Bradley again got partly out of his seat. "I was wondering—we know there has been a Manhattan Project, a Long Island Project, a Westchester Project and now a Brooklyn Project. Has there ever been a Bronx Project? I come from the Bronx; you know, civic pride."

"Quite. Very understandable. However, if there is a Bronx Project you may be assured that until its work has been successfully completed, the only individuals outside of it who will know of its existence are the President and the Secretary of Security. If—*if,* I say—there is such an institution, the world will learn of it with the same shattering suddenness that it learned of the Westchester Project. I don't think that the world will soon forget *that.*"

He chuckled in recollection and Culpepper echoed him a bit louder than the rest. The clock's hand was close to the red mark.

"Yes, the Westchester Project and now this; our nation shall yet be secure! Do you realize what a magnificent weapon chronar places in our democratic hands? To examine only one aspect—consider what happened to the Coney Island and Flatbush Subprojects (the events are mentioned in those sheets you've received) before the uses of chronar were fully appreciated.

"It was not yet known in those first experiments that Newton's third law of motion—action equalling reaction—held for time as well as it did for the other three dimensions of space. When the first chronar was excited backward into time for the length of a ninth of a second, the entire laboratory was propelled into the future for a like period and returned in an—uh, unrecognizable condition. That fact, by the way, has prevented excursions into the future. The equipment seems to suffer amazing alterations and no human could survive them. But do you realize what we could do to an enemy by virtue of that property alone? Sending an adequate mass of chronar into the past while it is adjacent to a hostile nation would force that nation into the future—all of it simultaneously—a future from which it would return populated only with corpses!"

He glanced down, placed his hands behind his back and teetered on his heels. "That is why you see two spheres on the floor. Only one of them, the ball on the right, is equipped with chronar. The other is a dummy, matching the other's mass perfectly and serving as a counterbalance. When the chronar is excited, it will plunge four billion years into our past and take photographs of an earth that was still a half-liquid, partly gaseous mass solidifying rapidly in a somewhat inchoate solar system.

"At the same time, the dummy will be propelled four billion years into the future, from whence it will return much changed but for reasons we don't completely understand. They will strike each other at what is to us *now* and bounce off again to approximately half the chronological distance of the first trip, where our chronar apparatus will record data of an almost solid planet, plagued by earthquakes and possibly holding forms of sublife in the manner of certain complex molecules.

"After each collision, the chronar will return roughly half the number of years covered before, automatically gathering information each time. The geological and historical periods we expect it to touch are listed from I to XXV in your sheets; there will be more than twenty-five, naturally, before both balls come to rest, but scientists feel that all periods after that number will be touched for such a short while as to be unproductive of photographs and other material. Remember, at the end, the balls will be doing little more than throbbing in place before coming to rest, so that even though they still ricochet centuries on either side of the present, it will be almost unnoticeable. A question, I see."

The thin woman in gray tweeds beside Culpepper got to her feet. "I—I know this is irrelevant," she began, "but I haven't been able to introduce my question into the discussion at any pertinent moment. Mr. Secretary—"

"Acting secretary," the chubby little man in the black suit told her genially. "I'm only the acting secretary. Go on."

"Well, I want to say—Mr. Secretary, is there any way at all that our post-experimental examination time may be reduced? Two years is a very long time to spend inside Pike's Peak simply out of fear that one of us may have seen enough and be unpatriotic enough to be dangerous to the nation. Once our stories have passed the censors, it seems to me that we could be allowed to return to our homes after a safety period of, say, three months. I have two small children and there are others here—"

"Speak for yourself, Mrs. Bryant!" the man from Security roared. "It *is* Mrs. Bryant, isn't it? Mrs. Bryant of the Women's Magazine Syndicate? Mrs. *Alexis* Bryant." He seemed to be making minute pencil notes across his brain.

Mrs. Bryant sat down beside Culpepper again, clutching her copy of the amended Security Code, the special pamphlet on the Brooklyn Project and the thin mimeographed sheet of paper very close to her breast. Culpepper moved hard against the opposite arm of his chair. Why did everything have to happen to him? Then, to make matters worse, the crazy woman looked tearfully at him as if expecting sympathy. Culpepper stared across the booth and crossed his legs.

"You must remain within the jurisdiction of the Brooklyn Project because that is the only way that Security can be *certain* that no important information leakage will occur before the apparatus has changed beyond your present recognition of it. You didn't have to come, Mrs. Bryant—you volunteered. You all volunteered. After your editors had designated you as their choices for covering this experiment, you all had the peculiarly democratic privilege of refusing. None of you did. You recognized that to refuse this unusual honor would have shown you incapable of thinking in terms of National Security, would have, in fact, implied a criticism of the Security Code itself from the standpoint of the usual two-year examination time. And now this! For someone who had hitherto been thought as able and trustworthy as yourself, Mrs. Bryant, to emerge at this late hour with such a request makes me, why it," the little man's voice dropped to a whisper, "—it almost makes me doubt the effectiveness of our Security screening methods."

Culpepper nodded angry affirmation at Mrs. Bryant who was biting her lips and trying to show a tremendous interest in the activities on the laboratory floor.

"The question *was* irrelevant. Highly irrelevant. It took up time which I had intended to devote to a more detailed discussion of the popular aspects of chronar and its possible uses in industry. But Mrs. Bryant must have her little feminine outburst. It makes no difference to Mrs. Bryant that our nation is daily surrounded by more and more hostility, more and more danger. These things matter not in the slightest to Mrs. Bryant. All she is concerned with are the two years of her life that her country asks her to surrender so that the future of her own children may be more secure."

The acting secretary smoothed his black jumper and became calmer. Tension in the booth decreased.

"Activation will occur at any moment now, so I will briefly touch upon those most interesting periods which the chronar will record for us and from which we expect the most useful data. I and II, of course, since they are the periods at which the earth was forming into its present shape. Then III, the Pre-Cambrian Period of the Proterozoic, one billion years ago, the first era in which we find distinct records of life—crustaceans and algae for the most part. VI, a hundred twenty-five million years in the past, covers the Middle Jurassic of the Mesozoic. This excursion into the so-called 'Age of Reptiles' may provide us with photographs of dinosaurs and solve the old riddle of their coloring, as well as photographs, if we are fortunate, of the first appearance of mammals and birds. Finally, VIII and IX, the Oligocene and Miocene Epochs of the Tertiary Period, mark the emergence of man's earliest ancestors. Unfortunately, the chronar will be oscillating back and forth so rapidly by that time that the chance of any decent recording—"

A gong sounded. The hand of the clock touched the red mark. Five of the technicians below pulled switches and, almost before the journalists could lean forward, the two spheres were no longer visible through the heavy plastic screen. Their places were empty.

"The chronar has begun its journey to four billion years in the past! Ladies and gentlemen, an historic moment—a profoundly historic moment! It will not return for a little while; I shall use the time in pointing up and exposing the fallacies of the—ah, *federation of chronic sighers!*"

Nervous laughter rippled at the acting secretary to the executive assistant on press relations. The twelve journalists settled down to hearing the ridiculous ideas torn apart.

"As you know, one of the fears entertained about travel to the past was that the most innocent-seeming acts would cause cataclysmic changes in the present. You are probably familiar with the fantasy in its most currently popular form—if Hitler had been killed in 1930, he would not have forced scientists in Germany and later occupied countries to emigrate, this nation might not have had the atomic bomb, thus no third atomic war, and Venezuela would still be part of the South American continent.

"The traitorous Shayson and his illegal federation extended this hypothesis to include much more detailed and minor acts such as shifting a molecule of hydrogen that in our past really was never shifted.

"At the time of the first experiment at the Coney Island Subproject, when the chronar was sent back for one-ninth of a second, a dozen different laboratories checked through every device imaginable, searched carefully for any conceivable change. There were none! Government officials concluded that the time stream was a rigid affair, past, present, and future, and nothing in it could be altered. But Shayson and his cohorts were not satisfied: they—"

I. Four billion years ago. The chronar floated in a cloudlet of silicon dioxide above the boiling earth and languidly collected its data with automatically operating instruments. The vapor it had displaced condensed and fell in great, shining drops.

"—insisted that we should do no further experimenting until we had checked the mathematical aspects of the problem yet again. They went so far as to state that it was possible that if changes occurred we would not notice them, that no instruments imaginable could detect them. They claimed we would accept these changes as things that had always existed. Well! This at a time when our country—and theirs, ladies and gentlemen of the press, *theirs,* too—was in greater danger than ever. Can you—"

Words failed him. He walked up and down the booth, shaking his head. All the reporters on the long, wooden bench shook their heads with him in sympathy.

There was another gong. The two dull spheres appeared briefly, clanged against each other and ricocheted off into opposite chronological directions.

"There you are." The government official waved his arms at the transparent laboratory floor above them. "The first oscillation has been completed; has anything changed? Isn't everything the same? But the dissidents would maintain that alterations have occurred and we haven't noticed them. With such faith-based, unscientific viewpoints, there can be no argument. People like these—"

II. Two billion years ago. The great ball clicked its photographs of the fiery, erupting ground below. Some red-hot crusts rattled off its sides. Five or six thousand complex molecules lost their basic structure as they impinged against it. A hundred didn't.

"—will labor thirty hours a day out of thirty-three to convince you that black isn't white, that we have seven moons instead of two. They are especially dangerous—"

A long, muted note as the apparatus collided with itself. The warm orange of the corner lights brightened as it started out again.

"—because of their learning, because they are sought for guidance in better ways of vegetation." The government official was slithering up and down rapidly now, gesturing with all of his pseudopods. "We are faced with a very difficult problem, at present—"

III. One billion years ago. The primitive triple tribolite the machine had destroyed when it materialized began drifting down wetly.

"—a very difficult problem. The question before us: should we *shllk* or shouldn't we *shllk?*" He was hardly speaking English now; in fact, for some time, he hadn't been speaking at all. He had been stating his thoughts by slapping one pseudopod against the other—as he always had. . . .

IV. A half-billion years ago. Many different kinds of bacteria died as the water changed temperature slightly.

"This, then, is no time for half measures. If we can reproduce well enough—"

V. Two hundred fifty million years ago. VI. A hundred twenty-five million years ago.

"—to satisfy the Five Who Spiral, we have—"

VII. Sixty-two million years. VIII. Thirty-one million. IX. Fifteen million. X. Seven and a half million.

"—spared all attainable virtue. Then—"

XI. XII. XIII. XIV. XV. XVI. XVII. XVIII. XIX. Bong—bong—bong bongbongbongongongngngngggg . . .

"—we are indeed ready for refraction. And that, I tell you, is good enough for those who billow and those who snap. But those who billow will be proven wrong as always, for in the snapping is the rolling and in the rolling is only truth. There need be no change merely because of a sodden cilium. The apparatus has rested at last in the fractional conveyance; shall we view it subtly?"

They all agreed, and their bloated purpled bodies dissolved into liquid and flowed up and around to the apparatus. When they reached its four square blocks, now no longer shrilling mechanically, they rose, solidified, and regained their slime-washed forms.

"See," cried the thing that had been the acting secretary to the executive assistant on press relations. "See, no matter how subtly! Those who billow were wrong: we haven't changed." He extended fifteen purple blobs triumphantly. "Nothing has changed!"

THE DARK STAR

So it's here again, is it? Another year and it's here again. The Day. Only this time it's the fiftieth anniversary. Your editors and program directors will be really spreading themselves tomorrow. Celebrations in every major city on Earth, a holiday on every planet of the Solar System, and on the Moon—*well!* Noisemakers for the schoolchildren, speeches in the parks, fireworks, drinking, dancing, parades—and you boys will have to cover it all. *The* Day.

Go ahead, sit down and make yourselves comfortable. I've been expecting you. I don't have very much that's new, I'm afraid. It will be just about the same old story everyone's heard for the past forty-nine years, but they never seen to get tired of it, do they?

Human interest, your editors call it. The story behind the news, the color behind the historical event. The strictly human side of today's holiday—that's all I am.

Those of you who want any refreshment, please help yourselves. I particularly recommend that Martian brandy; they're turning out some highly drinkable stuff in New Quebec these days. No, thank you, young fellow, I'm afraid I can't join you—a man's lining gets real soft at my time of life. But I still like to watch, so drink up, all of you, drink up and drink hearty.

The fiftieth anniversary. The years, the years! There I was, young and practically bubbling with high-test fuel like all of you, and here I am now, full of doddering, aimless talk. And in between, a full volume of history, but such history as the human race has not written for itself since it began climbing down from the trees.

And I was there on the very first page of that volume!

I was there, and Caldicott, Bresh, McGuire and Stefano. Just the five of us, five desperate and determined competitors, all that was left of an even hundred determined and brilliant young men that the best universities in the country had sent. We'd been examined mentally and examined physically, tested on our math and tested on our nerve, eliminated for this reason and for that reason, too tall, too slow, too heavy, too talkative—until only the pleased, happy, and shakingly tense five of us were left.

Then the finals began.

Picture it, five young men on a plane bound for the Arizona Research Station, looking at each other, wondering who it was going to be, who was going to end up the winner, the pilot of the first ship to land on the Moon. Each one of us wanting to be the man, the Columbus who would open up not a mere hemisphere but the incredible, infinite universe itself. Each of us wanting to be that man so bad that we had terrible little aches running up and down our insides.

Try to picture the world we'd grown up in. The first radio-controlled rocket to burst outside the Earth's atmosphere, the first piloted ship to go halfway to the Moon and back, the first robot craft to circle the Moon—interplanetary travel, *space* travel, getting closer all the time. The newspapers full of it, the television full of it, our very grammar-school textbooks chock-full of it.

And now, just as we'd graduated, the question was no longer exciting but remote news. It was as personal as a new neighbor moving next door. Who was he going to be, what would be his name—that first explorer—that hero of all-time heroes?

There were exactly five possibilities: Caldicott, Bresh,

McGuire, Stefano—and myself. The Moon ship had been built and was waiting for its pilot. One of us would be the modern Columbus.

I remember glancing around from face to face in that plane and thinking to myself that we could have been brothers. Cousins, anyway.

The ship had been built to exact specifications with regard to lift and mass, and there was only just so much room for the pilot. He had to fit into his cubicle like a machined part, which meant a maximum height and a maximum weight, but still nothing sacrificed in the way of strength and reflexes.

So we were all, all five of us, small, stern-bodied men with almost identical scholastic training behind us and almost identical psychological mechanisms inside us. The way we moved, the way we noticed things, even the way we talked—everything was remarkably, eerily similar. Especially considering that we'd each come from a different part of the country.

Any one of us would have been adequate. But the Moon ship had cost millions of dollars and nine years of painstaking construction. For that, they didn't want adequacy; they wanted the best that could be found.

We began talking to each other guardedly then, just before we landed at the Arizona Research Station. Not to make friends—hell, no!—but to get a line on relative weaknesses and strengths. Believe me, the differences were almost microscopic.

Stefano, for example. He had one more math course to his credit than I. Theory of Equations, I think it was—and how I bit my lip over skipping it for the sake of the Glee Club Tuesday afternoons! But it was on the record that he'd sprained his back in a high-school football game. Of course, the sprain was ancient history and long over with; still, it was on his record. How would *you* figure it?

And how would you figure, we wondered as we landed

at the hot, dusty Station and were led right into our first testing complex, how would you weigh the balances of sexual involvement? McGuire was married, a newlywed, Caldicott and I were more or less engaged, while Stefano and Bresh were carefree characters who took what they could where they could.

One way, engagement, marriage, pointed to an adjusted emotional life—and adjustment rated high. And someone to return to might provide that extra bit of incentive where the chances of return were considered no higher than two out of three.

On the other hand, McGuire's wife, my Irene and Caldicott's Edna might be looked upon by the powers-that-were as so much psychological dead weight, so much extra responsibility and worry that the men involved had to carry. Stefano and Bresh, I could just hear some jowl-heavy individual in a white smock argue, had nothing to concentrate on but themselves and the ship.

I tell you, I began to get awfully moody and regretful about Irene. Fine, I'd say to myself, I love the girl. But did I have to go and get engaged?

Yet there was no way to figure. You didn't know how they'd rate it.

Once we got into the routine at the Station, though, there was very little time to worry. Morning after morning, we'd be dragged out of bed and, pushing our yawns in front of us, made to go through a round of tests. Afternoon after afternoon, we'd get particularized instruction in the handling and maintenance of the Moon ship and made to go through the motions in a dummy model. Evening after evening, there'd be a light supper followed by a dessert of more tests, checkup tests, validation tests, and recapitulation tests.

Over and over again, they tested us where they had tested us before, mentally, physically, psychologically, always probing for a hair's-breadth of difference, for a third decimal place of advantage.

And then, when we had reached the point where our reflexes had become edgy, where our dreams were eight hours' worth of raising, flying and landing the ship, where we chewed bread in the mess-hall with the certain feeling that somewhere a stopwatch must be recording, the pressure came off abruptly.

And the results were announced.

I was first, by a millimicron. Bresh was second, by the same distance. Then came McGuire, Caldicott and Stefano.

I was first!

I would pilot the first ship to the Moon! *I* would be the new Columbus! *I* would start the era of space travel!

We didn't know who had invented the first crude tool, who had taken the first bareback ride on a horse, but as long as human history endured, the name of the first man to leave Earth and land on another world would be celebrated. And it would be *my* name—Emanuel Mengild.

I felt like the ten-year-old kid who is suddenly told, all right, tomorrow he can go out West and become a cowboy—like the man lying on a flophouse bed who opens a telegram informing him he's just inherited a million dollars—like the crackle-fingered, red-eyed seamstress who's invited to go out to Hollywood and become a film star. But much more than all of those, for someone of my generation and background, I would pilot the first Moon ship!

There were consolation prizes given out, too. If I dropped dead in the next week, or went crazy and refused to go, Bresh would be up. After him, of course, McGuire, Caldicott and Stefano, in that order. The way they looked at me!

When I got the order to report to Colonel Graves, the Commandant of the Station, I swaggered all the way into his office. I wasn't throwing any weight around. I just felt exactly that way.

Any time up to today that his eye fell on me, I'd pulled my shoulders back a little further, put a little extra snap into my step. As Commandant, he was a member of the testing board, and, for all I knew, the decisive one. There was always the possibility that he might notice me yawning a bit longer after breakfast than the others, that he might put that one extra question mark beside my name that would just make a vital difference.

But now! Now he was simply George Johnstown Graves, a super-annuated rocket pilot from the old days when men had thought it exciting to climb high enough to see the Earth as a curving horizon beneath. He was courageous enough and smart enough and fast enough, but he'd been born a mite too early. For all his rank, he was just a Portuguese fisherman, while I—well, as I said, I was Columbus.

He was middle height, a bit taller than I, and he was leaning back in his swivel chair with his collar open, his sleeves rolled up and a funny, faraway look in his eyes which I interpreted as envy.

I sat down alertly in the chair he nodded at.

He said "Um" at the opposite wall, as if he were agreeing with it. Then he looked at me.

"Mengild," he said, "you're engaged, aren't you? A Miss Rass?"

"Yes, sir," I told him snappily. The five of us were all civilians, but we'd gotten in the habit of saying "sir" to everyone, even the people who made up our beds. How did you know who would be contributing to the final, crucial decision?

He glanced flittingly across his desktop. The desktop held a single folderful of papers, but closed. I had the impression that he'd memorized everything in the folder.

"You've requested permission to have her enter the Station tonight on a four-hour civilian pass?"

I got a bit uncomfortable. "That's right, sir. When the results were posted, we were told we'd have a thirty-six-hour vacation from classes. We were told we could invite any one outsider to join us for this evening. I got in touch with Irene—Miss Rass—and she's flying down from Des Moines. I hope there's nothing wrong with—"

Colonel Graves shook his head sharply. "Nothing. Nothing wrong, Mengild. You don't expect to marry the lady before you take off, do you?"

"No-o-o. We'd pretty much set it up the other way, sir. That is, if I were picked and I got back in one piece, we'd do it the day I landed back on Earth. She sort of wanted to get married first, but I talked her out of it."

"She knows your chances of return in one piece are only slightly better than fifty percent?"

I felt relieved. I thought I understood what he was driving at. "Yes, sir. But she still wants me to go. She knows how I've grown up with the idea. Irene wouldn't want it any differently."

The colonel folded his hands under his chin and stared straight at me. "Miss Rass is a domestic type, isn't she? Wants the usual things—a home, babies, so on?"

"I guess so. She's a pretty normal girl."

"You want them, too?"

I looked off to one side and thought for a moment. "Well, sir, I've wanted one thing since I was a kid and another for the past three years—space flight and Irene. And whatever Irene wants in the way of a home, once I'm back, once I've made it, I guess I want that as well."

He examined the opposite wall again. When he got its opinion, he started talking at it in a low, soft voice. Didn't sound military at all.

"All right. I'll put it to you very briefly, Mengild. As you know, your engines are atomics and they have to be shielded. They are. Out in space, cosmic rays stream into the ship and it has to be shielded from them. It is. Thus far, except for a few unfortunate and preventable accidents, we've had no trouble on this matter. The shielding we've devised is good and it works. But this will be the longest trip that a man has taken under these conditions and the very latest poop from the lab is that the shielding, in all likelihood, will not be effective for its duration."

My lips suddenly weren't working too well. "Does this mean, sir, that—"

"It means that the pilot of the first Earth-Moon ship will probably be completely sterilized somewhere on the return journey. We could improve the shielding and no doubt will—in the future. To do it now would mean a long delay at best. At worst, it might mean completely redesigning and rebuilding the ship, which, as you know, has been figured for pretty close tolerances in terms of the equipment it can carry and the fuel it must carry. Our decision is therefore not to delay, but to put it up to the individual most concerned."

I thought it out for just a moment, for one emotion-churning moment. "I can give you my answer right now, sir. I've spent too much of my life dreaming of—"

He said "Um" to the wall once more. "Suppose you take twenty-four hours. We can wait till then. Talk it over with your girl, try to find out exactly how you feel."

"I *know* exactly how I feel, sir. There's nothing more important to me than this trip. And Irene will agree with me. If she doesn't—well, as I said, there's nothing more important than this trip. Why, do you think—do you think, sir, that after having come all this way, I'd let any risk, any risk at all, get in the way of my being the first man to make it to the Moon and back?"

You can imagine that I was pretty excited. But Colonel Graves knotted his tie and rolled down his sleeves and said firmly to the wall: "Suppose you take twenty-four hours, Mengild."

The moment I got out of his office, I understood what he meant. Irene was due tonight. I wasn't set to take off for close to three weeks. Plenty of time to get married, the way Irene had wanted to in the first place, and get a baby started.

Of course. That's what Colonel Graves had meant.

Bresh and McGuire were standing outside the administration building when I came down. They looked at me with carefully controlled eagerness.

"No," I told them, "it hasn't been suddenly discovered that my grandfather took sick on his first airplane ride. I still go."

Bresh socked his forehead with a thumb-knuckle, just under his spiky red hair. "Well," he grinned, "can you feel a heart murmur developing? Headaches? Vertigo?"

I pushed between the death watch with both hands, on my way to my quarters to shower and shave. I had to go through the same routine there with Caldicott and Stefano, although, being lower on the list, they were less grisly.

When Irene arrived at the gate in the sand-streaked taxi, I hauled her into my arms and let her soak there for a while. She looked so good, she felt so good!

We had a quickish snack at the recreation hall, while she filled me in on her mother's sciatica and her kid brother Lennie's art scholarship. Then she grabbed my hand and congratulated me on being selected for the Earth-Moon ship.

"Let me show you what it looks like," I suggested. "The next time you see it, it will be on the newscasts when I take off."

Irene glanced around as we left the rec hall. She pointed her little chin at the swarm of lab buildings rising in concrete squareness from the raw Arizona earth, at the guards pacing their intervals along the wire fence.

"Such a—" she thought for a moment—"such a *male* place."

I laughed. "What else should it be?"

She came in on the tail end of my laugh. "What else?" she repeated.

It was getting dark by the time we reached the ship. Irene gave a tiny and thoroughly feminine grunt of admiration. The ship stood on its tail, staring greedily, unswervingly at the enormous sky above. The lights from the station covered its sides with long thin glints and long thin shadows that seemed to be urging it to move, *move,* MOVE!

"The first one," she breathed. "And you're going to pilot it."

I figured it was exactly the right time. So I hoisted her up on the steps that led to the pilot's hatch, lit a cigarette for her—and started talking.

It took a surprisingly short time, even including the proposal. She had barely smoked one-third of the cigarette when I finished. But she kept on smoking the rest in quiet, long inhalations until it became a butt that burned her fingers and she had to throw it away.

I ground the butt into the sand and said, "Well?"

Her next words kind of astonished me. "Well what?"

"Well, we're going to get married, aren't we? Right away?"

"No, we're not," she said.

"Irene! But when I come back I may not be able to have children. You want to have children, don't you?"

A long pause. I wished it wasn't so dark: I couldn't see her face. "Yes, I want to have children. That's why we won't get married. Not before you go or after you come back."

I felt like saying *Oh, no!* I felt like grabbing her and

squeezing her until she was my sensible, lovable, loving Irene again. Instead, I stepped back away from her. I gave up talking and thought for a while.

"Look," I said at last. "Correct me if I'm wrong. You knew the risks I was running when I volunteered for this flight and you were with me all the way. You knew what it meant to me. You were willing to take the chance that I might not come back, and that if I did, it would be in three separate paper bags. This business is just some more of the same."

"No, it isn't." I could tell from her voice that she was crying. "I wasn't happy about the risks, but I knew you had to do it. You've been preparing for this moment since you were a little boy. But this—this is different, Mannie."

"How is it different? *How?"*

She wiped the sniffles off her nose-tip. "It's different, that's all. Maybe a man just can't understand these things. But it's different, altogether different for a woman."

"Baby, darling," I said, trying to take her in my arms, but she made a little away movement and I stopped. "I *want* to have a child. I want to have a child with *you.* Will you please tell me why we can't get married tonight, tomorrow, as soon as we can, and start a baby?"

"Suppose I don't get pregnant before you leave? And if I do—suppose I have a miscarriage?"

"Listen, Irene," I told her desperately. "In my position, we could have the best doctors in the world taking care of you. And if anything went wrong, we could adopt a baby. I know it isn't the same, but for all we know, one of us might be sterile to begin with! Lots of couples adopt babies and they're happy."

"Oh, Mannie, it wouldn't be the same thing with us, not if we started out this way. Besides, miscarriages, that sort of thing, that's not the real reason."

I put my fists on my hips and shoved my face close to

hers. "Well, will you kindly stop all this, woman, and *tell* me the real reason?"

She asked me for another cigarette. I lit it up and handed it to her.

"Mannie, I don't know if you can understand this, but I'll try. I wouldn't want to limit my childbearing powers in advance. And—I wouldn't want to marry a man who would deliberately give up his ability to become a father. He'd never be completely a man to me."

That took some absorption. "What would you think of a man," I asked slowly, "who gave up his ability to make the kind of trip I've been offered? Would *he* be completely a man?"

"I don't *know,*" she said, crying again. "But I don't think they're the same thing. I don't—I don't—and that's all!"

"But that's what you're asking me to do, Irene," I pointed out. "You're asking me to give up a dream that I've had since I was a—"

"I'm not asking you to do a single thing, Emanuel Mengild! I'm only telling you what I can and can't do. *I,* not *you*. You—*you* can go straight up in a rocket!"

And that's where we left it. I walked her back, walked her around, and, when her time was up, I walked her to the gate. We didn't hug when she left; we didn't even blow kisses at each other. I just stared after the cab until it sand-clouded around a big boulder and disappeared.

Then I walked myself around.

One way to look at it: I was in one Earth-Moon trip and out one woman. Rack up Fame and Fortune, scratch Family.

One way to look at it.

Another way: I could get mad at Irene for failing me at a crucial moment, for leaving when the going got rough. I got mad.

Then I got over it.

After all, I could see her point. It *wasn't* the same for a man as for a woman. A man had his work, his achievement; a woman had children. A woman grew up with the dream of kids the way I'd grown up with the dream of the stars. It wasn't the same for a man.

But wasn't it? I began to realize, walking myself around and around in a plodding, sweaty circle, how much I had counted on Irene to come through for me. I wanted kids—only I'd never said to myself two kids, five kids. I'd settle for one.

But *no* kids? Ever?

I'd taken it for granted, I now understood, when Colonel Graves had hit me with the problem, that Irene loved me enough to marry me right away and cancel out the chance of having no family. That's why I'd been so sure. That had been the little nubbin of security nestling comfortably at the back of my mind.

This, now, was a different matter.

It had taken a couple of billion years to produce me. In that couple of billion years, I had millions upon millions of ancestors. Slime-like ancestors, jelly-like ancestors, water-breathing ancestors, air-breathing ancestors, ancestors that floated, that swam, that crawled, that ran, that climbed, that finally walked. And all those ancestors, no matter how different, had one thing in common.

They had survived long enough to have descendants. Other species didn't and their lines were extinct, bare bones in rock strata. But no matter how scarce food got, no matter what enemies they faced, what unprecedented natural upheavals they had to adjust to, *my* ancestors somehow managed to pull through and have offspring. That's how I happen to be here.

If I didn't carry on, all their effort would come to nothing: I would be a biological dead-end. They might just as well not have bothered.

But that was only part of it, I decided, coming to the gate for the tenth time and starting off again.

What was it all about, for example? What was I here for? What was good, what was bad, what was right, what was wrong? What in the world was I sure of, with all my studies, with all my aspirations, with all my attitudes? Very damn little.

But while life continued, there was a chance of finding out, of getting a little closer, all the time a little closer. And my kind of life—me—could only find out if it went on.

It was like, I decided, my entering this competition for the Moon ship. I'd entered it partly because I wanted to very badly, but also because I felt I was the right man. I possessed inside me, I believed, the values necessary to make that difficult attempt which would initiate the age of interplanetary travel. Well, relative to life, I felt I was the right man, too. Both were conceits, but they were *fundamental* conceits. If I felt I was good enough, of value enough, I could not withdraw my entry.

That got me to the Moon ship. Life wasn't just reproduction—not human life. Life was achievement, too. Mankind pushed its collective nose past barrier after barrier, because one of its component individuals just *had* to, whether or not he reproduced. And I lived in a time of a major barrier and it had fallen to my lot to do the pushing. Wasn't that more important than children?

On the other hand, I couldn't fool myself—any of the other four men who had come out to the Station with me could do the job as well as I. And if this ship didn't make it, another would. I wasn't that necessary.

But I *wanted* to be.

So there I was, back again. I waved to the guard at the gate and kept going. By now, I'd worn a path for myself.

My mouth felt as if it were full of big teardrops that had fallen out of my eyes when I reported to Colonel Graves the next morning. He stared at my face with a good deal of interest as I sat down.

"It wasn't so easy, was it, Mengild?"

"No, sir," I told him unhappily, "it wasn't. But I've made up my mind. And I'll stick to the decision."

He waited.

"I've decided—maybe I'll regret this for the rest of my life, but, as I said, I stick by it—I've decided not to go."

"Um. The sterilization business?"

"Yes, sir."

"I take it the young lady said no."

I wiped my face with my wet handkerchief and shrugged. "She said no, all right, but that wasn't it. I thought it over all night and this is my personal decision. I'd rather have children than have the Moon ship."

He rocked back and forth in his chair. "You know, Mengild, there's such a thing as artificial insemination. And you still could be the father by being a donor before the take-off."

"I can see myself," I muttered, "running around with a test tube in my hand, trying to get women to marry me."

"Well, when you put it that way, I'll admit it isn't too romantic. However, there *are* women who would. Remember, Mengild, you'd be a hero, one of the greatest heroes of all time."

"Suppose it worked," I challenged. "Suppose I got married—to one of those women who would—and she were artificially inseminated and I were the father—what then if there were miscarriages? Or abnormal births? The frozen spermatozoa don't remain viable more than a year or two. But that's only part of it, sir. The rest would be that I had voluntarily and forever risked the chance of never becoming an ancestor. I've decided I don't want to."

Colonel Graves stood up. "Your business. And your decision. Certainly. I made these suggestions because, frankly, we would rather have you pilot the ship. You're a shade better than anyone else who competed with you. That would mean a shade better chance for the ship to get to the Moon and return. We want very much to have it return."

They offered the job to the next man in line and he jumped at it. They told him the problem and he laughed. They told him to take twenty-four hours to think it over, and he did, and he came back and said he still wanted to go.

Bresh, of course.

He took off three weeks later, landed on the Moon and returned safely to one of the greatest and most heroic receptions ever. That's why we celebrate Paul Bresh Day all over the Solar System. That's why you reporters are here today for some of the usual human-interest fill-in material.

And I can't tell you anything more than I've told you before.

No, that's not so. There's a new item.

As you know, I never married Irene. I married Frances, a year later, when I got the maintenance crew job. That's all I've ever done for interplanetary travel—keep the ships in good shape for the flight into space. I've made a good living, even made a name for myself as a ground-crew chief. Now, naturally, I'm retired.

I do regret that I never made a space flight when I was younger. Too old now, heart too weak, to be allowed even on one of those luxury passenger liners.

Not like Paul Bresh. Besides making the first flight to the Moon in history, he was a member of the Second Exploratory Party to Mars; the time he sort of wandered off into the desert and was never heard of again.

Me? All I have now is my son David and his wife in New Quebec on Mars, my daughter Ann and her family on Ganymede, my daughter Mildred and her family on Titan, and—oh, yes, the new item.

I got word last week that when the first star ship lifted from Pluto on its way to Alpha Centaurus, my grandson Aaron and his wife Phyllis were aboard. The trip will take thirty years, they tell me, so I'll probably have a great-grandson born on the way.

There it is, my side of the story. That's what I got out of it. Maybe I didn't become the new Columbus, but I'm an ancestor. Paul Bresh has his day. I have my millennia.

NULL-P

SEVERAL MONTHS after the Second Atomic War, when radioactivity still held one-third of the planet in desolation, Dr. Daniel Glurt of Fillmore Township, Wisc., stumbled upon a discovery which was to generate humanity's ultimate sociological advance.

Like Columbus, smug over his voyage to India; like Nobel, proud of the synthesis of dynamite which made combat between nations impossible, the doctor misinterpreted his discovery. Years later, he cackled to a visiting historian:

"Had no idea it would lead to this, no idea at all. You remember, the war had just ended: we were feeling mighty subdued what with the eastern and western coasts of the United States practically sizzled away. Well, word came down from the new capitol at Topeka in Kansas for us doctors to give all our patients a complete physical check. Sort of be on the lookout, you know, for radioactive burns and them fancy new diseases the armies had been tossing back and forth. Well, sir, that's absolutely all I set out to do. I'd known George Abnego for over thirty years—treated him for chicken-pox and pneumonia and ptomaine poisoning. I'd *never* suspected!"

Having reported to Dr. Glurt's office immediately after work in accordance with the proclamation shouted through the streets by the county clerk, and having waited patiently in line for an hour and a half, George Abnego was at last received into the small consulting room. Here he was thoroughly chest-thumped, X-rayed, blood-sampled, and urinanalyzed. His skin was examined carefully, and he was made to answer the five hundred questions prepared by the Department of Health in a pathetic attempt to cover the symptoms of the new ailments.

George Abnego then dressed and went home to the cereal supper permitted for that day by the ration board. Dr. Glurt placed his folder in a drawer and called for the next patient. He had noticed nothing up to this point; yet already he had unwittingly begun the Abnegite Revolution.

Four days later, the health survey of Fillmore, Wisc., being complete, the doctor forwarded the examination reports to Topeka. Just before signing George Abnego's sheet, he glanced at it cursorily, raised his eyebrows and entered the following note: "Despite the tendency to dental caries and athlete's foot, I would consider this man to be of average health. Physically, he is the Fillmore Township norm."

It was this last sentence which caused the government medical official to chuckle and glance at the sheet once more. His smile was puzzled after this; it was even more puzzled after he had checked the figures and statements on the form against standard medical references.

He wrote a phrase in red ink in the right-hand corner and sent it along to Research.

His name is lost to history.

Research wondered why the report on George Abnego had been sent up—he had no unusual symptoms portending exotic innovations like cerebral measles or arterial trichinosis. Then it observed the phrase in red ink and Dr. Glurt's remark. Research shrugged its anonymous shoulders and assigned a crew of statisticians to go further into the matter.

A week later, as a result of their findings, another

crew—nine medical specialists—left for Fillmore. They examined George Abnego with coordinated precision. Afterwards, they called on Dr. Glurt briefly, leaving a copy of their examination report with him when he expressed interest.

Ironically, the government copies were destroyed in the Topeka Hard-Shelled Baptist Riots a month later, the same riots which stimulated Dr. Glurt to launch the Abnegite Revolution.

This Baptist denomination, because of population shrinkage due to atomic and bacteriological warfare, was now the largest single religious body in the nation. It was then controlled by a group pledged to the establishment of a Hard-Shelled Baptist theocracy in what was left of the United States. The rioters were quelled after much destruction and bloodshed; their leader, the Reverend Hemingway T. Gaunt—who had vowed that he would remove neither the pistol from his left hand nor the Bible from his right until the Rule of God had been established and the Third Temple built—was sentenced to death by a jury composed of stern-faced fellow Baptists.

Commenting on the riots, the Fillmore, Wisc., *Bugle-Herald* drew a mournful parallel between the Topeka street battles and the destruction wreaked upon the world by atomic conflict.

"International communication and transportation having broken down," the editorial went on broodingly, "we now know little of the smashed world in which we live beyond such meager facts as the complete disappearance of Australia beneath the waves, and the contraction of Europe to the Pyrenees and Ural Mountains. We know that our planet's physical appearance has changed as much from what it was ten years ago, as the infant monstrosities and mutants being born everywhere as a result of radioactivity are unpleasantly different from their parents.

"Truly, in these days of mounting catastrophe and

change, our faltering spirits beg the heavens for a sign, a portent, that all will be well again, that all will yet be as it once was, that the waters of disaster will subside and we shall once more walk upon the solid ground of normalcy."

It was this last word which attracted Dr. Glurt's attention. That night, he slid the report of the special government medical crew into the newspaper's mail slot. He had penciled a laconic note in the margin of the first page:

"Noticed your interest in the subject."

Next week's edition of the Fillmore *Bugle-Herald* flaunted a page one five-column headline.

FILLMORE CITIZEN THE SIGN?

Normal Man of Fillmore May Be Answer From Above
Local Doctor Reveals Government Medical Secret

The story that followed was liberally sprinkled with quotations taken equally from the government report and the Psalms of David. The startled residents of Fillmore learned that one George Abnego, a citizen unnoticed in their midst for almost forty years, was a living abstraction. Through a combination of circumstances no more remarkable than those producing a royal flush in stud poker, Abnego's physique, psyche, and other miscellaneous attributes had resulted in that legendary creature—the statistical average.

According to the last census taken before the war, George Abnego's height and weight were identical with the mean of the American adult male. He had married at the exact age—year, month, day—when statisticians had estimated the marriage of the *average* man took place; he had married a woman the *average* number of years younger than himself; his income as declared on his last tax statement was the *average* income for that year. The very teeth in his mouth tallied in quantity and condition with those predicted by the American Dental Association to be found on a man extracted at random from the population. Abnego's metabolism and blood pressure, his bodily proportions and private neuroses, were all cross-sections of the latest available records. Subjected to every psychological and personality test available, his final, overall grade corrected out to show that he was both average and normal.

Finally, Mrs. Abnego had been recently delivered of their third child, a boy. This development had not only occurred at exactly the right time according to the population indices, but it had resulted in an entirely normal sample of humanity—unlike most babies being born throughout the land.

The *Bugle-Herald* blared its hymn to the new celebrity around a greasy photograph of the family in which the assembled Abnegos stared glassily out at the reader, looking, as many put it, "Average—average as hell!"

Newspapers in other states were invited to copy.

They did, slowly at first, then with an accelerating, contagious enthusiasm. Indeed, as the intense public interest in this symbol of stability, this refugee from the extremes, became manifest, newspaper columns gushed fountains of purple prose about the "Normal Man of Fillmore."

At Nebraska State University, Professor Roderick Klingmeister noticed that many members of his biology class were wearing extra-large buttons decorated with pictures of George Abnego. "Before beginning my lecture," he chuckled, "I would like to tell you that this 'normal man' of yours is no Messiah. All he is, I am afraid, is a bell-shaped curve with ambitions, the median made flesh—"

He got no further. He was brained with his own demonstration microscope.

Even that early, a few watchful politicians noticed that no one was punished for this hasty act.

The incident could be related to many others which followed: the unfortunate and unknown citizen of Duluth, for example, who—at the high point of that city's *Welcome Average Old Abnego* parade—was heard to remark in good-natured amazement, "Why, he's just an ordinary jerk like you and me," and was immediately torn into celebratory confetti by horrified neighbors in the crowd.

Developments such as these received careful consideration from men whose power was derived from the just, if well-directed, consent of the governed.

George Abnego, these gentry concluded, represented the maturation of a great national myth which, implicit in the culture for over a century, had been brought to garish fulfillment by the mass communication and entertainment media.

This was the myth that began with the juvenile appeal to be "A Normal Red-Blooded American Boy" and ended, on the highest political levels, with a shirt-sleeved, suspendered seeker after political office boasting. "Shucks, everybody knows who I am. I'm folks—just plain folks."

This was the myth from which were derived such superficially disparate practices as the rite of political baby-kissing, the cult of "keeping up with the Joneses," the foppish, foolish, forever-changing fads which went through the population with the monotonous regularity and sweep of a windshield wiper. The myth of styles and fraternal organizations. The myth of the "regular fellow."

There was a presidential election that year.

Since all that remained of the United States was the Middle West, the Democratic Party had disappeared. Its remnants had been absorbed by a group calling itself the Old Guard Republicans, the closest thing to an American Left. The party in power—the Conservative Republicans—so far right as to verge upon royalism, had acquired enough pledged theocratic votes to make them smug about the election.

Desperately, the Old Guard Republicans searched for a candidate. Having regretfully passed over the adolescent epileptic recently elected to the governorship of South Dakota in violation of the state constitution—and deciding against the psalm-singing grandmother from Oklahoma who punctuated her senatorial speeches with religious music upon the banjo—the party strategists arrived, one summer afternoon, in Fillmore, Wisconsin.

From the moment that Abnego was persuaded to accept the nomination and his last well-intentioned but flimsy objection was overcome (the fact that he was a registered member of the opposition party) it was obvious that the tide of battle had turned, that the fabled grass roots had caught fire.

Abnego ran for president on the slogan "Back to Normal with the Normal Man!"

By the time the Conservative Republicans met in convention assembled, the danger of loss by landslide was already apparent. They changed their tactics, tried to meet the attack head-on and imaginatively.

They nominated a hunchback for the presidency. This man suffered from the additional disability of being a distinguished professor of law in a leading university; he had married with no issue and divorced with much publicity; and finally, he had once admitted to a congressional investigating committee that he had written and published surrealist poetry. Posters depicting him leering horribly, his hump twice life-size, were smeared across the country over the slogan: "An Abnormal Man for an Abnormal World!"

Despite this brilliant political stroke, the issue was never in doubt. On Election Day, the nostalgic slogan defeated its medicative adversary by three to one. Four years later, with the same opponents, it had risen to five and a half to one. And there was no organized opposition when Abnego ran for a third term. . . .

Not that he had crushed it. There was more casual liberty of political thought allowed during Abnego's administrations than in many previous ones. But less political thinking and debating were done.

Whenever possible, Abnego avoided decision. When a decision was unavoidable, he made it entirely on the basis of precedent. He rarely spoke on a topic of current interest and never committed himself. He was garrulous and an exhibitionist only about his family.

"How can you lampoon a vacuum?" This had been the wail of many opposition newspaper writers and cartoonists during the early years of the Abnegite Revolution, when men still ran against Abnego at election time. They tried to draw him into ridiculous statements or admissions time and again without success. Abnego was simply incapable of saying anything that any major cross-section of the population would consider ridiculous.

Emergencies? "Well," Abnego had said, in the story every schoolchild knew, "I've noticed even the biggest forest fire will burn itself out. Main thing is not to get excited."

He made them lie down in low-blood-pressure areas. And, after years of building and destruction, of stimulation and conflict, of accelerating anxieties and torments, they rested and were humbly grateful.

It seemed to many, from the day Abnego was sworn in, that chaos began to waver and everywhere a glorious, welcome stability flowered. In some respects, such as the decrease in the number of monstrous births, processes were under way which had nothing at all to do with the Normal Man of Fillmore; in others—the astonished announcement by lexicographers, for example, that slang expressions peculiar to teen-agers in Abnego's first term were used by their children in exactly the same contexts eighteen years later in his fifth administration—the historical leveling-out and patting-down effects of the Abnegite trowel were obvious.

The verbal expression of this great calm was the Abnegism.

History's earliest record of these deftly phrased inadequacies relates to the administration in which Abnego, at last feeling secure enough to do so, appointed a cabinet without any regard to the wishes of his party hierarchy. A journalist, attempting to point up the absolute lack of color in the new official family, asked if any one of them—from Secretary of State to Postmaster-General—had ever committed himself publicly on any issue or, in previous positions, had been responsible for a single constructive step in any direction.

To which the President supposedly replied with a bland, unhesitating smile, "I always say there's no hard feelings if no one's defeated. Well, sir, no one's defeated in a fight where the referee can't make a decision."

Apocryphal though it may have been, this remark expressed the mood of Abnegite America perfectly. "As pleasant as a no-decision bout" became part of everyday language.

Certainly as apocryphal as the George Washington cherry-tree legend, but the most definite Abnegism of them all was the one attributed to the President after a performance of *Romeo and Juliet*. "It is better not to have loved at all, than to have loved and lost," he is reported to have remarked at the morbid end of the play.

At the inception of Abnego's sixth term—the first in which his oldest son served with him as Vice-President—a group of Europeans reopened trade with the United States by arriving in a cargo ship assembled from the salvaged parts of three sunken destroyers and one capsized aircraft carrier.

Received everywhere with undemonstrative cordiality,

they traveled the country, amazed at the placidity—the almost total absence of political and military excitement on the one hand, and the rapid technological retrogression on the other. One of the emissaries sufficiently mislaid his diplomatic caution to comment before he left:

"We came to America, to these cathedrals of industrialism, in the hope that we would find solutions to many vexing problems of applied science. These problems—the development of atomic power for factory use, the application of nuclear fission to such small arms as pistols and hand grenades—stand in the way of our postwar recovery. But you, in what remains of the United States of America, don't even see what we, in what remains of Europe, consider so complex and pressing. Excuse me, but what you have here is a national trance!"

His American hosts were not offended: they received his expostulations with polite smiles and shrugs. The delegate returned to tell his countrymen that the Americans, always notorious for their madness, had finally specialized in cretinism.

But another delegate who had observed widely and asked many searching questions went back to his native Toulouse (French culture had once more coagulated in Provence) to define the philosophical foundations of the Abnegite Revolution.

In a book which was read by the world with enormous interest, Michel Gaston Fouffnique, sometime Professor of History at the Sorbonne, pointed out that while twentieth-century man had escaped from the narrow Greek formulations sufficiently to visualize a non-Aristotelian logic and a non-Euclidean geometry, he had not yet had the intellectual temerity to create a non-Platonic system of politics. Not until Abnego.

"Since the time of Socrates," wrote Monsieur Fouffnique, "Man's political viewpoints have been in thrall to the conception that the best should govern. How to determine that 'best,' the scale of values to be used in order that the 'best' and not mere undifferentiated 'betters' should rule—these have been the basic issues around which have raged the fires of political controversy for almost three millennia. Whether an aristocracy of birth or intellect should prevail is an argument over values; whether rulers should be determined by the will of a god as determined by the entrails of a hog, or selected by the whole people on the basis of a ballot tally—these are alternatives in method. But hitherto no political system has ventured away from the implicit and unexamined assumption first embodied in the philosopher-state of Plato's *Republic*.

"Now, at last, America has turned and questioned the pragmatic validity of the axiom. The young democracy to the West, which introduced the concept of the Rights of Man to jurisprudence, now gives a feverish world the Doctrine of the Lowest Common Denominator in government. According to this doctrine as I have come to understand it through prolonged observation, it is *not* the worst who should govern—as many of my prejudiced fellow-delegates insist—but the mean: what might be termed the 'unbest' or the 'non-elite.' "

Situated amid the still-radioactive rubbish of modern war, the people of Europe listened devoutly to readings from Fouffnique's monograph. They were enthralled by the peaceful monotonies said to exist in the United States and bored by the academician's reasons thereto: that a governing group who knew to begin with that they were "unbest" would be free of the myriad jealousies and conflicts arising from the need to prove individual superiority, and that such a group would tend to smooth any major quarrel very rapidly because of the dangerous opportunities created for imaginative and resourceful people by conditions of struggle and strain.

There were oligarchs here and bosses there; in one nation an ancient religious order still held sway, in another, calculating and brilliant men continued to lead the people. But the word was preached. Shamans appeared in the population, ordinary-looking folk who were called "abnegos." Tyrants found it impossible to destroy these shamans, since they were not chosen for any special abilities but simply because they represented the median of a given group: the middle of any population grouping, it was found, lasts as long as the group itself. Therefore, through bloodshed and much time, the abnegos spread their philosophy and flourished.

Oliver Abnego, who became the first President of the World, was President Abnego VI of the United States of America. His son presided—as Vice-President—over a Senate composed mostly of his uncles and his cousins and his aunts. They and their numerous offspring lived in an economy which had deteriorated very, very slightly from the conditions experienced by the founder of their line.

As world president, Oliver Abnego approved only one measure—that granting preferential university scholarships to students whose grades were closest to their age-group median all over the planet. The President could hardly have been accused of originality and innovation unbecoming to his high office, however, since for some time now all reward systems—scholastic, athletic, and even industrial—had been adjusted to recognition of the most average achievement while castigating equally the highest and lowest scores.

When the usable oil gave out shortly afterwards, men turned with perfect calmness to coal. The last turbines were placed in museums while still in operating condition: the people they served felt their isolated and individual use of electricity was too ostentatious for good abnegism.

Outstanding cultural phenomena of this period were carefully rhymed and exactly metered poems addressed to the nondescript beauties and vague charms of a wife or old mother. Had not anthropology disappeared long ago, it would have become a matter of common knowledge that there was a startling tendency to uniformity everywhere in such qualities as bone structure, features and pigmentation, not to mention intelligence, musculature, and personality. Humanity was breeding rapidly and unconsciously in toward its center.

Nonetheless, just before the exhaustion of coal, there was a brief sputter of intellect among a group who established themselves on a site northwest of Cairo. These Nilotics, as they were known, consisted mostly of unreconstructed dissidents expelled by their communities, with a leavening of the mentally ill and the physically handicapped; they had at their peak an immense number of technical gadgets and yellowing books culled from crumbling museums and libraries the world over.

Intensely ignored by their fellowmen, the Nilotics carried on shrill and interminable debates while plowing their muddy fields just enough to keep alive. They concluded that they were the only surviving heirs of *homo sapiens,* the bulk of the world's population now being composed of what they termed *homo abnegus.*

Man's evolutionary success, they concluded, had been due chiefly to his lack of specialization. While other creatures had been forced to standardize to a particular and limited environment, mankind had been free for a tremendous spurt, until ultimately it had struck an environmental factor which demanded the fee of specialization. To avoid war, Man had to specialize in nonentity.

Having come this far in discussion, the Nilotics determined to use the ancient weapons at their disposal to save *homo abnegus* from himself. However, violent disagreements over the methods of re-education to be employed led them to a bloody internecine conflict with those same weapons in the course of which the entire colony was destroyed and its site made untenable for life. About this time, his coal used up, Man re-entered the broad, self-replenishing forests.

The reign of *homo abnegus* endured for a quarter of a million years. It was disputed finally—and successfully—by a group of Newfoundland retrievers who had been marooned on an island in Hudson Bay when the cargo vessel transporting them to new owners had sunk back in the twentieth century.

These sturdy and highly intelligent dogs, limited perforce to each other's growling society for several hundred millennia, learned to talk in much the same manner that mankind's simian ancestors had learned to walk when a sudden shift in botany destroyed their ancient arboreal homes—out of boredom. Their wits sharpened further by the hardships of their bleak island, their imaginations stimulated by the cold, the articulate retrievers built a most remarkable canine civilization in the Arctic before sweeping southward to enslave and eventually domesticate humanity.

Domestication took the form of breeding men solely for their ability to throw sticks and other objects, the retrieving of which was a sport still popular among the new masters of the planet, however sedentary certain erudite individuals might have become.

Highly prized as pets were a group of men with incredibly thin and long arms; another school of retrievers, however, favored a stocky breed whose arms were short, but extremely sinewy; while, occasionally, interesting results were obtained by inducing rickets for a few generations to produce a pet whose arms were sufficiently limber as to appear almost boneless. This last type, while intriguing both esthetically and scientifically, was generally decried as a sign of decadence in the owner as well as a functional insult to the animal.

Eventually, of course, the retriever civilization developed machines which could throw sticks farther, faster, and with more frequency. Thereupon, except in the most backward canine communities, Man disappeared.

EASTWARD HO!

THE NEW JERSEY Turnpike had been hard on the horses. South of New Brunswick the potholes had been so deep, the scattered boulders so plentiful, that the two men had been forced to move at a slow trot, to avoid crippling their three precious animals. And, of course, this far south, farms were nonexistent: they had been able to eat nothing but the dried provisions in the saddlebags, and last night they had slept in a roadside service station, suspending their hammocks between the tilted, rusty gas pumps.

But it was still the best, the most direct route, Jerry Franklin knew. The Turnpike was a government road: its rubble was cleared semiannually. They had made excellent time and come through without even developing a limp in the pack horse. As they swung out on the last lap, past the riven tree stump with the words TRENTON EXIT carved on its side, Jerry relaxed a bit. His father, his father's colleagues, would be proud of him. And he was proud of himself.

But the next moment, he was alert again. He roweled his horse, moved up alongside his companion, a young man of his own age.

"Protocol," he reminded. "I'm the leader here. You know better than to ride ahead of me this close to Trenton."

He hated to pull rank. But facts were facts, and if a subordinate got above himself he was asking to be set down. After all, he was the son—and the oldest son, at that—of the Senator from Idaho; Sam Rutherford's father was a mere Undersecretary of State and Sam's mother's family was pure post office clerk all the way back.

Sam nodded apologetically and reined his horse back the proper couple of feet. "Thought I saw something odd," he explained. "Looked like an advance party on the side of the road—and I could have sworn they were wearing buffalo robes."

"Seminole don't wear buffalo robes, Sammy. Don't you remember your sophomore political science?"

"I never had any political science, Mr. Franklin: I was an engineering major. Digging around in ruins has always been my dish. But, from the little I know, I didn't *think* buffalo robes went with the Seminole. That's why I was—"

"Concentrate on the pack horse," Jerry advised. "Negotiations are my job."

As he said this, he was unable to refrain from touching the pouch upon his breast with rippling fingertips. Inside it was his commission, carefully typed on one of the last precious sheets of official government stationery (and it was not one whit less official because the reverse side had been used years ago as a scribbled interoffice memo) and signed by the President himself. In ink!

The existence of such documents was important to a man in later life. He would have to hand it over, in all probability, during the conferences, but the commission to which it attested would be on file in the capital up north. And, when his father died, and he took over one of the two hallowed Idaho seats, it would give him enough stature to make an attempt at membership on the Appropriations Committee. Or, for that matter, why not go the whole hog—the Rules Committee itself? No Senator Franklin had ever been a member of the Rules Committee. . . .

The two envoys knew they were on the outskirts of

Trenton when they passed the first gangs of Jerseyites working to clear the road. Frightened faces glanced at them briefly, and quickly bent again to work. The gangs were working without any visible supervision. Evidently the Seminole felt that simple instructions were sufficient.

But as they rode into the blocks of neat ruins that were the city proper and still came across nobody more important than white men, another explanation began to occur to Jerry Franklin. This all had the look of a town still at war, but where were the combatants? Almost certainly on the other side of Trenton, defending the Delaware River—that was the direction from which the new rulers of Trenton might fear attack—not from the north where there was only the United States of America.

But if that were so, who in the world could they be defending against? Across the Delaware to the south there was nothing but more Seminole. Was it possible—was it possible that the Seminole had at last fallen to fighting among themselves?

Or was it possible that Sam Rutherford had been right? Fantastic. Buffalo robes in Trenton! There should be no buffalo robes closer than a hundred miles westward, in Harrisburg.

But when they turned onto State Street, Jerry bit his lip in chagrin. Sam had seen correctly, which made him one up.

Scattered over the wide lawn of the gutted state capitol were dozens of wigwams. And the tall, dark men who sat impassively, or strode proudly among the wigwams, all wore buffalo robes. There was no need even to associate the paint on their faces with a remembered lecture in political science: these were Sioux.

So the information that had come drifting up to the government about the identity of the invader was totally inaccurate—as usual. Well, you couldn't expect communication miracles over this long a distance. But that inaccuracy made things difficult. It might invalidate his commission for one thing: his commission was addressed directly to Osceola VII, Ruler of All the Seminoles. And if Sam Rutherford thought this gave him a right to preen himself—

He looked back dangerously. No, Sam would give no trouble. Sam knew better than to dare an I-told-you-so. At his leader's look, the son of the Undersecretary of State dropped his eyes groundwards to immediate humility.

Satisfied, Jerry searched his memory for relevant data on recent political relationships with the Sioux. He couldn't recall much—just the provisions of the last two or three treaties. It would have to do.

He drew up before an important-looking warrior and carefully dismounted. You might get away with talking to a Seminole while mounted, but not the Sioux. The Sioux were very tender on matters of protocol with white men.

"We come in peace," he said to the warrior standing as impassively straight as the spear he held, as stiff and hard as the rifle on his back. "We come with a message of importance and many gifts to your chief. We come from New York, the home of our chief." He thought a moment, then added: "You know, the Great White Father?"

Immediately, he was sorry for the addition. The warrior chuckled briefly; his eyes lit up with a lightning-stroke of mirth. Then his face was expressionless again, and serenely dignified as befitted a man who had counted coup many times.

"Yes," he said. "I have heard of him. Who has not heard of the wealth and power and far dominions of the Great White Father? Come. I will take you to our chief. Walk behind me, white man."

Jerry motioned Sam Rutherford to wait.

At the entrance to a large, expensively decorated tent, the Indian stood aside and casually indicated that Jerry should enter.

It was dim inside, but the illumination was rich enough to take Jerry's breath away. Oil lamps! Three of them! These people lived well.

A century ago, before the whole world had gone smash in the last big war, his people had owned plenty of oil lamps themselves. Better than oil lamps, perhaps, if one could believe the stories the engineers told around the evening fires. Such stories were pleasant to hear, but they were glories of the distant past. Like the stories of overflowing granaries and chock-full supermarkets, they made you proud of the history of your people, but they did nothing for you now. They made your mouth water, but they didn't feed you.

The Indians whose tribal organization had been the first to adjust to the new conditions, in the all-important present, the Indians had the granaries, the Indians had the oil lamps. And the Indians . . .

There were two nervous white men serving food to the group squatting on the floor. An old man, the chief, with a carved, chunky body. Three warriors, one of them surprisingly young for council. And a middle-aged Negro, wearing the same bound-on rags as Franklin, except that they looked a little newer, a little cleaner.

Jerry bowed low before the chief, spreading his arms apart, palms down.

"I come from New York, from our chief," he mumbled. In spite of himself, he was more than a little frightened. He wished he knew their names so that he could relate them to specific events. Although he knew what their names would be like—approximately. The Sioux, the Seminole, all the Indian tribes renaissant in power and numbers, all bore names garlanded with anachronism. That queer mixture of several levels of the past, overlaid always with the cocky, expanding present. Like the rifles *and* the spears, one for the reality of fighting, the other for the symbol that was more important than reality. Like the use of wigwams on campaign, when, according to the rumors that drifted smokily across country, their slave artisans could now build the meanest Indian noble a damp-free, draftproof dwelling such as the President of the United States, lying on his special straw pallet, did not dream about. Like paint-spattered faces peering through newly reinvented, crude microscopes. What had microscopes been like? Jerry tried to remember the Engineering Survey Course he'd taken in his freshman year—and drew a blank. All the same, the Indians were so queer, *and* so awesome. Sometimes you thought that destiny had meant them to be conquerors, with a conqueror's careless inconsistency. Sometimes . . .

He noticed that they were waiting for him to continue. "From our chief," he repeated hurriedly. "I come with a message of importance and many gifts."

"Eat with us," the old man said. "Then you will give us your gifts and your message."

Gratefully, Jerry squatted on the ground a short distance from them. He was hungry, and among the fruit in the bowls he had seen something that must be an orange. He had heard so many arguments about what oranges tasted like!

After a while, the old man said, "I am Chief Three Hydrogen Bombs. This"—pointing to the young man—"is my son, Makes Much Radiation. And this"—pointing to the middle-aged Negro—"is a sort of compatriot of yours."

At Jerry's questioning look, and the chief's raised finger of permission, the Negro explained. "Sylvester Thomas. Ambassador to the Sioux from the Confederate States of America."

"The Confederacy? She's still alive? We heard ten years ago—"

"The Confederacy is very much alive, sir. The Western Confederacy, that is, with its capital at Jackson, Mississippi. The Eastern Confederacy, the one centered at Richmond, Virginia, did go down under the Seminole. We have been more fortunate. The Arapahoe, the Cheyenne, and"—with a nod to the chief—"especially the Sioux, if I may say so, sir, have been very kind to us. They allow us to live in peace, so long as we till the soil quietly and pay our tithes."

"Then would you know, Mr. Thomas—" Jerry began eagerly. "That is . . . the Lone Star Republic—Texas— Is it possible that Texas, too . . . ?"

Mr. Thomas looked at the door of the wigwam unhappily. "Alas, my good sir, the Republic of the Lone Star Flag fell before the Kiowa and the Comanche long years ago when I was still a small boy. I don't remember the exact date, but I do know it was before even the last of California was annexed by the Apache and the Navajo, and well before the nation of the Mormons under the august leadership of—"

Makes Much Radiation shifted his shoulders back and forth and flexed his arm muscles. "All this talk," he growled. "Paleface talk. Makes me tired."

"Mr. Thomas is not a paleface," his father told him sharply. "Show respect! He's our guest and an accredited ambassador—you're not to use a word like paleface in his presence!"

One of the other, older warriors near the child spoke up. "In ancient days, in the days of the heroes, a boy of Makes Much Radiation's age would not dare raise his voice in council before his father. Certainly not to say the things he just has. I cite as reference, for those interested, Robert Lowie's definitive volume, *The Crow Indians*, and Lesser's fine piece of anthropological insight, *Three Types of Siouan Kinship*. Now, whereas we have not yet been able to reconstruct a Siouan kinship pattern on the classic model described by Lesser, we have developed a working arrangement that—"

"The trouble with you, Bright Book Jacket," the warrior on his left broke in, "is that you're too much of a classicist. You're always trying to live in the Golden Age instead of the present, and a Golden Age that really has little to do with the Sioux. Oh, I'll admit that we're as much Dakotan as the Crow, from the linguist's point of view at any rate, and that, superficially, what applies to the Crow should apply to us. But what happens when we quote Lowie in so many words and try to bring his precepts into daily life?"

"Enough," the chief announced. "Enough, Hangs A Tale. And you, too, Bright Book Jacket—enough, enough! These are private tribal matters. Though they do serve to remind us that the paleface was once great before he became sick and corrupt and frightened. These men whose holy books teach us the lost art of being real Sioux, men like Lesser, men like Robert H. Lowie, were not these men palefaces? And in memory of them should we not show tolerance?"

"A-ah!" said Makes Much Radiation impatiently. "As far as I'm concerned, the only good paleface is a dead paleface. And that's that." He thought a bit. "Except their women. Paleface women are fun when you're a long way from home and feel like raising a little hell."

Chief Three Hydrogen Bombs glared his son into silence. Then he turned to Jerry Franklin. "Your message and your gifts. First your message."

"No, Chief," Bright Book Jacket told him respectfully but definitely. "First the gifts. *Then* the message. That's the way it was done."

"I'll have to get them. Be right back." Jerry walked out of the tent backwards and ran to where Sam Rutherford had tethered the horses. "The presents," he said urgently. "The presents for the chief."

The two of them tore at the pack straps. With his arms loaded, Jerry returned through the warriors who had assembled to watch their activity with quiet arrogance. He entered the tent, set the gifts on the ground and bowed low again.

"Bright beads for the chief," he said, handing over two star sapphires and a large white diamond, the best that the engineers had evacuated from the ruins of New York in the past ten years.

"Cloth for the chief," he said, handing over a bolt of linen and a bolt of wool, spun and loomed in New Hampshire especially for this occasion and painfully, expensively carted to New York.

"Pretty toys for the chief," he said, handing over a large, only slightly rusty alarm clock and a precious typewriter, both of them put in operating order by batteries of engineers and artisans working in tandem (the engineers interpreting the brittle old documents to the artisans) for two and a half months.

"Weapons for the chief," he said, handing over a beautifully decorated cavalry saber, the prized hereditary possession of the Chief of Staff of the United States Air Force, who had protested its requisitioning most bitterly ("Damn it all, Mr. President, do you expect me to fight these Indians with my bare hands?" "No, I don't, Johnny, but I'm sure you can pick up one just as good from one of your eager junior officers").

Three Hydrogen Bombs examined the gifts, particularly the typewriter, with some interest. Then he solemnly distributed them among the members of his council, keeping only the typewriter and one of the sapphires for himself. The sword he gave to his son.

Makes Much Radiation tapped the steel with his fingernail. "Not so much," he stated. *"Not-so-much.* Mr. Thomas came up with better stuff than this from the Confederate States of America for my sister's puberty ceremony." He tossed the saber negligently to the ground. "But what can you expect from a bunch of lazy, good-for-nothing whiteskin stinkards?"

When he heard the last word, Jerry Franklin went rigid. That meant he'd have to fight Makes Much Radiation—and the prospect scared him right down to the wet hairs on his legs. The alternative was losing face completely among the Sioux.

"Stinkard" was a term from the Natchez system and was applied these days indiscriminately to all white men bound to field or factory under their aristocratic Indian overlords. A "stinkard" was something lower than a serf, whose one value was that his toil gave his masters the leisure to engage in the activities of full manhood: hunting, fighting, thinking.

If you let someone call you a stinkard and didn't kill him, why, then you *were* a stinkard—and that was all there was to it.

"I am an accredited representative of the United States of America," Jerry said slowly and distinctly, "and the oldest son of the Senator from Idaho. When my father dies, I will sit in the Senate in his place. I am a free-born man, high in the councils of my nation, and anyone who calls me a stinkard is a rotten, no-good, foul-mouthed liar!"

There—it was done. He waited as Makes Much Radiation rose to his feet. He noted with dismay the well-fed, well-muscled sleekness of the young warrior. He wouldn't have a chance against him. Not in hand-to-hand combat—which was the way it would be.

Makes Much Radiation picked up the sword and pointed it at Jerry Franklin. "I could chop you in half right now like a fat onion," he observed. "Or I could go into a ring with you knife to knife and cut your belly open. I've fought and killed Seminole, I've fought Apache, I've even fought and killed Comanche. But I've never dirtied my hands with paleface blood, and I don't intend to start now. I leave such simple butchery to the overseers of our estates. Father, I'll be outside until the lodge is clean again." Then he threw the sword ringingly at Jerry's feet and walked out.

Just before he left, he stopped, and remarked over his shoulder: "The oldest son of the Senator from Idaho! Idaho has been part of the estates of my mother's family for the past forty-five years! When will these romantic children stop playing games and start living in the world as it is now?"

"My son," the old chief murmured. "Younger generation. A bit wild. Highly intolerant. But he means well. Really does. Means well."

He signaled to the white serfs who brought over a large chest covered with great splashes of color.

While the chief rummaged in the chest, Jerry Franklin relaxed inch by inch. It was almost too good to be true: he wouldn't have to fight Makes Much Radiation, and he hadn't lost face. All things considered, the whole business had turned out very well indeed.

And as for the last comment—well, why expect an Indian to understand about things like tradition and the glory that could reside forever in a symbol? When his father stood up under the cracked roof of Madison Square Garden and roared across to the Vice-President of the United States: "The people of the sovereign state of Idaho will never and can never in all conscience consent to a tax on potatoes. From time immemorial, potatoes have been associated with Idaho, potatoes have been the pride of Idaho. The people of Boise say *no* to a tax on potatoes, the people of Pocatello say *no* to a tax on potatoes, the very rolling farmlands of the Gem of the Mountain say *no, never,* a thousand times *no,* to a tax on potatoes!"—when his father spoke like that, he *was* speaking for the people of Boise and Pocatello. Not the crushed Boise or desolate Pocatello of today, true, but the magnificent cities as they had been of yore . . . and the rich farms on either side of the Snake River. . . . And Sun Valley, Moscow,

Idaho Falls, American Falls, Weiser, Grangeville, Twin Falls. . . .

"We did not expect you, so we have not many gifts to offer in return," Three Hydrogen Bombs was explaining. "However, there is this one small thing. For you."

Jerry gasped as he took it. It was a pistol, a real, brand-new pistol! And a small box of cartridges. Made in one of the Sioux slave workshops of the Middle West that he had heard about. But to hold it in his hand, and to know that it belonged to him!

It was a Crazy Horse forty-five, and, according to all reports, far superior to the Apache weapon that had so long dominated the West, the Geronimo thirty-two. This was a weapon a General of the Armies, a President of the United States, might never hope to own—and it was his!

"I don't know how— Really, I—I—"

"That's all right," the chief told him genially. "Really it is. My son would not approve of giving firearms to palefaces, but I feel that palefaces are like other people—it's the individual that counts. You look like a responsible man for a paleface: I'm sure you'll use the pistol wisely. Now your message."

Jerry collected his faculties and opened the pouch that hung from his neck. Reverently, he extracted the precious document and presented it to the chief.

Three Hydrogen Bombs read it quickly and passed it to his warriors. The last one to get it, Bright Book Jacket, wadded it up into a ball and tossed it back at the white man.

"Bad penmanship," he said. "And 'receive' is spelled three different ways. The rule is: '*i* before *e*, except after *c*.' But what does it have to do with us? It's addressed to the Seminole chief, Osceola VII, requesting him to order his warriors back to the southern bank of the Delaware River, or to return the hostage given him by the Government of the United States as an earnest of good will and peaceful intentions. We're not Seminole: why show it to us?"

As Jerry Franklin smoothed out the wrinkles in the paper with painful care and replaced the document in his pouch, the Confederate ambassador, Sylvester Thomas, spoke up. "I think I might explain," he suggested, glancing inquiringly from face to face. "If you gentlemen don't mind . . . ? It is obvious that the United States Government has heard that an Indian tribe finally crossed the Delaware at this point, and assumed it was the Seminole. The last movement of the Seminole, you will recall, was to Philadelphia, forcing the evacuation of the capital once more and its transfer to New York City. It was a natural mistake: the communications of the American States, whether Confederate or United"—a small, coughing, diplomatic laugh here—"have not been as good as might have been expected in recent years. It is quite evident that neither this young man nor the government he represents so ably and so well, had any idea that the Sioux had decided to steal a march on his majesty, Osceola VII, and cross the Delaware at Lambertville."

"That's right," Jerry broke in eagerly. "That's exactly right. And now, as the accredited emissary of the President of the United States, it is my duty formally to request that the Sioux nation honor the treaty of eleven years ago as well as the treaty of fifteen—I *think* it was fifteen—years ago, and retire once more behind the banks of the Susquehanna River. I must remind you that when we retired from Pittsburgh, Altoona, and Johnstown, you swore that the Sioux would take no more land from us and would protect us in the little we had left. I am certain that the Sioux want to be known as a nation that keeps its promises."

Three Hydrogen Bombs glanced questioningly at the faces of Bright Book Jacket and Hangs A Tale. Then he leaned forward and placed his elbows on his crossed legs.

"You speak well, young man," he commented. "You are a credit to your chief. . . . Now, then. Of course the Sioux want to be known as a nation that honors its treaties and keeps its promises. And so forth and so forth. But we have an expanding population. You don't have an expanding population. We need more land. You don't use most of the land you have. Should we sit by and see the land go to waste—worse yet, should we see it acquired by the Seminole who already rule a domain stretching from Philadelphia to Key West? Be reasonable. You can retire to—to other places. You have most of New England left and a large part of New York State. Surely you can afford to give up New Jersey."

In spite of himself, in spite of his ambassadorial position, Jerry Franklin began yelling. All of a sudden it was too much. It was one thing to shrug your shoulders unhappily back home in the blunted ruins of New York, but here on the spot where the process was actually taking place—no, it was too much.

"What else can we afford to give up? Where else can we retire to? There's nothing left of the United States of America but a handful of square miles, and still we're supposed to move back! In the time of my forefathers, we were a great nation, we stretched from ocean to ocean, so say the legends of my people, and now we are huddled in a miserable corner of our land, starving, filthy, sick, dying, and ashamed. In the North, we are oppressed by the Ojibway and the Cree, we are pushed southward relentlessly by the Montaignais; in the South, the Seminole climb up our land yard by yard; and in the West, the Sioux take a piece more of New Jersey, and the Cheyenne come up and nibble yet another slice out of Elmira and Buffalo. When will it stop—where are we to go?"

The old man shifted uncomfortably at the agony in his voice. "It *is* hard; mind you, I don't deny that it *is* hard. But facts are facts, and weaker peoples always go to the wall. . . . Now, as to the rest of your mission. If we don't retire as you reouest, you're supposed to ask for the return of your hostage. Sounds reasonable to me. You ought to get something out of it. However, I can't for the life of me remember a hostage. Do we have a hostage from you people?"

His head hanging, his body exhausted, Jerry muttered in misery, "Yes. All the Indian nations on our borders have hostages. As earnests of our good will and peaceful intentions."

Bright Book Jacket snapped his fingers. "That girl. Sarah Cameron—Canton—what's-her-name."

Jerry looked up. "Calvin?" he asked. "Could it be *Calvin?* Sarah Calvin? The Daughter of the Chief Justice of the United States Supreme Court?"

"Sarah Calvin. That's the one. Been with us for five, six years. You remember, chief? The girl your son's been playing around with?"

Three Hydrogen Bombs looked amazed. "Is *she* the hostage? I thought she was some paleface female he had imported from his plantations in southern Ohio. Well, well, well. Makes Much Radiation is just a chip off the old block, no doubt about it." He became suddenly serious. "But that girl will never go back. She rather goes for Indian loving. Goes for it all the way. And she has the idea that my son will eventually marry her. Or some such."

He looked Jerry Franklin over. "Tell you what, my boy. Why don't you wait outside while we talk this over? And take the saber. Take it back with you. My son doesn't seem to want it."

Jerry wearily picked up the saber and trudged out of the wigwam.

Dully, uninterestedly, he noticed the band of Sioux warriors around Sam Rutherford and his horses. Then the group parted for a moment, and he saw Sam with a bottle in his hand. Tequila! The damned fool had let the Indians give him tequila—he was drunk as a pig.

Didn't he know that white men couldn't drink, didn't dare drink? With every inch of their unthreatened arable land under cultivation for foodstuffs, they were all still on the edge of starvation. There was absolutely no room in their economy for such luxuries as intoxicating beverages—and no white man in the usual course of a lifetime got close to so much as a glassful of the stuff. Give him a whole bottle of tequila and he was a stinking mess.

As Sam was now. He staggered back and forth in dipping semicircles, holding the bottle by its neck and waving it idiotically. The Sioux chuckled, dug each other in the ribs and pointed. Sam vomited loosely down the rags upon his chest and belly, tried to take one more drink, and fell over backwards. The bottle continued to pour over his face until it was empty. He was snoring loudly. The Sioux shook their heads, made grimaces of distaste, and walked away.

Jerry looked on and nursed the pain in his heart. Where could they go? What could they do? And what difference did it make? Might as well be as drunk as Sammy there. At least you wouldn't be able to feel.

He looked at the saber in one hand, the bright new pistol in the other. Logically, he should throw them away. Wasn't it ridiculous when you came right down to it, wasn't it pathetic—a white man carrying weapons?

Sylvester Thomas came out of the tent. "Get your horses ready, my dear sir," he whispered. "Be prepared to ride as soon as I come back. Hurry!"

The young man slouched over to the horses and followed instructions—might as well do that as anything else. Ride where? Do what?

He lifted Sam Rutherford up and tied him upon his horse. Go back home? Back to the great, the powerful, the respected capital of what had once been the United States of America?

Thomas came back with a bound and gagged girl in his grasp. She wriggled madly. Her eyes crackled with anger and rebellion. She kept trying to kick the Confederate Ambassador.

She wore the rich robes of an Indian princess. Her hair was braided in the style currently fashionable among Sioux women. And her face had been stained carefully with some darkish dye.

Sarah Calvin. The daughter of the Chief Justice. They tied her to the pack horse.

"Chief Three Hydrogen Bombs," the Negro explained. "He feels his son plays around too much with paleface females. He wants this one out of the way. The boy has to settle down, prepare for the responsibilities of chieftainship. This may help. And listen, the old man likes you. He told me to tell you something."

"I'm grateful. I'm grateful for every favor, no matter how small, how humiliating."

Sylvester Thomas shook his head decisively. "Don't be bitter, young sir. If you want to go on living you have to be alert. And you can't be alert and bitter at the same time. The Chief wants you to know there's no point in your going home. He couldn't say it openly in council, but the reason the Sioux moved in on Trenton has nothing to do with the Seminole on the other side. It has to do with the Ojibway-Cree-Montaignais situation in the North. They've decided to take over the Eastern Seaboard—that includes what's left of your country. By this time, they're probably in Yonkers or the Bronx, somewhere inside New York City. In a matter of hours, your government will no longer be in existence. The Chief had advance word of this and felt it necessary for the Sioux to establish some sort of bridgehead on the coast before matters were permanently stabilized. By occupying New Jersey he is preventing an Ojibway-Seminole junction. But he likes you, as I said, and wants you warned against going home."

"Fine, but where *do* I go? Up a rain cloud? Down a well?"

"No," Thomas admitted without smiling. He hoisted Jerry up on his horse. "You might come back with me to the Confederacy—" He paused, and when Jerry's sullen expression did not change, he went on, "Well, then, may I suggest—and mind you, this is my advice, not the Chief's—head straight out to Asbury Park. It's not far away—you can make it in reasonable time if you ride hard. According to reports I've overheard, there should be units of the United States Navy there, the Tenth Fleet, to be exact."

"Tell me," Jerry asked, bending down. "Have you heard any other news? Anything about the rest of the world? How has it been with those people—the Russkies, the Sovietskis, whatever they were called—the ones the United States had so much to do with years and years ago?"

"According to several of the chief's councilors, the Soviet Russians were having a good deal of difficulty with people called Tatars. I *think* they were called Tatars. But, my good sir, you should be on your way."

Jerry leaned down further and grasped his hand. "Thanks," he said. "You've gone to a lot of trouble for me. I'm grateful."

"That's quite all right," said Mr. Thomas earnestly. "After all, by the rocket's red glare, and all that. We were a single nation once."

Jerry moved off, leading the other two horses. He set a fast pace, exercising the minimum of caution made necessary by the condition of the road. By the time they reached Route 33, Sam Rutherford, though not altogether sober or well, was able to sit in his saddle. They could then untie Sarah Calvin and ride with her between them.

She cursed and wept. "Filthy paleface! Foul, ugly, stinking whiteskins! I'm an Indian, can't you see I'm an Indian? My skin isn't white—it's brown, brown!"

They kept riding.

Asbury Park was a dismal clatter of rags and confusion and refugees. There were refugees from the north, from Perth Amboy, from as far as Newark. There were refugees from Princeton in the west, flying before the Sioux invasion. And from the south, from Atlantic City—even, unbelievably, from distant Camden—were still other refugees, with stories of a sudden Seminole attack, an attempt to flank the armies of Three Hydrogen Bombs.

The three horses were stared at enviously, even in their lathered, exhausted condition. They represented food to the hungry, the fastest transportation possible to the fearful. Jerry found the saber very useful. And the pistol was even better—it had only to be exhibited. Few of these people had ever seen a pistol in action: they had a mighty, superstitious fear of firearms.

With this fact discovered, Jerry kept the pistol out nakedly in his right hand when he walked into the United States Naval Depot on the beach at Asbury Park. Sam Rutherford was at his side; Sarah Calvin walked sobbing behind.

He announced their family backgrounds to Admiral Milton Chester. The son of the Undersecretary of State. The daughter of the Chief Justice of the Supreme Court. The oldest son of the Senator from Idaho. "And now. Do you recognize the authority of this document?"

Admiral Chester read the wrinkled commission slowly, spelling out the harder words to himself. He twisted his head respectfully when he had finished, looking first at the seal of the United States on the paper before him, and then at the glittering pistol in Jerry's hand.

"Yes," he said at last. "I recognize its authority. Is that a real pistol?"

Jerry nodded. "A Crazy Horse forty-five. The latest. *How* do you recognize its authority?"

The admiral spread his hands. "Everything is confused out here. The latest word I've received is that there are Ojibway warriors in Manhattan—that there is no longer any United States Government. And yet this"—he bent over the document once more—"this is a commission by the President himself, appointing you full plenipotentiary. To the Seminole, of course. But full plenipotentiary. The last official appointment, to the best of my knowledge, of the President of the United States of America."

He reached forward and touched the pistol in Jerry Franklin's hand curiously and inquiringly. He nodded to himself, as if he'd come to a decision. He stood up, and saluted with a flourish.

"I hereby recognize you as the last legal authority of the United States Government. And I place my fleet at your disposal."

"Good." Jerry stuck the pistol in his belt. He pointed with the saber. "Do you have enough food and water for a long voyage?"

"No, sir," Admiral Chester said. "But that can be arranged in a few hours at most. May I escort you aboard, sir?"

He gestured proudly down the beach and past the surf to where the three, forty-five-foot gaff-rigged schooners rode at anchor. "The United States Tenth Fleet, sir. Awaiting your orders."

Hours later when the three vessels were standing out to sea, the admiral came to the cramped main cabin where Jerry Franklin was resting. Sam Rutherford and Sarah Calvin were asleep in the bunks above.

"And the orders, sir . . . ?"

Jerry Franklin walked out on the narrow deck, looked up at the taut, patched sails. "Sail east."

"East, sir? *Due* east?"

"Due east all the way. To the fabled lands of Europe. To a place where a white man can stand at last on his own two legs. Where he need not fear persecution. Where he need not fear slavery. Sail east, Admiral, until we discover a new and hopeful world—a world of freedom!"

THE DESERTER

November 10, 2039—

Terran Supreme Command communiqué No. 18-673 for the twenty-four hours ending 0900 Monday, Terran capital time:

. . . whereupon sector HQ on Fortress Satellite Five ordered a strategic withdrawal of all interceptor units. The withdrawal was accomplished without difficulty and with minimal loss.

The only other incident of interest in this period was the surrender of an enemy soldier of undetermined rank, the first of these creatures from Jupiter to be taken alive by our forces. The capture was made in the course of defending Cochabamba, Bolivia, from an enemy commando raid. Four Jovians were killed in this unsuccessful assault upon a vital tin-supplying area after which the fifth laid down his arms and begged that his life be spared. Upon capture by our forces, the Jovian claimed to be a deserter and requested a safe-conduct to . . .

MARDIN HAD been briefed on what to expect by the MP officer who'd escorted him into the cave. Inevitably, though, his first view of the tank in which the alien floated brought out a long, whimpering grunt of disbelief and remembered fear. It was at least sixty feet long by forty wide, and it reared off the rocky floor to twice the height of a man. Whatever incredible material its sides had been composed of had hours ago been covered by thick white layers of ice.

Cold air currents bouncing the foul, damp smell of methane back from the tank tweaked his nose and pricked at his ears. *Well, after all,* Mardin thought, *those things have a body temperature somewhere in the neighborhood of minus 200° Fahrenheit!*

And he had felt this cold once before . . .

He shivered violently in response to the memory and zipped shut the fur-lined coveralls he'd been issued at the entrance. "Must have been quite a job getting that thing in here." The casualness of his voice suprised him and made him feel better.

"Oh, a special engineer task force did it in—let me see, now—" The MP lieutenant, a Chinese girl in her late teens, pursed soft, coral lips at his graying hair. "Less than five hours, figuring from the moment they arrived. The biggest problem was finding a cell in the neighborhood that was big enough to hold the prisoner. This cave was perfect."

Mardin looked up at the ledge above their heads. Every ten feet, a squad of three men, highly polished weapons ready for instant action. Atomic cannon squads alternating with men bent down under the weight of dem-dem grenades. Grim-faced young subalterns, very conscious of the bigness of the brass that occupied the platform at the far end of the cave, stamped back and forth along the ledge from squad to squad, deadly little Royster pistolettos tinkling and naked in their sweating hands. *Those kids,* he thought angrily, *so well adjusted to it all!*

The ledge ran along three sides of the cave; on the fourth, the low entrance from which Mardin had just come, he had seen five steel Caesars implanted, long, pointed snouts throbbingly eager to throw tremendous gusts of nuclear energy at the Jovian's rear. And amid the immense rock folds of the roof, a labyrinth of slender, pencil-like bombs had been laid, held in place by clamps that would all open simultaneously the moment a certain colonel's finger pressed a certain green button. . . .

"If our friend in the tank makes one wrong move," Mardin muttered, "half of South America goes down the drain."

The girl started to chuckle, then changed her mind and frowned. "I'm sorry, Major Mardin, but I don't like that. I don't like hearing them referred to as 'friends.' Even in a joke. Over a million and a half people—three hundred thousand of them Chinese—have been wiped out by those—those ammoniated flatworms!"

"And the first fifty of which," he reminded her irritably, "were my relatives and neighbors. If you're old enough to remember Mars and the Three Watertanks Massacre, young lady."

She swallowed and looked stricken. An apology seemed to be in the process of composition, but Mardin moved past her in a long, disgusted stride and headed rapidly for the distant platform. He had a fierce dislike, he had discovered long ago, for people who were unable to hate wholesomely and intelligently, who had to jog their animus with special symbols and idiotic negations. Americans, during the War of 1914–18, changing sauerkraut into liberty cabbage; mobs of Turks, in the Gibraltar Flare-up of 1985, lynching anyone in Ankara caught eating oranges. How many times had he seen aged men in the uniform of the oldsters' service, the Infirm Civilian Corps, make the socially accepted gesture of grinding out a worm with their heels whenever they referred to the enemy from Jupiter!

He grimaced at the enormous expanse of ice-covered tank in which a blanket of living matter large enough to cover a city block pursued its alien processes. "Let me see you lift your foot and step on *that!*" he told the astonished girl behind him. *Damn all simplicity-hounds, anyway,* he thought. *A week on the receiving end of a Jovian question-machine is exactly what they need. Make them nice and thoughtful and give them some inkling of how crazily complex this universe can be!*

That reminded him of his purpose in this place. He became thoughtful himself and—while the circular scar on his forehead wrinkled—very gravely reminiscent of how crazily complex the universe actually was. . . .

So thoughtful, in fact, that he had to take a long, relaxing breath and wipe his hands on his coveralls before climbing the stairs that led up to the hastily constructed platform.

Colonel Liu, Mardin's immediate superior, broke away from the knot of men at the other end and came up to him with arms spread wide. "Good to see you, Mardin," he said rapidly. "Now listen to me. Old Rockethead himself is here—you know how *he* is. So put a little snap into your salute and kind of pull back on those shoulders when you're talking to him. Know what I mean? Try to show him that when it comes to military bearing, we in Intelligence don't take a—Mardin, are you listening to me? This is *very* important."

With difficulty, Mardin took his eyes away from the transparent un-iced top of the tank. "Sorry, sir," he mumbled. "I'll—I'll try to remember."

"This the interpreter, Colonel Liu? Major Mardin, eh?" the very tall, stiffly erect man in the jeweled uniform of a Marshal of Space yelled from the railing. "Bring him over. On the double, sir!"

Colonel Liu grabbed Mardin's left arm and pulled him rapidly across the platform. Rockethead Billingsley cut the colonel's breathless introduction short. "Major *Igor* Mardin, is it? Sounds Russian. You wouldn't be Russian now, would you? I hate Russians."

Mardin noticed a broad-shouldered vice-marshal standing in Billingsley's rear stiffen angrily. "No, sir," he replied. "Mardin is a Croat name. My family is French and Yugoslav with possibly a bit of Arab."

The Marshal of Space inclined his fur-covered head. "Good! Couldn't stand you if you were Russian. Hate Russians, hate Chinese, hate Portuguese. Though the Chinese are worst of all, I'd say. Ready to start working on this devil from Jupiter? Come over here, then. And move, man, move!" As he swung around, the dozen or so sapphire-studded Royster pistolettos that swung picturesquely from his shoulder straps clinked and clanked madly, making him seem like a gigantic cat that the mice had belled again and again.

Hurrying after him, Mardin noticed with amusement that the stiff, angry backs were everywhere now. Colonel Liu's mouth was screwed up into a dark pucker in his face; at the far end of the platform, the young lieutenant who'd escorted him from the jet base was punching a tiny fist into an open palm. Marshal of Space Rudolfo Billingsley enjoyed a rank high enough to make tact a function of the moment's whim—and it was obvious that he rarely indulged such moments. "Head thick as a rocket wall and a mouth as filthy as a burned-out exhaust, but he can figure out, down to the smallest wound on the greenest corporal, exactly how much blood any attack is going to cost." That was what the line officers said of him.

And that, after all, Mardin reflected, was just the kind of man needed in the kind of world Earth had become in eighteen years of Jovian siege. He, himself, owed this man a very special debt. . . .

"You probably don't remember me, sir," he began hesitantly as they paused beside a metal armchair that was suspended from an overhead wire. "But we met once before, about sixteen years ago. It was aboard your spaceship, the *Euphrates*, that I—"

"The *Euphrates* wasn't a spaceship. It was an interceptor, third class. Learn your damned terminology if you're going to dishonor a major's uniform, mister! And pull that zipper up tight. Of course, you were one of that mob of mewling civilians I pulled out of Three Watertanks right under the Jovians' noses. Let's see: that young archaeologist fellow. Didn't know then that we were going to get a real, first-class, bang-up, slaughter-em-dead war out of that incident, did we? Hah! You thought you had an easy life ahead of you, eh? Didn't suspect you'd be spending the rest of it in uniform, standing up straight and jumping when you got an order! This war's made men out of a lot of wet jellyfish like you, mister, and you can be grateful for the privilege."

Mardin nodded with difficulty, sardonically conscious of the abrupt stiffness of his own back, of the tightly clenched fingers scraping his palm. He wondered about the incidence of courts-martial, for striking a superior officer, in Billingsley's personal staff.

"All right, hop into it. Hop *in,* man!" Mardin realized the significance of the cupped hands being extended to him. A Marshal of Space was offering him a boost! Billingsley believed nobody could do *anything* better than Billingsley. Very gingerly, he stepped into it, was lifted up so that he could squirm into the chair. Automatically, he fastened the safety belt across his middle, strapped the headset in place.

Below him, Old Rockethead pulled the clamps tight around his ankles and called up: "You've been briefed? Arkhnatta contacted you?"

"Yes. I mean yes, *sir*. Professor Arkhnatta traveled with me all the way from Melbourne Base. He managed to cover everything, but of course it wasn't the detail he'd have liked."

"Hell with the detail. Listen to me, Major Mardin. Right there in front of you is the only Jovian flatworm we've managed to take alive. I don't know how much longer we can *keep* him alive—engineers are building a methane plant in another part of the cave so he'll have some stink to breathe when his own supply runs out, and the chemistry johnnies are refrigerating ammonia for him to drink—but I intend to rip every bit of useful military information out of his hide before he caves in. And your mind is the only chisel I've got. Hope I don't break the chisel, but the way I figure it you're not worth as much as a secondary space fleet. And I sacrificed one of those day before yesterday—complement of two thousand men—just to find out what the enemy was up to. So, mister, you pay attention to me and keep asking him questions. And shout out your replies good and loud for the recording machines. Swing him out, Colonel! Didn't you *hear* me? How the hell long does it take to swing him out?"

As the cable pulled the chair away from the platform and over the immense expanse of monster, Mardin felt something in his belly go far away and something in his brain try to hide. In a few moments—at the thought of what he'd be doing in a minute or two he shut his eyes tightly as he had in childhood, trying to wish the bad thing away.

He should have done what all his instincts urged way back in Melbourne Base when he'd gotten the orders and realized what they meant. He should have deserted. Only trouble, where do you desert in a world under arms, on a planet where every child has its own military responsibilities? But he should have done something. *Something.* No man should have to go through this twice in one lifetime.

Simple enough for Old Rockethead. This was *his* life, negative as its goals were; moments like these of incipient destruction were the fulfillment for which he'd trained and worked and studied. He remembered something else now about Marshal of Space Billingsley. The beautiful little winged creatures of Venus—*Griggoddon,* they'd been called—who'd learned human languages and begun pestering the early colonists of that planet with hundreds of questions. Toleration of their high-pitched, ear-splitting voices had turned into annoyance and they'd been locked out of the settlements, whereupon they'd made the nights hideous with their curiosity. Since they'd refused to leave, and since the hard-working colonists found themselves losing more and more sleep, the problem had been turned over to the resident military power on Venus. Mardin recalled the uproar even on Mars when a laconic order of the day—"Venus has been rendered permanently calm: Commodore R. Billingsley."—announced that the first intelligent extra-terrestrial life to be discovered had been destroyed down to the last crawling segmented infant by means of a new insecticide spray.

Barely six months later the attack on sparsely settled Mars had underlined with human corpses the existence of another intelligent race in the solar system—and a much more powerful one. Who remembered the insignificant *Griggoddon* when Commodore Rudolfo Billingsley slashed back into the enemy-occupied capital of Southern Mars and evacuated the few survivors of Jupiter's initial assault? Then the Hero of Three Watertanks had even gone back and rescued one of the men captured alive by the Jovian monsters—a certain Igor Mardin, proud possessor of the first, and, as it eventually turned out, also the only Ph.D. in Martian archaeology.

No, for Old Rockethead this horrendous planet-smashing was more than fulfillment, much more than a wonderful opportunity to practice various aspects of his trade: it represented reprieve. If mankind had not blundered into and alerted the outposts of Jovian empire in the asteroid belt, Billingsley would have worked out a miserable career as a police officer in various patrol posts, chained for the balance of his professional life to a commodore's rank by the *Griggoddon* blunder. Whenever he appeared at a party some fat woman would explain to her escort in a whisper full of highly audible sibilants that this was the famous Beast of Venus—and every uniformed man in the place would look uncomfortable. The Beast of Venus it would have been instead of the Hero of Three Watertanks, Defender of Luna, the Father of the Fortress Satellite System.

As for himself—well, Dr. Mardin would have plodded out the long years tranquilly and usefully, a scholar among scholars, not the brightest and best, possibly—here, a stimulating and rather cleverly documented paper, there a startling minor discovery of interest only to specialists—but a man respected by his colleagues, doing work he was fitted for and liked, earning a secure place for himself in the textbooks of another age as a secondary footnote or additional line in a bibliography. But instead the Popa Site Diggings were disintegrated rubble near the ruins of what had once been the human capital of Southern Mars and Major Igor Marden's civilian skills had less relevance and value than those of a dodo breeder or a veterinarian to mammoths and mastodons. He was now a mildly incompetent field grade officer in an unimportant section of Intelligence whose attempts at military bearing and deportment amused his subordinates and caused his superiors a good deal of pain. He didn't like the tasks he was assigned; frequently he didn't even understand them. His value lay only in the two years of psychological hell he'd endured as a prisoner of the Jovians and even that could be realized only in peculiarly fortuitous circumstances such as those of the moment. He could never be anything but an object of pathos to the snappy, single-minded generation grown up in a milieu of no-quarter interplanetary war: and should the war end tomorrow with humanity, by some unimaginable miracle, victorious, he would have picked up nothing in the eighteen years of conflict but uncertainty about himself and a few doubtful moments for some drab little memoirs.

He found that, his fears forgotten, he had been glaring down at the enormous hulk of the Jovian rippling gently under the transparent tank-surface. This quiet-appearing sea of turgid scarlet soup in which an occasional bluish-white dumpling bobbed to the surface only to dwindle in size and disappear—this was one of the creatures that had robbed him of the life he should have had and had hurled him into a by-the-numbers purgatory. And why? So that their own peculiar concepts of mastery might be maintained, so that another species might not arise to challenge their dominion of the outer planets. No attempt at arbitration, at treaty-making, at any kind of discussion—instead an overwhelming and relatively sudden onslaught, as methodical and irresistible as the attack of an anteater on an anthill.

A slender silvery tendril rose from the top of the tank to meet him and the chair came to an abrupt halt in its swaying journey across the roof of the gigantic cave. Mardin's shoulders shot up against his neck convulsively, he found himself trying to pull his head down into his chest—just as he had scores of times in the prison cell that had once been the Three Watertanks Public Library.

At the sight of the familiar questing tendril, a panic eighteen years old engulfed and nauseated him.

It's going to hurt inside, his mind wept, twisting and turning and dodging in his brain. *The thoughts are going to be rubbed against each other so that the skin comes off them and they hurt and hurt and hurt. . . .*

The tendril came to a stop before his face and the tip curved interrogatively. Mardin squirmed back against the metal chair back.

I won't! This time I don't have to! You can't make me—this time you're our prisoner—you can't make me—you can't make me—

"Mardin!" Billingsley's voice bellowed in his headphones. "Put the damn thing on and let's get going! Move, man, *move!*"

And almost before he knew he had done it, as automatically as he had learned to go rigid at the sound of *atten-shun!* Mardin's hand reached out for the tendril and placed the tip of it against the old scar on his forehead.

There was that anciently familiar sensation of inmost rapport, of new-found completeness, of belonging to a higher order of being. There were the strange double memories: a river of green fire arching off a jet-black trembling cliff hundreds of miles high, somehow blending in with the feel of delighted shock as Dave Weiner's baseball hit the catcher's mitt you'd gotten two hours ago for a birthday present; a picture of a very lovely and very intent young female physicist explaining to you just how somebody named Albert Fermi Vannevar derived $E=MC^2$, getting all confused with the time to begin the many-scented dance to the surface because of the myriad of wonderful soft spots you could feel calling to each other on your back.

But, Mardin realized with amazement in some recess of autonomy still left in his mind, this time there was a difference. This time there was no feeling of terror as of thorough personal violation, there was no incredibly ugly sensation of tentacles armed with multitudes of tiny suckers speeding through his nervous system and feeding, feeding, greedily feeding. . . . This time none of his thoughts were dissected, kicking and screaming, in the operating theater of his own skull while his ego shuddered fearfully at the bloody spectacle from a distant psychic cranny.

This time he was *with*—not *of*.

Of course, a lot of work undoubtedly had been done on the Jovian question-machine in the past decade. The single tendril that contained all of the intricate mechanism for telepathic communion between two races had probably been refined far past the coarse and blundering gadget that had gouged at his mind eighteen years ago.

And, of course, this time *he* was the interrogator. This time it was a Jovian that lay helpless before the probe, the weapons, the merciless detachment of an alien culture. This time it was a Jovian, not Igor Mardin, who had to find the right answers to the insistent questions—and the right symbols with which to articulate those answers.

All that made a tremendous difference. Mardin relaxed and was amused by the feeling of power that roared through him.

Still—there was something else. This time he was dealing with a totally different personality.

There was a pleasant, undefinable quality to this individual from a world whose gravity could smear Mardin across the landscape in a fine liquid film. A character trait like—no, not simple tact—certainly not timidity—and you couldn't just call it gentleness and warmth—

Mardin gave up. Certainly, he decided, the difference between this Jovian and his jailer on Mars was like the difference between two entirely different breeds. Why, it was a pleasure to share part of his mental processes temporarily with this kind of person! As from a distance, he heard the Jovian reply that the pleasure was mutual. He felt instinctively they had much in common.

And they'd have to—if Billingsley were to get the information he wanted. Superficially, it might seem that a mechanism for sharing thoughts was the ideal answer to communication between races as dissimilar as the Jovian and Terrestrial. In practice, Mardin knew from long months of squeezing his imagination under orders in Three Watertanks, a telepathy machine merely gave you a communication potential. An individual thinks in pictures and symbols based on his life experiences—if two individuals have no life experiences in common, all they can share is confusion. It had taken extended periods of desperate effort before Mardin and his Jovian captor had established that what passed for the digestive process among humans was a combination of breathing and strenuous physical exercise to a creature born on Jupiter, that the concept of taking a bath could be equated with a Jovian activity so shameful and so overlaid with pain that Mardin's questioner had been unable to visit him for five weeks after the subject came up and thenceforth treated him with the reserve one might maintain toward an intelligent blob of fecal matter.

But mutually accepted symbols eventually had been established—just before Mardin's rescue. And ever since then, he'd been kept on ice in Intelligence, for a moment like this. . . .

"Mardin!" Old Rockethead's voice ripped out of his earphones. "Made contact yet?"

"Yes. I think I have, sir."

"Good! Feels like a reunion of the goddam old regiment, eh? All set to ask questions? The slug's cooperating? Answer me, Mardin! Don't sit there gaping at him!"

"Yes, sir," Mardin said hurriedly. "Everything's all set."

"Good! Let's see now. First off, ask him his name, rank and serial number."

Mardin shook his head. The terrifying, straight-faced orderliness of the military mind! The protocol was unalterable: you asked a Japanese prisoner-of-war for his name, rank and serial number; obviously, you did the same when the prisoner was a Jovian! The fact that there was no interplanetary Red Cross to notify his family that food packages might now be sent . . .

He addressed himself to the immense blanket of quiescent living matter below him, phrasing the question in as broad a set of symbols as he could contrive. Where would the answer be worked out, he wondered? On the basis of their examination of dead Jovians, some scientists maintained that the creatures were really vertebrates, except that they had nine separate brains and spinal columns; other biologists insisted that the "brains" were merely the kind of ganglia to be found in various kinds of invertebrates and that thinking took place on the delicately convoluted surface of their bodies. And no one had ever found anything vaguely resembling a mouth or eyes, not to mention appendages that could be used in locomotion.

Abruptly, he found himself on the bottom of a noisy sea of liquid ammonia, clustered with dozens of other newborn around the neuter "mother." Someone flaked off the cluster and darted away; he followed. The two of them met in the appointed place of crystallization and joined into one individual. The pride he felt in the increase of self was worth every bit of effort.

Then he was humping along a painful surface. He was much larger now—and increased in self many times over. The Council of Unborn asked him for his choice. He chose to become a male. He was directed to a new fraternity.

Later, there was a mating with tiny silent females and enormous, highly active neuters. He was given many presents. Much later, there was a songfest in a dripping cavern that was interrupted by a battle scene with rebellious slaves on one of Saturn's moons. With a great regret he seemed to go into suspended animation for a number of years. *Wounded?* Mardin wondered. *Hospitalized?*

In conclusion, there was a guided tour of an undersea hatchery which terminated in a colorful earthquake.

Mardin slowly assimilated the information in terms of human symbology.

"Here it is, sir," he said at last hesitantly into the mouthpiece. "They don't have any actual equivalents in this area, but you might call him Ho-Par XV, originally of the Titan garrison and sometime adjutant to the commanders of Ganymede." Mardin paused a moment before going on. "He'd like it on the record that he's been invited to reproduce five times—and twice in public."

Billingsley grunted. "Nonsense! Find out why he didn't fight to the death like the other four raiders. If he still claims to be a deserter, find out why. Personally, I think these Jovians are too damn fine soldiers for that sort of thing. They may be worms, but I can't see one of them going over to the enemy."

Mardin put the question to the prisoner. . . .

Once more he wandered on worlds where he could not have lived for a moment. He superintended a work detail of strange dustmotes, long ago conquered and placed under Jovian hegemony. He found himself feeling about them the way he had felt about the *Griggoddon* eighteen years ago: they were too wonderful to be doomed, he protested. Then he realized that the protest was not his, but that of the sorrowing entity who had lived these experiences. And they went on to other garrisons, other duties.

The reply he got this time made Mardin gasp. "He says all five of the Jovians were deserting! They had planned it for years, all of them being both fraternity-brothers and brood-brothers. He says that they—well, you might say *parachuted* down together—and not one of them had a weapon. They each tried in different ways, as they had planned beforehand, to make their surrender known. Ho-Par XV was the only successful one. He brings greetings from clusters as yet unsynthesized."

"Stick to the facts, Mardin. No romancing. Why did they desert?"

"I am sticking to the facts, sir: I'm just trying to give you the flavor as well as the substance. According to Ho-Par XV, they deserted because they were all violently opposed to militarism."

"Wha-at?"

"That, as near as I can render it, is exactly what he

says. He says that militarism is ruining their race. It has resulted in all kinds of incorrect choices on the part of the young as to which sex they will assume in the adult state (I don't understand that part at all myself, sir)—it has thrown confusion into an art somewhere between cartography and horticulture that Ho-Par thinks is very important to the future of Jupiter—and it has weighed every Jovian down with an immense burden of guilt because of what their armies and military administration have done to alien life-forms on Ganymede, Titan and Europa, not to mention the half-sentient bubbles of the Saturnian core."

"To hell with the latrine-blasted half-sentient bubbles of the Saturnian core!" Billingsley bellowed.

"Ho-Par XV feels," the man in the suspended metal armchair went on relentlessly, staring down with delight at the flat stretch of red liquid whose beautifully sane, delicately balanced mind he was paraphrasing, "that his race needs to be stopped for its own sake as well as that of the other forms of life in the Solar System. Creatures trained in warfare are what he calls 'philosophically anti-life.' The young Jovians had just about given up hope that Jupiter *could* be stopped, when humanity came busting through the asteroids. Only trouble is that while we do think and move about three times as fast as they do, the Jovian females—who are the closest thing they have to theoretical scientists—know a lot more than we, dig into a concept more deeply than we can imagine and generally can be expected to keep licking us as they have been, until we are either extinct or enslaved. Ho-Par XV and his brood-brothers decided after the annual smelling session in the Jovian fleet this year to try to change all this. They felt that with our speedier metabolism, we might be able to take a new weapon, which the Jovians have barely got into production, and turn it out fast enough to make a slight—"

At this point there was a certain amount of noise in the headphones. After a while, Old Rockethead's voice, suavity gone, came through more or less distinctly: "—and if you don't start detailing that weapon immediately, you mangy son of a flea-bitten cur, I will have you broken twelve grades below Ordinary Spaceman and strip the skin off your pimply backside with my own boot the moment I get you back on this platform. I'll personally see to it that you spend all of your leaves cleaning the filthiest latrines the space fleet can find! Now jump to it!"

Major Mardin wiped the line of sweat off his upper lip and began detailing the weapon. *Who does he think he's talking to?* his mind asked bitterly. *I'm no kid, no apple-cheeked youngster, to be snapped at and dressed down with that line of frowsy, ugly, barracks-corporal humor! I got a standing ovation from the All-Earth Archaeological Society once, and Dr. Emmanuel Hozzne himself congratulated me on my report.*

But his mouth began detailing the weapon, his mouth went on articulating the difficult ideas which Ho-Par XV and his fellow deserters had painfully translated into faintly recognizable human terms, his mouth dutifully continued to explicate mathematical and physical concepts into the black speaking cone near his chin.

His mouth went about its business and carried out its orders—but his mind lay agonized at the insult. And then, in a corner of his mind where tenancy was joint, so to speak, a puzzled, warm, highly sensitive and extremely intelligent personality asked a puzzled, tentative question.

Mardin stopped in mid-sentence, overcome with horror at what he'd almost given away to the alien. He tried to cover up, to fill his mind with memories of contentment, to create *non-sequiturs* as psychological camouflage. What an idiot to forget that he wasn't alone in his mind!

And the question was asked again. *Are you not the*

representative of your people? Are—are there others . . . unlike you?

Of course not! Mardin told him desperately. *Your confusion is due entirely to the fundamental differences between Jovian and Terrestrial thinking—*

"Mardin! Will you stop drooling out of those near-sighted eyes and come the hell to attention? Keep talking, chowderhead, we want the rest of that flatworm's brain picked!"

What fundamental differences? Mardin asked himself suddenly, his skull a white-hot furnace of rage. There were more fundamental differences between someone like Billingsley and himself, than between himself and this poetic creature who had risked death and become a traitor to his own race—to preserve the dignity of the life-force. What did he have in common with that Cain come to judgment, this bemedaled swaggering boor who rejoiced in having reduced all the subtleties of conscious thought to rigidly simple, unavoidable alternatives: kill or be killed! damn or be damned! be powerful or be overpowered! The monster who had tortured his mind endlessly, dispassionately, in the prison on Mars would have found Old Rockethead much more of a friend than Ho-Par XV.

That is true, that is so! The Jovian's thought came down emphatically on his mind. *And now, friend, blood-brother, whatever you may choose to call yourself, please let me know what kind of creature I have given this weapon to. Let me know what he has done in the past with power, what he may be expected to do in hatching cycles yet to come. Let me know through your mind and your memories and your feelings—for you and I understand each other.*

Mardin let him know.

. . . to the nearest legal representative of the entire human race. As the result of preliminary interrogation by the military authorities a good deal was learned about the life and habits of the enemy. Unfortunately, in the course of further questioning, the Jovian evidently came to regret being taken alive and opened the valves of the gigantic tank which was his space suit, thus committing suicide instantly and incidentally smothering his human interpreter in a dense cloud of methane gas. Major Igor Mardin, the interpreter, has been posthumously awarded the Silver Lunar Circlet with doubled jets. The Jovian's suicide is now being studied by space fleet psychologists to determine whether this may not indicate an unstable mental pattern which will be useful to our deep-space armed forces in the future. . . .

BETELGEUSE BRIDGE

YOU TELL them, Alvarez, old boy; you know how to talk to them. This isn't my kind of Public Relations. All I care about is that they get the pitch exactly right with all the implications and complications and everything just the way they really were.

If it hurts, well, let them yell. Just use your words and get it right. Get it all.

You can start with the day the alien spaceship landed outside Baltimore. Makes you sick to think how we never tumbled, doesn't it, Alvarez? No more than a hop, skip and a jet from the Capitol dome, and we thought it was just a lucky accident.

Explain why we thought it was so lucky. Explain about the secrecy it made possible, how the farmer who telephoned the news was placed in special and luxurious custody, how a hand-picked cordon of M.P.'s paced five square miles off into an emergency military reservation a few hours later, how Congress was called into secret session and the way it was all kept out of the newspapers.

How and why Trowson, my old sociology prof, was consulted once the problem became clear. How he blinked at the brass hats and striped pants and came up with the answer.

Me. I was the answer.

How my entire staff and I were plucked out of our New York offices, where we were quietly earning a million bucks, by a flying squad of the F. B. I. and air-mailed to Baltimore. Honestly, Alvarez, even after Trowson explained the situation to me, I was still irritated. Government hush-hush always makes me uncomfortable. Though I don't have to tell you how grateful I was for it later.

The spaceship itself was such a big surprise that I didn't even wet my lips when the first of the aliens *slooshed* out. After all those years of streamlined cigar-shapes the Sunday Supplement artists had dreamed up, that colorful and rococo spheroid rearing out of a barley field in Maryland looked less like an interplanetary vessel than an oversized ornament for a what-not table. Nothing that seemed like a rocket jet anywhere.

"And there's your job," the prof pointed. "Those two visitors."

They were standing on a flat metal plate surrounded by the highest the republic had elected or appointed. Nine feet of slimy green trunk tapering up from a rather wide base to a pointed top, and crested with a tiny pink and white shell. Two stalks with eyes on them that swung this way and that, and seemed muscular enough to throttle a man. And a huge wet slash of a mouth that showed whenever an edge of the squirming base lifted from the metal plate.

"Snails," I said. *"Snails!"*

"Or slugs," Trowson amended. "Gastropodal molluscs in any case." He gestured at the roiling white bush of hair that sprouted from his head. "But, Dick, that vestigial bit of coiled shell is even less an evolutionary memento than this. They're an older—and smarter—race."

"Smarter?"

He nodded. "When our engineers got curious, they were very courteously invited inside to inspect the ship. They came out with their mouths hanging."

I began to get uncomfortable. I ripped a small piece off

my hangnail. "Well, naturally, prof, if they're so alien, so different—"

"Not only that. Superior. Get that, Dick, because it'll be very important in what you have to do. The best engineering minds that this country can assemble in a hurry are like a crowd of Caribbean Indians trying to analyze the rifle and compass from what they know of spears and windstorms. These creatures belong to a galaxy-wide civilization composed of races *at least* as advanced as they; we're a bunch of backward hicks in an unfrequented hinterland of space that's about to be opened to exploration. Exploitation, perhaps, if we can't measure up. We have to give a very good impression and we have to learn fast."

A dignified official with a briefcase detached himself from the nodding, smiling group around the aliens and started for us.

"Whew!" I commented brilliantly. "1492, repeat performance." I thought for a moment, not too clearly. "But why send the army and navy after *me?* I'm not going to be able to read blueprints from—from—"

"Betelgeuse. Ninth planet of the star Betelgeuse. No, Dick, we've already had Dr. Warbury out here. They learned English from him in two hours, although he hasn't identified a word of theirs in three days! And people like Lopez, like Mainzer, are going quietly psychotic trying to locate their power source. We have the best minds we can get to do the learning. Your job is different. We want you as a top-notch advertising man, a public relations executive. You're the good impression part of the program."

The official plucked at my sleeve and I shrugged him away. "Isn't that the function of government gladhanders?" I asked Trowson.

"No. Don't you remember what you said when you first saw them? *Snails!* How do you think this country is going to take to the idea of snails—giant snails—who sneer condescendingly at our skyscraper cities, our atomic bombs, our most advanced mathematics? We're a conceited kind of monkey. Also, we're afraid of the dark."

There was a gentle official tap on my shoulder. I said *"Please!"* impatiently. I watched the warm little breeze ruffle Professor Trowson's slept-in clothes and noticed the tiny red streaks in his weary eyes.

"Mighty Monsters from Outer Space. Headlines like that, prof?"

"Slugs with Superiority Complexes. *Dirty* Slugs, more likely. We're lucky they landed in this country, and so close to the Capitol, too. In a few days, we'll have to call in the heads of other nations. Then, sometime soon after, the news will be out. We don't want our visitors attacked by mobs drunk on superstition, planetary isolation or any other form of tabloid hysteria. We don't want them carrying stories back to their civilization of being shot at by a suspendered fanatic who screamed, 'Go back where you came from, you furrin seafood!' We want to give them the impression that we are a fairly amiable, fairly intelligent race, that we can be dealt with reasonably well."

I nodded. "Yeah. So they'll set up trading posts on this planet instead of garrisons. But what do I do in all this?"

He punched my chest gently. "You, Dick—you do a job of public relations. You sell these aliens to the American people!"

The official had maneuvered around in front of me. I recognized him. He was the Undersecretary of State.

"Would you step this way, please?" he said. "I'd like to introduce you to our distinguished guests."

So I stepped this way please, and we went all across the field and clanked across the steel plate and stood next to our gastropodal guests.

"Ahem," said the Undersecretary politely.

The nearer snail bent an eye toward us. The other eye drew a bead on the companion snail, and then the great slimy head arched and came down to our level. The creature raised, as it were, one cheek of its foot and said, with all the mellowness of air being pumped through a torn inner tube, "Can it be that you wish to communicate with my unworthy self, respected sir?"

I was introduced. The thing brought two eyes to bear on me. The place where its chin should have been dropped to my feet and snaked around there for a second. Then it said, "You, honored sir, are our touchstone, the link with all that is great in your noble race. Your condescension is truly a tribute."

All this tumbled out while I was muttering "How," and extending a diffident hand. The snail put one eyeball in my palm and the other on the back of my wrist. It didn't shake; it just put the things there and took them away again. I had the wit not to wipe my hands on my pants, which was my immediate impulse. The eyeball wasn't exactly dry, either.

I said, "I'll do my best. Tell me, are you—uh—ambassadors, sort of? Or maybe just explorers?"

"Our small worth justifies no titles," said the creature, "yet we are both; for all communication is ambassadorship of a kind, and any seeker after knowledge is an explorer."

I was suddenly reminded of an old story with the punchline, "Ask a foolish question and you get a foolish answer." I also wondered suddenly what snails eat.

The second alien glided over and eyed me. "You may depend upon our utmost obedience," it said humbly. "We understand your awesome function and we wish to be liked to whatever extent it is possible for your admirable race to like such miserable creatures as ourselves."

"Stick to that attitude and we'll get along," I said.

By and large they were a pleasure to work with. I mean there was no temperament, no upstaging, no insistence on this camera angle or that mention of a previously published book or the other wishful biographical apocrypha about being raised in a convent, like most of my other clients.

On the other hand they weren't easy to talk to. They'd take orders, sure. But ask them a question. Any question:

"How long did the trip take you?"

" 'How long' in your eloquent tongue indicates a frame of reference dealing with duration. I hesitate to discuss so complex a problem with one as learned as yourself. The velocities involved make it necessary to answer in relative terms. Our lowly and undesirable planet recedes from this beauteous system during part of its orbital period, advances toward it during part. Also we must take into consideration the direction and velocity of our star in reference to the cosmic expansion of this portion of the continuum. Had we come from Cygnus, say, or Bootes, the question could be answered somewhat more directly; for those bodies travel in a contiguous arc skewed from the ecliptic plane in such a way that—"

Or a question like, "Is your government a democracy?"

"A democracy is a rule of the people, according to your rich etymology. We could not, in our lowly tongue, have expressed it so succinctly and movingly. One must govern oneself, of course. The degree of governmental control on the individual must vary from individual to individual and in the individual from time to time. This is so evident to as comprehensive a mind as yours that I trust you forgive me my inanities. The same control applies, naturally, to individuals considered in the mass. When faced with a universal necessity, the tendency exists among civilized species to unite to fill the need. Therefore, when no such necessity exists, there is less reason for concerted effort. Since this applies to all species, it applies even to such as us. On the other hand—"

See what I mean? A little of that got old quickly with me. I was happy to keep my nose to my own grindstone.

The government gave me a month for the preparatory propaganda. Originally, the story was to break in two weeks, but I got down on my hands and knees and bawled that a publicity deadline required at least five times that. So they gave me a month.

Explain that carefully, Alvarez. I want them to understand exactly what a job I faced. All those years of lurid magazine covers showing extremely nubile females being menaced in three distinct colors by assorted monstrosities; those horror movies, those invasion-from-outer-space novels, those Sunday Supplement fright-splashes—all those sturdy psychological ruts I had to retrack. Not to mention the shudders elicited by mention of "worms," the regulation distrust of even human foreigners, the superstitious dread of creatures who had no visible place to park a soul.

Trowson helped me round up the men to write the scientific articles, and I dug up the boys who could pseudo them satisfactorily. Magazine mats were ripped apart to make way for yarns speculating gently on how far extraterrestrial races might have evolved beyond us, how much more ethical they might have become, how imaginary seven-headed creatures could still apply the Sermon on the Mount. Syndicated features popped up describing "Humble Creatures Who Create our Gardens," "Snail-Racing, the Spectacular New Spectator Sport," and so much stuff on "The Basic Unity of all Living Things" that I began to get uncomfortable at even a vegetarian dinner. I remember hearing there was a perceptible boom in mineral waters and vitamin pills. . . .

And all this, mind you, without a word of the real story breaking. A columnist did run a cute and cryptic item about someone having finally found meat on the flying saucers, but half an hour of earnest discussion in an abandoned fingerprint-file room prejudiced him against further comment along this line.

The video show was the biggest problem. I don't think I could have done it on time with anything less than the resources and influence of the United States government behind me. But a week before the official announcement I had both the video show and the comic strip in production.

I think fourteen—though maybe it was more—of the country's best comedy writers collaborated on the project, not to mention the horde of illustrators and university psychologists who combined to sweat out the delightful little drawings. We used the drawings as the basis for the puppets on the TV show and I don't think anything was ever so gimmicked up with Popular Appeal—and I do mean *Popular*—as "Andy and Dandy."

Those two fictional snails crept into the heart of America like a virus infection: overnight, everybody was talking about their anthropomorphic antics, repeating their quotable running gags and adjuring each other not to miss the next show. ("You *can't* miss it, Steve; it's on every channel anyway. Right after supper.") I had the tie-ins, too: Andy and Dandy dolls for the girls, snail scooters for the boys, everything from pictures on cocktail glasses to kitchen decalcomanias. Of course, a lot of the tie-ins didn't come off the production line till after the Big Announcement.

When we gave the handouts to the newspapers, we "suggested" what headlines to use. They had a choice of ten. Even *The New York Times* was forced to shriek "REAL ANDY AND DANDY BLOW IN FROM BETELGEUSE," and under that a four-column cut of blonde Baby Ann Joyce with the snails.

Baby Ann had been flown out from Hollywood for the photograph. The cut showed her standing between the two aliens and clutching an eye-stalk of each in her trusting, chubby hands.

The nicknames stuck. Those two slimy intellectuals

from another star became even more important than the youthful evangelist who was currently being sued for bigamy.

Andy and Dandy had a ticker-tape reception in New York. They obligingly laid a cornerstone for the University of Chicago's new library. They posed for the newsreels everywhere, surrounded by Florida oranges, Idaho potatoes, Milwaukee beer. They were magnificently cooperative.

From time to time, I wondered what they thought of us. They had no facial expressions, which was scarcely odd since they had no faces. Their long eye-stalks swung this way and that as they rode down shrieking Broadway in the back seat of the Mayor's car; their gelatinous body-foot would heave periodically and the mouth under it make a smacking noise, but when the photographers suggested that they curl around the barely clad beauties, the time video rigged up a Malibu Beach show, Andy and Dandy wriggled over and complied without a word. Which is more than I can say for the barely clad beauties.

And when the winning pitcher presented them with an autographed baseball at that year's World Series, they bowed gravely, their pink shell-tops glistening in the sunlight, and said throatily into the battery of microphones: "We're the happiest fans in the universe!"

The country went wild over them.

"But we can't keep them here," Trowson predicted. "Did you read about the debate in the U. N. General Assembly yesterday? We were accused of making secret alliances with non-human aggressors against the best interests of our own species."

I shrugged. "Well, let them go overseas. I don't think anyone else will be more successful extracting information from them than we were."

Professor Trowson wriggled his short body up on a corner of his desk. He lifted a folder of typewritten notes and grimaced as if his tongue were wrapped in wool.

"Four months of careful questioning," he grumbled. "Four months of painstaking interrogation by trained sociologists using every free moment the aliens had, which admittedly wasn't much. Four months of organized investigation, of careful data-sifting." He dropped the folder disgustedly to the desk and some of the pages splashed out. "And we know more about the social structure of Atlantis than Betelgeuse IX."

We were in the wing of the Pentagon assigned to what the brass hats, in their own cute way, had christened Mission Encyclopedia. I strolled across the large, sunny office and glanced at the very latest organizational wall-chart. I pointed to a small rectangle labeled "Power Source Sub-Section" depending via a straight line from a larger rectangle marked "Alien Physical Science Inquiry Section." In the small rectangle, very finely printed, were the names of an army major, a WAC corporal, and Drs. Lopez, Vinthe and Mainzer.

"How're they doing?" I asked.

"Not much better, I'm afraid." Trowson turned away with a sigh from peering over my shoulder. "At least, I deduce that from the unhappy way Mainzer bubbles into his soup spoon at lunch. Conversation between subsections originating in different offices on the departmental level is officially discouraged, you know. But I remember Mainzer from the university cafeteria. He bubbled into his soup the very same way when he was stuck on his solar refraction engine."

"Think Andy and Dandy are afraid we're too young to play with matches? Or maybe ape-like creatures are too unpleasant-looking to be allowed to circulate in their refined and esthetic civilization?"

"I don't *know,* Dick." The prof ambled back to his desk and leafed irritably through his sociological notes. "If anything like that is true, why would they give us free run of their ship? Why would they reply so gravely and courteously to every question? If only their answers weren't so vague in our terms! But they are such complex and artistically minded creatures, so chockful of poetic sentiment and good manners that it's impossible to make mathematical or even verbal sense out of their vast and circumlocutory explanations. Sometimes, when I think of their highly polished manners and their seeming lack of interest in the structure of their society, when I put that together with their spaceship which looks like one of those tiny jade carvings that took a lifetime to accomplish . . ."

He trailed off and began riffling the pages like a Mississippi steamboat gambler going over somebody else's deck of cards.

"Isn't it possible we just don't have enough stuff as yet to understand them?"

"Yes. In fact, that's what we always come back to. Warbury points to the tremendous development in our language since the advent of technical vocabularies. He says that this process, just beginning with us, already affects our conceptual approach as well as our words. And, naturally, in a race so much further along— But if we could only find a science of theirs which bears a faint resemblance to one of ours!"

I felt sorry for him, standing there blinking futilely out of gentle, academic eyes.

"Cheer up, prof. Maybe by the time old Suckfoot and his pal come back from the Grand Tour, you'll have unsnarled a sophistry and we'll be off this 'Me, friend; you come from across sea in great bird with many wings' basis that we seemed to have wandered into."

And there you are, Alvarez: a cheap, advertising small brain like me, and I was that close. I should have said something then. Bet you wouldn't have nodded at me heavily and said, "I hope so, Dick. I desperately hope so." But, come to think of it, not only Trowson was trotting up that path. So was Warbury. So were Lopez, Vinthe and Mainzer. So was I, among others.

I had a chance to relax when Andy and Dandy went abroad. My job wasn't exactly over, but the Public Relations end was meshing right along, with me needed only once in a while to give a supervisory spin. Chiefly, I maintained close contact with my opposite number in various other sovereign states, giving out with experienced advice on how to sell the Boys from Betelgeuse. They had to adjust it to their own mass phobias and popular myths; but they were a little happier about it than I had been, without any clear idea of what public behavior to expect of our visitors.

Remember, when *I'd* started, I hadn't even been sure those snails were housebroken.

I followed them in the newspapers. I pasted the pictures of the Mikado receiving them next to their nice comments on the Taj Mahal. They weren't nearly so nice to the Akhund of Swat; but, then, when you think of what the Akhund said about them—

They tended to do that everywhere, giving just a little better than they got. For example, when they were presented with those newly created decorations in Red Square (Dandy got The Order of Extraterrestrial Friends of Soviet Labor, while, for some abstruse reason, The Order of Heroic Interstellar Champion of the Soviet People was conferred upon Andy) they came out with a long, ringing speech about the scientific validity of communist government. It made for cheering, flower-tossing crowds in the Ukraine and Poland, but a certain amount of restiveness in these United States.

But before I had to run my staff into overtime hours, whipping up press releases which recapitulated the aliens' statement before the joint houses of Congress and their lovely, sentimental comments at Valley Forge, the aliens were in Berne, telling the Swiss that only free enterprise could have produced the yodel, the Incabloc escapement in watches, and such a superb example of liberty; hadn't they had democracy long enough to have had it first, and wasn't it wonderful?

By the time they reached Paris, I had the national affection pretty much under control again, although here and there a tabloid still muttered peevishly in its late city final. But, as always, Andy and Dandy put the clincher on. Even then I wondered whether they really liked DeRoges' latest abstraction for itself alone.

But they bought the twisted sculpture, paying for it, since they had no cash of their own, with a thumb-sized gadget which actually melted marble to any degree of pattern-delicacy the artist desired, merely by being touched to the appropriate surface. DeRoges threw away his chisels blissfully, but six of the finest minds in France retired to intensive nervous breakdowns after a week of trying to solve the tool's working principles.

It went over big here:

ANDY AND DANDY PAY
AS THEY GO

Betelgeuse Business Men
Show Appreciation for
Value Received

This newspaper notes with pleasure the sound shopper's ethics behind the latest transaction of our distinguished guests from the elemental void. Understanding the inexorable law of supply and demand, these representatives of an advanced economic system refuse to succumb to the "gimmies." If certain other members of the human race were to examine carefully the true implications of . . .

So when they returned to the United States after being presented at the British Court, they got juicy spreads in all the newspapers, a tug-whistle reception in New York harbor and the mayor's very chiefest deputy there on City Hall steps to receive them.

And even though people were more or less accustomed to them now, they were somehow never shoved off page one. There was the time a certain furniture polish got a testimonial out of them in which the aliens announced that they'd had particularly happy and glossy results on their tiny shell toppers with the goo; and they used the large financial rewards of the testimonial to buy ten extremely rare orchids and have them sunk in plastic. And there was the time—

I missed the television show on which it broke. I had gone to a sidestreet movie theater that night to see a revival of one of my favorite Chaplin pictures; and I'd never enjoyed the ostentatious greet-the-great hysterics of *Celebrity Salon* anyway. I hadn't any idea of how long the M.C., Bill Bancroft, had waited to get Andy and Dandy on his program, and how much he was determined to make it count when the big night arrived.

Reconstructed and stripped of meaningless effusion, it went something like this:

Bancroft asked them if they weren't anxious to get home to the wife and kiddies. Andy explained patiently, for perhaps the thirty-fourth time, that, since they were hermaphrodites, they had no family in any humanly acceptable sense. Bancroft cut into the explanation to ask them what ties they *did* have. Chiefly the revitalizer, says Andy politely.

Revitalizer? What's a revitalizer? Oh, a machine they have to expose themselves to every decade or so, says Dandy. There's at least one revitalizer in every large city on their home planet.

Bancroft makes a bad pun, waits for the uproarious

audience to regain control, then asks: And this revitalizer—just what does it do? Andy goes into a long-winded explanation, the gist of which is that the revitalizers stir up cytoplasm in all animal cells and refresh them.

I see, cracks Bancroft; the pause every decade that refreshes. And then, after being refreshed, you have what as a result? "Oh," muses Dandy, "you might say we have no fear of cancer or any degenerative disease. Besides that, by exposing ourselves to revitalizers at regular intervals throughout our lifetime and refreshing our body cells, we quintuple our life expectancy. We live five times longer than we should. That's about what the revitalizer does, you might say," says Dandy. Andy, after thinking a bit, agrees. "That's about it."

Pandemonium, and not mild. Newspaper extras in all languages, including the Scandinavian. Lights burning late at night in the U. N. Headquarters with guards twenty deep around the site.

When President of the Assembly Ranvi asked them why they'd never mentioned revitalizers before, they did the snail equivalent of shrugging and said the Betelgeuse IX equivalent of nobody ever asked them.

President Ranvi cleared his throat, waved all complications aside with his long brown fingers and announced, "That is not important. Not now. We must have revitalizers."

It seemed to take the aliens a while to understand that. When they finally became convinced that we, as a species, were utterly entranced with the prospect of two to four centuries of life instead of fifty or sixty years, they went into a huddle.

But their race didn't make these machines for export, they explained regretfully. Just enough to service their population. And, while they *could* see as how we might like and must obviously deserve to have these gadgets, there were none to ferry back from Betelgeuse.

Ranvi didn't even look around for advice. 'What would your people want?" he asked. "What would they like in exchange for manufacturing these machines for us? We will pay almost any price within the power of this entire planet." A rumbling, eager "yes" in several languages rolled across the floor of the Assembly.

Andy and Dandy couldn't think of a thing. Sadhu begged them to try. He personally escorted them to their spaceship, which was now parked in a restricted area in Central Park. "Good night, gentlemen," said President of the Assembly Ranvi. "Try—please try hard to think of an exchange."

They stayed inside their ship for almost six days while the world almost went insane with impatience. When I think of all the fingernails bitten that week by two billion people. . . .

"Imagine!" Trowson whispered to me. He was pacing the floor as if he fully intended to walk all the way to Betelgeuse. "We'd just be children on a quintupled life-scale, Dick. All my achievement and education, all yours, would be just the beginning! A man could learn five professions in such a life—and think what he could accomplish in one!"

I nodded, a little numb. I was thinking of the books I could read, the books I might write, if the bulk of my life stretched ahead of me and the advertising profession were just a passing phase in the beginning of it. Then, again, somehow I'd never married, never had had a family. Not enough free time, I had felt. And now, at forty, I was so set in my ways. But a man can undo a lot in a century—

In six days the aliens came out. With a statement of price.

They believed they could persuade their people to manufacture a supply of revitalizers for us if . . . An IF writ very large indeed.

Their planet was woefully short of radioactive minerals,

they explained apologetically. Barren worlds containing radium, uranium and thorium had been discovered and claimed by other races, but the folk of Betelgeuse IX were forbidden by their ethics to wage aggressive war for territorial purposes. We had plenty of radioactive ore, which we used chiefly for war and biological research. The former was patently undesirable and the latter would be rendered largely unnecessary by the revitalizers.

So, in exchange, they wanted our radioactive elements. All of them, they stated humbly.

All right, we were a little surprised, even stunned. But the protests never *started* to materialize. There was an overwhelming chorus of "Sold!" from every quadrant of the globe. A couple of generals here, a few militaristic statesmen there managed to raise direly pointing forefingers before they were whisked out of position. A nuclear physicist or two howled about the future of sub-atomic research, but the peoples of the earth howled louder.

"Research? How much research can you do in a lifetime of three hundred years?"

Overnight, the United Nations became the central office of a planet-wide mining concession. National boundaries were superseded by pitchblende deposits and swords were beaten into pickaxes. Practically anyone with a good, usable arm enlisted in the mining brigades for two or more months out of the year. Camaraderie flew on the winds of the world.

Andy and Dandy politely offered to help. They marked out on detail-contour maps the spots to be excavated: that included areas never suspected of radioactivity. They supplied us with fantastic but clear line drawings of devices for extracting the stuff from the ores in which it assayed poorly, and taught us the exact use of these devices, if not their basic principle.

They hadn't been joking. They wanted it all.

Then, when everything was running smoothly, they

buzzed off for Betelgeuse to handle their part of the bargain.

Those two years were the most exhilarating of my life. And I'd say everyone feels the same, don't they, Alvarez? The knowledge that the world was working together, cheerfully, happily, for life itself. I put *my* year in at The Great Slave Lake and I don't think anyone of my age and weight lifted more pitchblende.

Andy and Dandy came back in two huge ships, manned by weird snail-like robots. The robots did everything, while Andy and Dandy went on being lionized. From the two ships, almost covering the sky, the robots ferried back and forth in strange, spiral aircraft, bringing revitalizers down, carrying refined radioactive elements aloft. No one paid the slightest attention to their methods of instantaneous extraction from large quantities of ore: we were interested in just one throbbing thought—the revitalizers.

They worked. And that, so far as most of us were concerned, was that.

The revitalizers *worked*. Cancer disappeared; heart and kidney disease were instantaneously arrested. Insects which were introduced into the square one-story lab structures lived for a year instead of a few months. And humans—doctors shook their heads in wonder over people who had gone through.

All over the planet, near every major city, the long, patient, slowly moving lines stood outside the revitalizers, which were rapidly becoming something else.

"Temples!" shouted Mainzer. "They look on them as temples. A scientist investigating their operation is treated like a dangerous lunatic trying to break into a nursery. Not that a man can find a clue in those ridiculously small motors. I no longer ask what their power source can be—instead, I ask if they have a power source *at all!*"

"The revitalizers are very precious now, in the beginning," Trowson soothed him. "After a while, the novelty will wear off and you'll be able to investigate at your leisure. Could it be solar power?"

"No!" Mainzer shook his huge head positively. "Not solar power—solar power I am sure I could recognize. As I am sure that the power supply of their ships and whatever runs these—these revitalizers are two entirely separate things. On the ships I have given up. But the revitalizers I believe I could solve. If only they would let me examine them. Fools! So terribly afraid I might damage one, and they would have to travel to another city for their elixir!"

We patted his shoulder, but we weren't really interested. Andy and Dandy left that week, after wishing us well in their own courteous and complex fashion. Whole population groups blew kisses at their mineral-laden ships.

Six months after they left, the revitalizers stopped.

"Am I certain?" Trowson nodded at my dismayed face. "One set of statistics proves it: look at your death rate. It's back to pre-Betelgeuse normal. Or ask any doctor. Any doctor who can forget his U. N. security oath, that is. There'll be really wild riots when the news breaks, Dick."

"But *why?*" I asked him. "Did we do something wrong?"

He started a laugh that ended with his teeth clicking frightenedly together. He rose and walked to the window, staring out into the star-diseased sky. "We did something wrong, all right. We trusted. We made the same mistake all natives have made when they met a superior civilization. Mainzer and Lopez have taken one of the revitalizer engine units apart. There was just a trace of it left, but this time they found the power source. Dick, my boy, the revitalizers were run on the fuel of completely pure radioactive elements!"

I needed a few moments to file that properly. Then I sat down in the easy chair very, very carefully. I made some hoarse, improbable sounds before croaking: "Prof, do you mean they wanted that stuff for themselves, for their *own* revitalizers? That everything they did on this planet was carefully planned so that they could con us with a maximum of friendliness all around? It doesn't seem—it just can't—why, with their superior science, they could have conquered us if they'd cared to. They could have—"

"No, they couldn't have," Trowson whipped out. He turned to face me and crossed his arms upon his chest. "They're a decadent, dying race; they wouldn't have attempted to conquer us. Not because of their ethics—this huge, horrible swindle serves to illustrate *that* aspect of them—but because they haven't the energy, the concentration, the interest. Andy and Dandy are probably representative of the few remaining who have barely enough git-up-and-go to *trick* backward peoples out of the all-important, life-sustaining revitalizer fuel."

The implications were just beginning to soak in my brain. Me, the guy who did the most complete and colossal public relations job of all time—I could just see what my relations with the public would be like if I was ever connected with this shambles.

"And without atomic power, prof, we won't have space travel!"

He gestured bitterly. "Oh, we've been taken, Dick; the whole human race has been had. I know what you're going through, but think of me! I'm the failure, the man responsible. I'm supposed to be a sociologist! How could I have missed? *How?* It was all there: the lack of interest in their own culture, the overintellectualization of esthetics, the involved methods of thought and expression, the exaggerated etiquette, even the very first thing of theirs we saw—their ship—was too heavily stylized and intricately designed for a young, thrusting civilization.

"They *had* to be decadent; every sign pointed to that conclusion. And, of course, the fact that they resort to the methods of fueling their revitalizers that we've experienced—when if we had their science, what might we not do, what substitutes might we not develop! No wonder they couldn't explain their science to us; I doubt if they understand it fully themselves. They are the profligate, inadequate and sneak-thief heirs of what was once a soaring race!"

I was following my own unhappy images. "And we're still hicks. Hicks who've been sold the equivalent of the Brookyln Bridge by some dressed-up sharpies from Betelgeuse."

Trowson nodded. "Or a bunch of poor natives who have sold their island home to a group of European explorers for a handful of brightly colored glass beads."

But of course we were both wrong, Alvarez. Neither Trowson nor I had figured on Mainzer or Lopez or the others. Like Mainzer said, a few years earlier and we would have been licked. But Man had entered the atomic age sometime before 1945 and people like Mainzer and Vinthe had done nuclear research back in the days when radioactive elements abounded on Earth. We had data and we had such tools as the cyclotron, the betatron. And, if our present company will pardon the expression, Alvarez, we are a young and vigorous race.

All we had to do was the necessary research.

The research was done. With a truly effective world government, with a population not only interested in the problem, but recently experienced in working together—and with the grim incentive we had, Alvarez—the problem, as you know, was solved.

We developed artificial radioactives and refueled the revitalizers. We developed atomic fuels out of the artificial radioactives and we got space travel. We did it comparatively fast, and we weren't interested in a ship that just went to the Moon or Mars. We wanted a star ship. And we wanted it so bad, so fast, that we have it now, too.

Here we are. Explain the situation to them, Alvarez, just the way I told it to you, but with all the knee-bending and double-talk that a transplanted Brazilian with twelve years Oriental trading experience can put into it. You're the man to do it—I can't talk like that. It's the only language those decadent slugs understand, so it's the only way we can talk to them. So talk to them, these slimy snails, these oysters on the quarter shell, these smart-alecky slugs. Don't forget to mention to them that the supply of radioactives they got from us won't last forever. Get that down in fine detail.

Then stress the fact that we've got artificial radioactives, and that they've got some things we know we want and lots of other things we mean to find out about.

Tell them, Alvarez, that we've come to collect tolls on that Brooklyn Bridge they sold us.

"WILL YOU WALK A LITTLE FASTER"

ALL RIGHT. So maybe I should be ashamed of myself.

But I'm a writer and this is too good a story to let go. My imagination is tired, and I'm completely out of usable plots; I'm down to the gristle of truth. I'll use it.

Besides, someone's bound to blab sooner or later—as Forkbeard pointed out, we're that kind of animal—and I might as well get some private good out of the deal.

Why, for all I know, there is a cow on the White House lawn this very moment. . . .

Last August, to be exact, I was perspiring over an ice-cold yarn that I never should have started in the first place, when the door bell rang.

I looked up and yelled, "Come in! Door's open!"

The hinges squeaked a little the way they do in my place. I heard feet slap-slapping up the long corridor which makes the rent on my apartment a little lower than most of the others in the building. I couldn't recognize the walk as belonging to anyone I knew, so I waited with my fingers on the typewriter keys and my face turned to the study entrance.

After a while, the feet came around the corner. A little man, not much more than two feet high, dressed in a green knee-length tunic, walked in. He had a very large head, a short pointed red beard, a long pointed green cap, and he was talking to himself. In his right hand, he carried a golden pencil-like object; in his left, a curling strip of what seemed to be parchment.

"Now, you," he said with a guttural accent, pointing both the beard and the pencil-like object at me, "now you must be a writer."

I closed my mouth carefully around a lump of air. Somehow, I noted with interest, I seemed to be nodding.

"Good." He flourished the pencil and made a mark at the end of a line halfway down the scroll. "That completes the enrollment for this session. Come with me, please."

He seized the arm with which I had begun an elaborate gesture. Holding me in a grip that had all the resiliency of a steel manacle, he smiled benevolently and walked back down my entrance hall. Every few steps he walked straight up in the air, and then—as if he'd noticed his error—calmly strode down to the floor again.

"What—who—" I said, stumbling and tripping and occasionally getting walloped by the wall, "you wait, you—who—*who*—"

"Please do not make such repetitious noises," he admonished me. "You are supposed to be a creature of civilization. Ask intelligent questions if you wish, but only when you have them properly organized."

I brooded on that while he closed the door of my apartment behind him and began dragging me up the stairs. His heart may or may not have been pure, but I estimated his strength as being roughly equivalent to that of ten. I felt like a flag being flapped from the end of my own arm.

"We're going up?" I commented tentatively as I swung around a landing.

"Naturally. To the roof. Where we're parked."

"Parked, you said?" I thought of a helicopter, then of a broomstick. Who was it that rode around on the back of an eagle?

Mrs. Flugelman, who lived on the floor above, had

come out of her apartment with a canful of garbage. She opened the door of the dumbwaiter and started to nod good-morning at me. She stopped when she saw my friend.

"Yes, parked. What you call our flying saucer." He noticed Mrs. Flugelman staring at him and jutted his beard at her as we went by. "Yes, I said flying saucer!" he spat.

Mrs. Flugelman walked back into her apartment with the canful of garbage and closed the door behind her very quietly.

Maybe the stuff I write for a living prepared me for such experiences, but—somehow—as soon as he told me that, I felt better. Little men and flying saucers, they seemed to go together. Just so halos and pitchforks didn't wander into the continuity.

When we reached the roof, I wished I'd had time to grab a jacket. It was evidently going to be a breezy ride.

The saucer was about thirty feet in diameter and, colorful magazine articles to the contrary, had been used for more than mere sightseeing. In the center, where it was deepest, there was a huge pile of boxes and packages lashed down with criss-crossing masses of gleaming thread. Here and there, in the pile, was the unpackaged metal of completely unfamiliar machinery.

Still using my arm as a kind of convenient handle to the rest of me, the little man whirled me about experimentally once or twice, then scaled me accurately end over end some twenty feet through the air to the top of the pile. A moment before I hit, golden threads boiled about me, cushioning like a elastic net, and tying me up more thoroughly than any three shipping clerks. My shot-putting pal grunted enthusiastically and prepared to climb aboard.

Suddenly he stopped and looked back along the roof. "Irngl!" he yelled in a voice like two ocean liners arguing. "Irngl! Bordge modgunk!"

There was a tattoo of feet on the roof so rapid as to be almost one sound, and a ten-inch replica of my strong-arm guide—minus the beard, however—leaped over the railing and into the craft. Young Irngl, I decided, bordge modgunking.

His father (?) stared at him very suspiciously, then walked back slowly in the direction from which he had run. He halted and shook a ferocious finger at the youngster. Beside me, Irngl cowered.

Just behind the chimney were a cluster of television antennae. But the dipoles of these antennae were no longer parallel. Some had been carefully braided together; others had been tied into delicate and perfect bows. Growling ferociously, shaking his head so that the pointed red beard made like a metronome, the old man untied the knots and smoothed the dipoles out to careful straightness with his fingers. Then, he bent his legs slightly at their knobby knees and performed one of the more spectacular standing broad jumps of all time.

And, as he hit the floor of the giant saucer, we took off. Straight up.

When I'd recovered sufficiently to regurgitate my larynx, I noticed that old redbeard was controlling the movement of the disc beneath us by means of an egg-shaped piece of metal in his right hand. After we'd gone up a goodly distance, he pointed the egg south and we headed that way.

Radiant power, I wondered? No information—not much that was useful—had been volunteered. *Of course,* I realized suddenly: I hadn't asked any questions! Grabbed from my typewriter in the middle of the morning by a midget of great brain and greater muscle—I couldn't be blamed, though: few men in my position would have been able to put their finger on the nub of the problem and make appropriate inquiries. *Now,* however—

"While there's a lull in the action," I began breezily

enough, "and as long as you speak English, I'd like to clear up a few troublesome matters. For example—"

"Your questions will be answered later. Meanwhile, you will shut up." Golden threads filled my mouth with the taste of antiseptics, and I found myself unable to part my jaws. Redbeard stared at me as I grunted impotently. "How hateful are humans!" he said, beaming. "And how fortunate that they are hateful!"

The rest of the trip was uneventful, except for a few moments when the Miami-bound plane came abreast of us. People inside pointed excitedly, seemed to yell, and one extremely fat man held up an expensive camera and took six pictures very rapidly. Unfortunately, I noticed, he had neglected to remove the lens cap.

The saucer skipper shook his metal egg, there was a momentary feeling of acceleration—and the airplane was a disappearing dot behind us. Irngl climbed to the top of what looked like a giant malted milk machine and stuck his tongue out at me. I glared back.

It struck me then that the little one's mischievous quality was mighty reminiscent of an elf. And his pop—the parentage seemed unmistakable by then—was like nothing else than a gnome of Germanic folklore. Therefore, didn't these facts mean that—that—that—I let my brain have ten full minutes, before giving up. Oh, well, sometimes that method works. Reasoning by self-hypnotic momentum, I call it.

I was cold, but otherwise quite content with my situation and looking forward to the next development with interest and even pride. I had been selected, alone of my species, by this race of aliens for some significant purpose. I couldn't help hoping, of course, that purpose was not vivisection.

It wasn't.

We arrived, after a while, at something so huge that it could only be called a flying dinner plate. I suspected that a good distance down, under all those belly-soft clouds, was the State of South Carolina. I also suspected that the clouds were artificial. Our entire outfit entered through a hole in the bottom. The flying dinner plate was covered with another immense plate, upside-down, the whole making a hollow disc close to a quarter of a mile in diameter. Flying saucers stacked with goods and people—both long and short folk—were scattered up and down its expanse between great masses of glittering machinery.

Evidently I was wrong about having been selected as a representative sample. There were lots of us, men and women, all over the place—one to a flying saucer. It was to be a formal meeting between the representatives of two great races, I decided. Only why didn't our friends do it right—down at the U.N.? Possibly not so formal after all. Then I remembered Redbeard's comment on humanity and I began worrying.

On my right, an army colonel, with a face like a keg of butter, was chewing on the pencil with which he had been taking notes. On my left, a tall man in a gray sharkskin suit flipped back his sleeve, looked at his watch and expelled his breath noisily, impatiently. Up ahead, two women were leaning toward each other at the touching edges of their respective saucers, both talking at the same time and both nodding vehemently as they talked.

Each of the flying saucers also had at least one equivalent of my redbearded pilot. I observed that while the females of this people had beards too, they were exactly one-half as motherly as our women. But they balanced, they balanced. . . .

Abruptly, the image of a little man appeared on the ceiling. His beard was pink and it forked. He pulled on each fork and smiled down at us.

"To correct the impression in the minds of many of you," he said, chuckling benignly, "I will paraphrase your great poet, Shakespeare. I am here to bury humanity, not to praise it."

A startled murmur broke out all around me. *"Mars,"* I heard the colonel say, "bet they're from Mars. H. G. Wells predicted it. Dirty little, red little Martians. Well, just let them try!"

"Red," the man in the gray sharkskin suit repeated, *"red?"*

"Did you ever—" one of the women started to ask. "Is that a way to begin? No manners! A real foreigner."

"However," Forkbeard continued imperturbably from the ceiling, "in order to bury humanity properly, I need your help. Not only yours, but the help of others like you, who, at this moment, are listening to this talk in ships similar to this one and in dozens of languages all over the world. We need your help—and, knowing your peculiar talents so well, we are fairly certain of getting it!"

He waited until the next flurry of fist-waving and assorted imprecations had died down; he waited until the anti-Negroes and the anti-Jews, the anti-Catholics and the anti-Protestants, the Anglophobes and the Russophobes, the vegetarians and the fundamentalists, in the audience had all identified him colorfully with their peculiar concepts of the Opposition and had excoriated him soundly.

Then, once relative quiet had been achieved, we got the following blunt tale, rather contemptuously told, with mighty few explanatory flourishes:

There was an enormous and complex galactic civilization surrounding our meager nine-planet system. This civilization, composed of the various intelligent species throughout the galaxy, was organized into a peaceful federation for trade and mutual advancement.

A special bureau in the federation discharged the biological duty of more advanced races to new arrivals on the cerebral scene. Thus, quite a few millennia ago, the bureau had visited Earth to investigate tourist accounts of a remarkably ingenious animal that had lately been noticed wandering about. The animal having been certified as intelligent with a high cultural potential, Earth was closed to tourist traffic and sociological specialists began the customary close examination.

"And, as a result of this examination," the forked pink beard smiled gently down from above, "the specialists discovered that what you call the human race was nonviable. That is, while the individuals composing it had strongly developed instincts of self-preservation, the species as a whole was suicidal."

"Suicidal!" I found myself breathing up with rest.

"Quite. This is a matter on which there can be little argument from the more honest among you. High civilization is a product of communal living and Man, in groups, has always tended to wipe himself out. In fact, a large factor in the development of what little civilization you do experience has been the rewards contingent upon the development of mass-destruction weapons."

"We have had peaceful, brotherly periods," a hoarse voice said on the opposite side of the ship.

The large head shook slowly from side to side. The eyes, I saw suddenly and irrelevantly, were all black iris. "You have not. You *have* occasionally developed an island of culture here, an oasis of cooperation there; but these have inevitably disintegrated upon contact with the true standard-bearers of your species—the warrior-races. And when, as happened occasionally, the warrior-races were defeated, the conquerors in their turn became warriors, so that the suicidal strain was ever rewarded and became more dominant. Your past is your complete indictment, and your present—your present is about to become your executed sentence. But enough of this peculiar bloody nonsense—let me return to *living* history."

He went on to explain that the Federation felt a suicidal species should be allowed to fulfill its destiny unhampered. In fact, so long as overt acts were avoided, it was quite permissible to help such a creature along to the doom it desired—"Nature abhors self-destruction even more than a vacuum. The logic is simple: both cease almost as soon as they come into existence."

The sociologists having extrapolated the probable date on which humanity might be expected to extinguish itself, the planet was assigned—as soon as it should be vacated—to the inhabitants of an Earth-like world for the use of such surplus population as they might then have. These were the redbeards.

"We sent representatives here to serve as caretakers, so to speak, of our future property. But about nine hundred years ago, when your world still had six thousand years to run, we decided to hurry the process a bit as we experienced a rising index of population on our own planet. We therefore received full permission from the Galactic Federation to stimulate your technological development into an earlier suicide. The Federation stipulated, however, that each advance be made the moral responsibility of an adequate representative of your race, that he be told the complete truth of the situation. This we did: we would select an individual to be the discoverer of a revolutionary technique or scientific principle; then we would explain both the value of the technique and the consequences to his species in terms of accelerated mass destruction."

I found it hard to continue looking into his enormous eyes. "In every case"—the booming rattle of the voice had softened perceptibly—"in every case, sooner or later, the individual announced the discovery as his own, giving it to his fellows and profiting substantially. In a few cases, he later endowed great foundations which awarded prizes to those who advanced the cause of peace or the brotherhood of man. This resulted in little beyond an increase in the amount of currency being circulated. Individuals, we found, always chose to profit at the expense of their race's life-expectancy."

Gnomes, elves, kobolds! Not mischievous sprites—I glanced at Irngl sitting quietly under his father's heavy hand—nor the hoarders of gold, but helping man for their own reasons: teaching him to smelt metals and build machinery, showing him how to derive the binomial theorem in one part of the world and how to plow a field more efficiently in another.

To the end that people might perish from the Earth . . . sooner.

"Unfortunately—ah, something has developed."

We looked up at that, all of us—housewives and handymen, preachers and professional entertainers—looked up from the tangle of our reflections and prejudices, and *hoped*.

As D-day drew nigh, those among the kobolds who intended to emigrate filled their flying saucers with possessions and families. They scooted across space in larger craft such as the one we were now in and took up positions in the stratosphere, waiting to assume title to the planet as soon as its present occupants used their latest discovery—nuclear fission—as they had previously used ballistics and aeronautics.

The more impatient wandered down to survey homesites. They found to their annoyance that an unpleasant maggot of error had crawled into the pure mathematics of extrapolated sociology. Humanity should have wiped itself out shortly after acquiring atomic power. But—possibly as a result of the scientific stimulation we had been receiving recently—our technological momentum had carried us past uranium-plutonium fission up to the so-called hydrogen bomb.

Whereas a uranium-bomb Armageddon would have disposed of us in a most satisfactory and sanitary fashion, the explosion of several hydrogen bombs, it would seem, will result in the complete sterilization of our planet as the result of a subsidiary reaction at present unknown to us. If we go to war with this atomic refinement, Earth will not only be cleansed oı all present life-forms, but it will also become uninhabitable for several millions of years in the future.

Naturally, the kobolds view this situation with a certain amount of understandable unhappiness. According to Galactic Law, they may not actively intervene to safeguard their legacy. Therefore, they would like to offer a proposition—

Any nation which guarantees to stop making hydrogen bombs and to dispose of those it has already made—and the little redbeards have, they claim, satisfactory methods of enforcing these guarantees—such a nation will be furnished by them with a magnificently murderous weapon. This weapon is extremely simple to operate and is so calibrated that it can be set to kill instantaneously and painlessly any number of people at one time up to a full million.

"The advantage to any terrestrial military establishment of such a weapon over the unstable hydrogen bomb, which is not only hard to handle but must be transported physically to its target," the genial face on the ceiling commented, "should be obvious to all of you! And, as far as we are concerned, anything which will dispose of human beings on a wholesale basis while not injuring—"

At this point, there was so much noise that I couldn't hear a word he was saying. For that matter, I was yelling quite loudly myself.

"—while not injuring useful and compatible life-forms —"

"Ah-h," screamed a deeply tanned stout man in a flowerful red sports shirt and trunks, "whyn't you go back where you came from?"

"Yeah!" someone else added wrathfully. "Can't yuh see yuh not wanted? Shut up, huh? Shut *up!*"

"Murderers," one of the women in front of me quavered. "That's all you are—murderers trying to kill inoffensive people who've never done you any harm. Killing would be just too good for you."

The colonel was standing on his toes and oscillating a portentous forefinger at the roof. "We were doing all right," he began apoplectically, then stopped to allow himself to unpurple, "We were doing *well* enough, I can tell you, without—without—"

Forkbeard waited until we began to run down.

"Look at it this way," he urged in a wheedling voice: "You're going to wipe yourselves out—you know it, we know it and so does everybody else in the galaxy. What difference can it possibly make to you whether you do it one way or another? At least by our method you confine the injury to yourselves. You don't damage the highly valuable real estate—to wit, Earth—which will be ours after you've ceased to use it. And you go out with a weapon which is much more worthy of your destructive propensities than any you have used hitherto, including atomic bombs."

He paused and spread knobbed hands down at our impotent hatred. "Think of it—*just think of it:* a million deaths at one plunge of a lever! What other weapon can make that claim?"

Skimming back northwards with Redbeard and Irngl, I pointed to the flying saucers radiating away from us through the delicate summer sky. "These people are all fairly responsible citizens. Isn't it silly to expect them to advertise a more effective way of having their throats cut?"

There was a shrug of the green-wrapped shoulders. "With any other species, yes. But not you. The Galactic

Federation insists that the actual revelation of the weapon, either to your public or your government, must be made by a fairly intelligent representative of your own species, in full possession of the facts, and after he or she has had an adequate period to reflect on the consequences of disclosure."

"And you think we will? In spite of everything?"

"Oh, yes," the little man told me with tranquil assurance. *"Because* of everything. For example, you have each been selected with a view to the personal advantage you would derive from the revelation. Sooner or later, one of you will find the advantage so necessary and tempting that the inhibiting scruple will disappear; eventually, all of you would come to it. As Shulmr pointed out, each member of a suicidal race contributes to the destruction of the whole even while attentively safeguarding his own existence. Disagreeable creatures, but fortunately short-lived!"

"One million," I mused. "So arbitrary. I bet we make—"

"Quite correct. You are an ingenious race. Now if you wouldn't mind stepping back onto your roof? We're in a bit of a hurry, Irngl and I, and we have to disinfect after— Thank you."

I watched them disappear upwards into a cloud bank. Then, noticing a television dipole tied in a hangman's noose which Irngl's father had overlooked, I trudged downstairs.

For a while, I was very angry. Then I was glum. Then I was angry again. I've thought about it a lot since August.

I've read some recent stuff on flying saucers, but not a word about the super-weapon we'll get if we dismantle our hydrogen bombs. But, if someone had blabbed, how would I know about it?

That's just the point. Here I am a writer, a science-fiction writer no less, with a highly salable story that I'm not supposed to use. Well, it happens that I need money badly right now; and it further happens that I am plumb out of plots. How long am I supposed to go on being a sucker?

Somebody's probably told by now. If not in this country, in one of the others. And I *am* a writer, and I have a living to make. And this is fiction, and who asked you to believe it anyhow?

Only— Only I did intend to leave out the signal. The signal, that is, by which a government can get in touch with the kobolds, can let them know it's interested in making the trade, in getting that weapon. I did intend to leave out the signal.

But I don't have a satisfactory ending to this story. It needs some sort of tag-line. And the signal makes a perfect one. Well—it seems to me that if I've told *this* much—and probably anyhow—

The signal's the immemorial one between man and kobold: Leave a bowl of milk outside the White House door.

IT ENDS WITH A FLICKER

IT WAS a good job and Max Alben knew whom he had to thank for it—his great-grandfather.

"Good old Giovanni Albeni," he muttered as he hurried into the laboratory slightly ahead of the escorting technicians, all of them, despite the excitement of the moment, remembering to bob their heads deferentially at the half-dozen full-fleshed and hard-faced men lolling on the couches that had been set up around the time machine.

He shrugged rapidly out of his rags, as he had been instructed in the anteroom, and stepped into the housing of the enormous mechanism. This was the first time he had seen it, since he had been taught how to operate it on a dummy model, and now he stared at the great transparent coils and the susurrating energy bubble with much respect.

This machine, the pride and the hope of 2089, was something almost outside his powers of comprehension. But Max Alben knew how to run it, and he knew, roughly, what it was supposed to accomplish. He knew also that this was the first backward journey of any great duration and, being scientifically unpredictable, might well be the death of him.

"Good old Giovanni Albeni," he muttered again affectionately.

If his great-grandfather had not volunteered for the earliest time-travel experiments way back in the nineteen-seventies, back even before the Blight, it would never have been discovered that he and his seed possessed a great deal of immunity to extra-temporal blackout.

And if that had not been discovered, the ruling powers ot Earth, more than a century later, would never have plucked Max Alben out of an obscure civil-service job as a relief guard at the North American Chicken Reservation to his present heroic and remunerative eminence. He would still be patrolling the barbed wire that surrounded the three white leghorn hens and two roosters—about one-sixth of the known livestock wealth of the Western Hemisphere—thoroughly content with the half-pail of dried apricots he received each and every payday.

No, if his great-grandfather had not demonstrated long ago his unique capacity for remaining conscious during time travel, Max Alben would not now be shifting from foot to foot in a physics laboratory, facing the black market kings of the world and awaiting their final instructions with an uncertain and submissive grin.

Men like O'Hara, who controlled mushrooms, Levney, the blackberry tycoon, Sorgasso, the packaged-worm monopolist—would black marketeers of their tremendous stature so much as waste a glance on someone like Alben ordinarily, let alone confer a lifetime pension on his wife and five children of a full spoonful each of non-synthetic sugar a day?

Even if he didn't come back, his family was provided for like almost no other family on Earth. This was a damn good job and he was lucky.

Alben noticed that Abd Sadha had risen from the straight chair at the far side of the room and was approaching him with a sealed metal cylinder in one hand.

"We've decided to add a further precaution at the last moment," the old man said. "That is, the scientists have suggested it and I have—er—I have given my approval."

The last remark was added with a slight questioning

note as the Secretary-General of the United Nations looked about rapidly at the black market princes on the couches behind him. Since they stared back stonily, but offered no objection, he coughed in relief and returned to Alben.

"I am sure, young man, that I don't have to go into the details of your instructions once more. You enter the time machine and go back the duration for which it has been preset, a hundred and thirteen years, to the moment after the Guided Missile of 1976 was launched. It *is* 1976, isn't it?" he asked, suddenly uncertain.

"Yes, sir," one of the technicians standing by the time machine said respectfully. "The experiment with an atomic warhead guided missile that resulted in the Blight was conducted on this site on April 18, 1976." He glanced proudly at the unemotional men on the couches, very much like a small boy after completing a recitation before visiting dignitaries from the Board of Education.

"Just so." Abd Sadha nodded. "April 18, 1976. And on this site. You see, young man, you will materialize at the very moment and on the very spot where the remote-control station handling the missile was—er—handling the missile. You will be in a superb position, a superb position, to deflect the missile in its downward course and alter human history for the better. Yes."

He paused, having evidently stumbled out of his thought sequence.

"And he pulls the red switch toward him," Gomez, the dandelion-root magnate, reminded him sharply, impatiently.

"Ah, yes, the red switch. He pulls the little red switch toward him. Thank you, Mr. Gomez, thank you very much, sir. He pulls the little red switch on the green instrument panel toward him, thus preventing the error that caused the missile to explode in the Brazilian jungle and causing it, instead, to explode somewhere in the mid-Pacific, as originally planned."

The Secretary-General of the United Nations beamed. "Thus preventing the Blight, making it nonexistent, as it were, producing a present-day world in which the Blight never occurred. That is correct, is it not, gentlemen?" he asked, turning anxiously again.

None of the half-dozen men on couches deigned to answer him. And Alben kept his eyes deferentially in their direction, too, as he had throughout this period of last-minute instruction.

He knew who ruled his world—these stolid, well-fed men in clean garments with a minimum of patches, and where patches occurred, at least they were the color of the surrounding cloth.

Sadha might be Secretary-General of the United Nations, but that was still a civil-service job, only a few social notches higher than a chicken guard. His clothes were fully as ragged, fully as multi-colored, as those that Alben had stepped out of. And the gnawing in his stomach was no doubt almost as great.

"You understand, do you not, young man, that if anything goes wrong," Abd Sadha asked, his head nodding tremulously and anticipating the answer, "if anything unexpected, unprepared for occurs, you are not to continue with the experiment but return immediately?"

"He understands everything he has to understand," Gomez told him. "Let's get this thing moving."

The old man smiled again. "Yes. Of course, Mr. Gomez." He came up to where Alben stood in the entrance of the time machine and handed the sealed metal cylinder to him. "This is the precaution the scientists have just added. When you arrive at your destination, just before materializing, you will release it into the surrounding temporal medium. Our purpose here, as you no doubt—"

Levney sat up on his couch and snapped his fingers

peremptorily. "I just heard Gomez tell you to get this thing moving, Sadha. And it isn't moving. We're busy men. We've wasted enough time."

"I was just trying to explain a crucial final fact," the Secretary General apologized. "A fact which may be highly—"

"You've explained enough facts." Levney turned to the man inside the time machine. "Hey, fella. You. *Move!*"

Max Alben gulped and nodded violently. He darted to the rear of the machine and turned the dial which activated it.

flick!

It was a good job and Mac Albin knew whom he had to thank for it—his great-grandfather.

"Good old Giovanni Albeni," he laughed as he looked at the morose faces of his two colleagues. Bob Skeat and Hugo Honek had done as much as he to build the tiny time machine in the secret lab under the helicopter garage, and they were fully as eager to go, but—unfortunately for them—they were not descended from the right ancestor.

Leisurely, he unzipped the richly embroidered garment that, as the father of two children, he was privileged to wear, and wriggled into the housing of the complex little mechanism. This was hardly the first time he had seen it, since he'd been helping to build the device from the moment Honek had nodded and risen from the drafting board, and now he barely wasted a glance on the thumb-size translucent coils growing out of the almost microscopic energy bubbles which powered them.

This machine was the last hope of 2089, even if the world of 2089, as a whole, did not know of its existence and would try to prevent its being put into operation. But it meant a lot more to Mac Albin than merely saving a world. It meant an adventurous mission with the risk of death.

"Good old Giovanni Albeni," he laughed again happily.

If his great-grandfather had not volunteered for the earliest time-travel experiments way back in the nineteen-seventies, back even before the Epidemic, it would never have been discovered that he and his seed possessed a great deal of immunity to extra-temporal blackout.

And if that had not been discovered, the Albins would not have become physicists upon the passage of the United Nations law that everyone on Earth—absolutely without exception—had to choose a branch of research science in which to specialize. In the flabby, careful, life-guarding world the Earth had become, Mac Albin would never have been reluctantly selected by his two co-workers as the one to carry the forbidden banner of dangerous experiment.

No, if his great-grandfather had not demonstrated long ago his unique capacity for remaining conscious during time travel, Mac Albin would probably be a biologist today like almost everyone else on Earth, laboriously working out dreary gene problems instead of embarking on the greatest adventure Man had known to date.

Even if he didn't come back, he had at last found a socially useful escape from genetic responsibility to humanity in general and his own family in particular. This was a damn good job and he was lucky.

"Wait a minute, Mac," Skeat said and crossed to the other side of the narrow laboratory.

Albin and Honek watched him stuff several sheets of paper into a small metal box which he closed without locking.

"You will take care of yourself, won't you, Mac?" Hugo Honek pleaded. "Any time you feel like taking an unnecessary risk, remember that Bob and I will have to stand trial if you don't come back. We might be sentenced to complete loss of professional status and spend the rest of our lives supervising robot factories."

"Oh, it won't be that bad," Albin reassured him absent-mindedly from where he lay contorted inside the time machine. He watched Skeat coming toward him with the box.

Honek shrugged his shoulders. "It might be a lot worse than even that and you know it. The disappearance of a two-time father is going to leave an awful big vacancy in the world. One-timers, like Bob and me, are all over the place; if either of us dropped out of sight, it wouldn't cause nearly as much uproar."

"But Bob and you both tried to operate the machine," Albin reminded him. "And you blacked out after a fifteen-second temporal displacement. So I'm the only chance, the only way to stop the human race from dwindling and dwindling till it hits absolute zero, like the tired old Security Council seems willing for it to do."

"Take it easy, Mac," Bob Skeat said as he handed the metal box to Albin. "The Security Council is just trying to solve the problem in their way, the conservative way: a worldwide concentration on genetics research coupled with the maximum preservation of existing human lives, especially those that have a high reproductive potential. We three disagree with them; we've been skulking down here nights to solve it *our* way, and ours is a radical approach and plenty risky. That's the reason for the metal box—trying to cover one more explosive possibility."

Albin turned it around curiously. "How?"

"I sat up all last night writing the manuscript that's inside it. Look, Mac, when you go back to the Guided Missile Experiment of 1976 and push that red switch away from you, a lot of other things are going to happen than just deflecting the missile so that it will explode in the Brazilian jungle instead of the Pacific Ocean."

"Sure. I know. If it explodes in the jungle, the Epidemic doesn't occur. No Shapiro's Mumps."

Skeat jiggled his pudgy little face impatiently. "That's not what I mean. The Epidemic doesn't occur, but something else does. A new world, a different 2089, an alternate time sequence. It'll be a world in which humanity has a better chance to survive, but it'll be one with problems of its own. Maybe tough problems. Maybe the problems will be tough enough so that they'll get the same idea we did and try to go back to the same point in time to change them."

Albin laughed. "That's just looking for trouble."

"Maybe it is, but that's my job. Hugo's the designer of the time machine and you're the operator, but I'm the theoretical man in this research team. It's my job to look for trouble. So, just in case, I wrote a brief history of the world from the time the missile exploded in the Pacific. It tells why ours is the worst possible of futures. It's in that box."

"What do I do with it—hand it to the guy from the alternate 2089?"

The small fat man exasperatedly hit the side of the time machine with a well-cushioned palm. "You know better. There won't be any alternate 2089 until you push that red switch on the green instrument panel. The moment you do, our world, with all its slow slide to extinction, goes out and its alternate goes on—just like two electric light bulbs on a push-pull circuit. We and every single one of our artifacts, including the time machine, disappear. The problem is how to keep that manuscript from disappearing.

"Well, all you do, if I have this figured right, is shove the metal box containing the manuscript out into the surrounding temporal medium a moment before you materialize to do your job. That temporal medium in which you'll be traveling is something that exists independent of and autonomous to all possible futures. It's my hunch that something that's immersed in it will not be altered by a new time sequence."

"Remind him to be careful, Bob," Honek rumbled. "He

thinks he's Captain Blood and this is his big chance to run away to sea and become a swashbuckling pirate."

Albin grimaced in annoyance. "I *am* excited by doing something besides sitting in a safe little corner working out safe little abstractions for the first time in my life. But I know that this is a first experiment. Honestly, Hugo, I really have enough intelligence to recognize that simple fact. I know that if anything unexpected pops up, anything we didn't foresee, I'm supposed to come scuttling back and ask for advice."

"I hope you do," Bob Skeat sighed. "I hope you do know that. A twentieth century poet once wrote something to the effect that the world will end not with a bang, but a whimper. Well, our world is ending with a whimper. Try to see that it doesn't end with a bang, either."

"That I'll promise you," Albin said a trifle disgustedly. "It'll end with neither a bang *nor* a whimper. So long, Hugo. So long, Bob."

He twisted around, reaching overhead for the lever which activated the forces that drove the time machine.

flick!

It was strange, Max Alben reflected, that this time travel business, which knocked unconscious everyone who tried it, only made him feel slightly dizzy. That was because he was descended from Giovanni Albeni, he had been told. There must be some complicated scientific explanation for it, he decided—and that would make it none of his business. Better forget about it.

All around the time machine, there was a heavy gray murk in which objects were hinted at rather than stated definitely. It reminded him of patrolling his beat at the North American Chicken Reservation in a thick fog.

According to his gauges, he was now in 1976. He cut speed until he hit the last day of April, then cut speed again, drifting slowly backward to the eighteenth, the day of the infamous Guided Missile Experiment. Carefully,

carefully, like a man handling a strange bomb made on a strange planet, he watched the center gauge until the needle came to rest against the thin etched line that indicated the exactly crucial moment. Then he pulled the brake and stopped the machine dead.

All he had to do now was materialize in the right spot, flash out and pull the red switch toward him. Then his well-paid assignment would be done.

But . . .

He stopped and scratched his dirt-matted hair. Wasn't there something he was supposed to do a second before materialization? Yes, that useless old windbag, Sadha, had given him a last instruction.

He picked up the sealed metal cylinder, walked to the entrance of the time machine and tossed it into the gray murk. A solid object floating near the entrance caught his eye. He put his arm out—whew, it was cold!—and pulled it inside.

A small metal box. Funny. What was it doing out there? Curiously, he opened it, hoping to find something valuable. Nothing but a few sheets of paper, Alben noted disappointedly. He began to read them slowly, very slowly, for the manuscript was full of a lot of long and complicated words, like a letter from one bookworm scientist to another.

The problems all began with the Guided Missile Experiment of 1976, he read. There had been a number of such experiments, but it was the one of 1976 that finally did the damage the biologists had been warning about. The missile with its deadly warhead exploded in the Pacific Ocean as planned, the physicists and the military men went home to study their notes, and the world shivered once more over the approaching war and tried to forget about it.

But there was fallout, a radioactive rain several hundred miles to the north, and a small fishing fleet got thoroughly soaked by it. Fortunately, the radioactivity in the rain was sufficiently low to do little obvious physical damage: All it did was cause a mutation in the mumps virus that several of the men in the fleet were incubating at the time, having caught it from the children of the fishing town, among whom a minor epidemic was raging.

The fleet returned to its home town, which promptly came down with the new kind of mumps. Dr. Llewellyn Shapiro, the only physician in town, was the first man to note that, while the symptoms of this disease were substantially milder than those of its unmutated parent, practically no one was immune to it and its effects on human reproductivity were truly terrible. Most people were completely sterilized by it. The rest were rendered much less capable of fathering or bearing offspring.

Shapiro's Mumps spread over the entire planet in the next few decades. It leaped across every quarantine erected; for a long time, it successfully defied all the vaccines and serums attempted against it. Then, when a vaccine was finally perfected, humanity discovered to its dismay that its generative powers had been permanently and fundamentally impaired.

Something had happened to the germ plasm. A large percentage of individuals were born sterile, and, of those who were not, one child was usually the most that could be expected, a two-child parent being quite rare and a three-child parent almost unknown.

Strict eugenic control was instituted by the Security Council of the United Nations so that fertile men and women would not be wasted upon non-fertile mates. Fertility was the most important avenue to social status, and right after it came successful genetic research.

Genetic research had the very best minds prodded into it; the lesser ones went into the other sciences. Everyone on Earth was engaged in some form of scientific research to some extent. Since the population was now so limited in proportion to the great resources available, all physical labor had long been done by robots. The government saw to it that everybody had an ample supply of goods and, in return, asked only that they experiment without any risk to their own lives—every human being was now a much-prized, highly guarded rarity.

There were less than a hundred thousand of them, well below the danger point, it had been estimated, where a species might be wiped out by a new calamity. Not that another calamity would be needed. Since the end of the Epidemic, the birth rate had been moving further and further behind the death rate. In another century . . .

That was why a desperate and secret attempt to alter the past was being made. This kind of world was evidently impossible.

Max Alben finished the manuscript and sighed. What a wonderful world! What a comfortable place to live!

He walked to the rear dials and began the process of materializing at the crucial moment on April 18, 1976.

flick!

It was odd, Mac Albin reflected, that these temporal journeys, which induced coma in everyone who tried it, only made him feel slightly dizzy. That was because he was descended from Giovanni Albeni, he knew. Maybe there was some genetic relationship with his above-average fertility—might be a good idea to mention the idea to a biologist or two when he returned. *If* he returned.

All around the time machine, there was a soupy gray murk in which objects were hinted at rather than stated definitely. It reminded him of the problems of landing a helicopter in a thick fog when the robot butler had not been told to turn on the ground lights.

According to the insulated register, he was now in 1976. He lowered speed until he registered April, then maneuvered slowly backward through time to the eighteenth, the day of the infamous Guided Missile Experiment. Carefully, carefully, like an obstetrician supervising surgical robots at an unusually difficult birth, he watched the register until it rolled to rest against the notch that indicated the exactly crucial moment. Then he pushed a button and froze the machine where it was.

All he had to do now was materialize in the right spot, flash out and push the red switch from him. Then his exciting adventure would be over.

But . . .

He paused and tapped at his sleek chin. He was supposed to do something a second before materialization. Yes, that nervous theoretician, Bob Skeat, had given him a last suggestion.

He picked up the small metal box, twisted around to face the opening of the time machine and dropped it into the gray murk. A solid object floating near the opening attracted his attention. He shot his arm out—it was *cold,* as cold as they had figured—and pulled the object inside.

A sealed metal cylinder. Strange. What was it doing out there? Anxiously, he opened it, not daring to believe he'd find a document inside. Yes, that was exactly what it was, he saw excitedly. He began to read it rapidly, very rapidly, as if it were a newly published paper on neutrinos. Besides, the manuscript was written with almost painful simplicity, like a textbook composed by a stuffy pedagogue for the use of morons.

The problems all began with the Guided Missile Experiment of 1976, he read. There had been a number of such experiments, but it was the one of 1976 that finally did the damage the biologists had been warning about. The missile with its deadly warhead exploded in the Brazilian jungle through some absolutely unforgivable error in the remote-control station: the officer in charge of the station was reprimanded and the men under him court-martialed, and the Brazilian government was paid a handsome compensation for the damage.

But there had been more damage than anyone knew at the time. A plant virus, similar to the tobacco mosaic, had mutated under the impact of radioactivity. Five years later, it burst out of the jungle and completely wiped out every last rice plant on Earth. Japan and a large part of Asia became semi-deserts inhabited by a few struggling nomads.

Then the virus adjusted to wheat and corn—and famine howled in every street of the planet. All attempts by botanists to control the Blight failed because of the swiftness of its onslaught. And after it had fed, it hit again at a new plant and another and another.

Most of the world's non-human mammals had been slaughtered for food long before they could starve to death. Many insects, too, before they became extinct at the loss of their edible plants, served to assuage hunger to some small extent.

But the nutritive potential of Earth was steadily diminishing in a horrifying geometric progression. Recently, it had been observed, plankton—the tiny organism on which most of the sea's ecology was based—had started to disappear, and with its diminution, dead fish had begun to pile up on the beaches.

Mankind had lunged out desperately in all directions in an effort to survive, but nothing had worked for any length of time. Even the other planets of the Solar System, which had been reached and explored at a tremendous cost in remaining resources, had yielded no edible vegetation. Synthetics had failed to fill the prodigious gap.

In the midst of the sharply increasing hunger, social controls had pretty much dissolved. Pathetic attempts at rationing still continued, but black markets became the only markets, and black marketeers the barons of life. Starvation took the hindmost, and only the most agile economically lived in comparative comfort. Law and order were had only by those who could afford to pay for them and children of impoverished families were sold on the open market for a bit of food.

But the Blight was still adjusting to new plants and the food supply kept shrinking. In another century . . .

That was why the planet's powerful individuals had been persuaded to pool their wealth in a desperate attempt to alter the past. This kind of world was manifestly impossible.

Mac Albin finished the document and sighed. What a magnificent world! What an exciting place to live!

He dropped his hand on the side levers and began the process of materializing at the crucial moment on April 18, 1976.

flick!

As the equipment of the remote-control station began to take on a blurred reality all around him, Max Alben felt a bit of fear at what he was doing. The technicians, he remembered, the Secretary-General, even the black market kings, had all warned him not to go ahead with his instructions if anything unusual turned up. That was an awful lot of power to disobey: he knew he should return with this new information and let better minds work on it.

They with their easy lives, what did they know what existence had been like for such as he? Hunger, always hunger, scrabbling, servility, and more hunger. Every time things got really tight, you and your wife looking sideways at your kids and wondering which of them would bring the best price. Buying security for them, as he was now, at the risk of his life.

But in this other world, this other 2089, there was a state that took care of you and that treasured your children. A man like himself, with *five* children—why, he'd be a big man, maybe the biggest man on Earth! And he'd have robots to work for him and lots of food. Above all, lots and lots of food.

He'd even be a scientist—*everyone* was a scientist

there, weren't they?—and he'd have a big laboratory all to himself. This other world had its troubles, but it was a lot nicer place than where he'd come from. He wouldn't return. He'd go through with it.

The fear left him and, for the first time in his life, Max Alben felt the sensation of power.

He materialized the time machine around the green instrument panel, sweating a bit at the sight of the roomful of military figures, despite the technicians' reassurances that all this would be happening too fast to be visible. He saw the single red switch pointing upward on the instrument panel. The switch that controlled the course of the missile. Now! Now to make a halfway decent world!

Max Alben pulled the little red switch toward him.

flick!

As the equipment of the remote-control station began to oscillate into reality all around him, Mac Albin felt a bit of shame at what he was doing. He'd promised Bob and Hugo to drop the experiment at any stage if a new factor showed up. He knew he should go back with this new information and have all three of them kick it around.

But what would they be able to tell him, they with their blissful adjustment to their thoroughly blueprinted lives? They, at least, had been ordered to marry women they could live with; he'd drawn a female with whom he was completely incompatible in any but a genetic sense. Genetics! He was tired of genetics and the sanctity of human life, tired to the tips of his uncalloused fingers, tired to the recesses of his unused muscles. He was tired of having to undertake a simple adventure like a thief in the night.

But in this other world, this other 2089, someone like himself would be a monarch of the black market, a suzerain of chaos, making his own rules, taking his own women. So what if the weaklings, those unfit to carry on the race, went to the wall? His kind wouldn't.

He'd formed a pretty good idea of the kind of men who

ruled that other world, from the document in the sealed metal cylinder. The black marketeers had not even read it. Why, the fools had obviously been duped by the technicians into permitting the experiment; they had not grasped the idea that an alternate time track would mean their own non-existence.

This other world had its troubles, but it was certainly a livelier place than where he'd come from. It deserved a chance. Yes, that was how he felt: his world was drowsily moribund; this alternate was starving but managing to flail away at destiny. It *deserved* a chance.

Albin decided that he was experiencing renunciation and felt proud.

He materialized the time machine around the green instrument panel, disregarding the roomful of military figures since he knew they could not see him. The single red switch pointed downward on the instrument panel. That was the device that controlled the course of the missile. Now! Now to make a halfway interesting world!

Mac Albin pushed the little red switch from him.

flick!

Now! Now to make a halfway decent world!

Max Alben pulled the little red switch toward him.

flick!

Now! Now to make a halfway interesting world!

Mac Albin pushed the little red switch from him.

flick!

. . . pulled the little red switch toward him.

flick!

. . . pushed the little red switch from him.

flick!

. . . toward him.

flick!

. . . from him.

flick!

LISBON CUBED

THE TELEPHONE rang. Alfred Smith, who had been hauling clothes out of his valise and stuffing them into a typical hotel room bureau, looked up startled.

"Now, who—" he began, and shook his head.

Obviously it must be a wrong number. Nobody knew he was in New York, and nobody—this for a certainty—knew he had checked into this particular hotel. Or come to think of it, somebody did.

The room clerk at the desk where he had just registered.

Must be some hotel business. Something about don't use the lamp on the end table: it tends to short-circuit.

The telephone rang again. He dropped the valise and walked around the bed. He picked up the phone.

"Yes?" he said.

"Mr. Smith?" came a thick voice from the other end.

"Speaking."

"This is Mr. Jones. Mr. Cohen and Mr. Kelly are with me in the lobby. So is Jane Doe. Do you want us to come up or shall we wait for you?"

"I beg your pardon?"

"Well, then, we'll come up. 504, isn't it?"

"Yes, but wait a minute! *Who* did you say?" He realized they had hung up.

Alfred Smith put down the telephone and ran his fingers through his crew-cut. He was a moderately tall, moderately athletic, moderately handsome young man with the faintest hint at jowl and belly of recent prosperity.

"Mr. *Jones? Cohen? Kelly?* And for suffering Pete's sake, *Jane Doe?*"

It must be a joke. Any Smith was used to jokes on his name. What was your name before it was Smith? *Alfred* Smith? Whatever happened to good old Johnnie?

Then he remembered that his caller had just asked for Mr. Smith. Smith *was* a common name, like it or not.

He picked up the phone again. "Desk," he told the operator.

"Yes, Desk?" a smooth voice said after a while.

"This is Mr. Smith in Room 504. Was there another Smith registered here before me?"

A long pause. "Are you having any trouble, sir?"

Alfred Smith grimaced. "That's not what I'm asking. Was there or wasn't there?"

"Well, sir, if you could tell me if it is causing you inconvenience in any way. . . ."

He got exasperated. "I asked you a simple question. Was there a Smith in this room before me? What's the matter, did he kill himself?"

"We have no right to believe he committed suicide, sir!" the desk clerk said emphatically. "There are many, *many* circumstances under which a guest might disappear after registering for a room!"

There was a peremptory knock on the door. Alfred Smith grunted, "Okay. That's all I wanted to know," and hung up.

He opened the door, and before he could say anything, four people came in. Three were men; the last was a mildly attractive woman.

"Now, look—" he began.

"Hello, Gar-Pitha," one of the men said. "I'm Jones. This is Cohen, this is Kelly. And, of course, Jane Doe."

"There's been a mistake," Alfred told him.

"And how there's been a mistake!" said Cohen, locking the door behind him carefully. "Jones, you called Smith by his right name! When the corridor door was open! That's unpardonable stupidity."

Jane Doe nodded. "Open or closed, we must remember that we are on Earth. We will use only Earth names. Operating Procedure Regulations XIV-XXII."

Alfred took a long, slow look at her. "On Earth?"

She smiled shamefacedly. "There I go, myself. I did practically the same thing. You're right. In *America.* Or rather, to put it more exactly and less suspiciously, in New York City."

Mr. Kelly had been walking around him, staring at Alfred. "You're perfect," he said at last. "Better than any of us. That disguise took a lot of hard, patient work. Don't tell me, I know. You're perfect, Smith, perfect."

What in the world were they, Alfred wondered frantically—lunatics? No, *spies!* Should he say something, should he give the mistake away, or should he start yelling his head off for help? But maybe they weren't spies—maybe they were detectives on the trail of spies. He was in New York, after all. New York wasn't Grocery Corners, Illinois.

And that suggested another possibility. New York, the home of the sharpie, the smart aleck. It could be a simple practical joke being played by some city slickers on a new little hayseed.

If it were . . .

His visitors had found seats for themselves. Mr. Kelly opened the briefcase he was carrying and grubbed around in it with his fingers. A low hum filled the room.

"Not enough power," Mr. Kelly apologized. "This is a small sun, after all. But give the rig a few minutes: it'll build up."

Mr. Jones leaned forward. "Listen, do you folks mind if I slip out of my disguise? I'm hot."

"You're not supposed to," Jane Doe reminded him. "The uniform is to be worn at all times when we're on duty."

"I know, I know, but Sten-Durok—*oops,* I mean Cohen, locked the door. Nobody comes in through windows in this particular place, and we don't have to worry about materialization. So how about I relax for a second or two?"

Alfred had perched on the edge of the dresser. He looked Mr. Jones over with great amusement. The pudgy little man was wearing a cheap gray sharkskin suit. He was bald; he wore no eyeglasses; he had no beard. He didn't even have a mustache.

Disguise, huh?

"I say let him," Alfred suggested with an anticipatory chuckle. "We're all alone—he might as well be comfortable. Go ahead, Jones, *take* off your disguise."

"Thanks," Jones said with feeling. "I'm suffocating in this outfit."

Alfred chuckled again. He'd show these New Yorkers.

"Take it off. Be comfortable. Make yourself at home."

Jones nodded and unbuttoned the jacket of his gray sharkskin suit. Then he unbuttoned the white shirt under it. Then he put his two forefingers into his chest, all the way in, and pulled his chest apart. He kept pulling until there was a great dark hole about ten inches wide.

A black spider squirmed out of the opening. Its round little body was about the size of a man's fist, its legs about the size and length of pipe stems. It crouched on Jones' chest, while the body from which it had emerged maintained its position in a kind of paralysis, the fingers still holding the chest apart, the back and legs still resting comfortably in the chair.

"Whew!" said the spider. "That feels good."

Alfred found he couldn't stop chuckling. He finally managed to halt the noise from his mouth, but it kept on going in his head. He stared at the spider, at the stiff body from which it had come. Then, frantically, he stared at the others in the room, at Cohen, at Kelly, at Jane Doe.

They couldn't have looked less interested.

The hum from the briefcase on Kelly's knees abruptly resolved itself into words. Alfred's visitors stopped looking bored and leaned forward attentively.

"Greetings, Special Emissaries," said the voice. "This is Command Central speaking. Robinson, to you. Are there any reports of significance?"

"None from me," Jane Doe told it.

"Nor me," from Kelly.

"Nothing new yet," said Cohen.

The spider stretched itself luxuriously. "Same here. Nothing to report."

"Jones!" ordered the voice from the briefcase. "Get back into your uniform!"

"It's *hot,* chief. And we're all alone in here, sitting behind what they call a locked door. Remember, they've got a superstition on Earth about locked doors? We don't have anything to worry about."

"I'll tell you what to worry about. You get into that uniform, Jones! Or maybe you're tired of being a Special Emissary? Maybe you'd like to go back to General Emissary status?"

The spider stretched its legs and performed what could only be described as a shrug. Then it backed carefully into the hole in the chest. The hole closed behind it. The body of Jones came to life and buttoned his shirt and jacket.

"That's better," said the voice from the briefcase on Kelly's knee. "Don't ever do that again while you're on duty."

"Okay, chief, okay. But couldn't we cool down this

planet? You know, bring on winter, start a new ice age? It would make it a lot easier to work."

"And a lot easier to be detected, stupid. You worry about the big things like conventions and beauty contests. We'll worry about the little things here, in Command Central, like arbitrarily changing the seasons and starting new ice ages. All right, Smith, how about you? What's your report?"

Alfred Smith shook the thick gathered wool out of his head, slid off the dresser, and on to his feet. He looked around wildly.

"Re-re*port?"* A breath. "Why, nothing—nothing to report."

"Took you a long time to make up your mind about it. You're not holding anything back, are you? Remember, it's our job to evaluate information, not yours."

Alfred wet his lips. "N-no. I'm not holding anything back."

"You'd better not. One beauty contest you forget to tell us about and you're through, Smith. We still haven't forgotten that boner you pulled in Zagreb."

"Oh, chief," Jane Doe intervened. "It was only a local stunt to discover who was the tallest card-carrying Communist in Croatia. You can't blame Smith for missing *that.*"

"We certainly can blame Smith for that. It was a beauty contest, within the definition of the term you were given. If Cohen hadn't stumbled across a mention of it in the Kiev *Pravda,* all hell could have broken loose. Remember that, Smith. And stop calling me *chief,* all of you. The name is Robinson. Remember it."

They all nodded, Alfred with them. He shot a mixed look of uncertainty and gratitude at Jane Doe.

"All right," the voice went on, somewhat mollified. "And to show you that I can hand out the boosts as well as the knocks, I want to commend Smith on his disguise.

It's a little offbeat, but it rings true—and that's the main thing. If the rest of you only spent as much time and care on your uniform, we'd be in the home stretch in no time." The voice paused and took on an oily, heavily whimsical quality. "Before you could say 'Jack Robinson.' "

They all laughed dutifully at that one, even Alfred.

"You think Smith did a good job on his disguise, don't you, chief, I mean, Mr. Robinson?" Jane Doe asked eagerly, as if she wanted to underline the fact for everyone.

"I certainly do. Look at that suit: it's not just any old suit, but a tweed jacket and flannel pants. Now that's what I call using your imagination. His chin isn't just a chin, it's a *cleft* chin. Very good. The color of his hair—first-rate. The only thing I might possibly object to is the bow tie. I'd say a good solid rep tie, regular length, would be a little less chancey, a little less likely to attract attention. But it feels right, and that's the main thing—the *feel* of the disguise. In this business, you either have an instinct for merging with the population of the planet, or you don't. I think Smith has it. Good work, Smith."

"Thank you," Alfred mumbled.

"All right, oh—er, Robinson," Mr. Jones said impatiently. "It's a good uniform-disguise. But it's not that important. Our work is more important than how we look."

"Your work *is* how you look. If you look right, you work right. Take yourself, for example, Jones. A more nondescript, carelessly assembled human being, I don't think I've ever come across before. What are you supposed to be—Mr. American-Man-in-the-Street?"

Mr. Jones looked deeply hurt. "I'm supposed to be a Brooklyn druggist. And believe me, the uniform is plenty good enough. I know. You should see some of these druggists."

"Some, Jones, but not most. And that's my point."

There was a throat-clearing sound from Mr. Cohen.

"Don't want to interrupt you, Robinson, but this isn't supposed to be a long visit we're having with Smith. We just dropped up, kind of."

"Right, Cohen, right on the old button. All right, everybody ready for instructions?"

"Ready," they all chorused, Alfred coming in raggedly on the last syllable.

"Here we go then. Cohen, you're back on your old assignment, keeping careful check on any new beauty contests scheduled anywhere in the country, with special attention to be paid to New York, of course. Kelly, you're to do the same with conventions. Jane Doe and John Smith will continue to look into anything that might be a camouflaged attempt."

"Anything particular in mind?" Jane Doe asked.

"Not for you at the moment. You just keep making the rounds of beauty parlors and see if you stumble across something. Smith, we have a special item we'd like you to look into. There's a fancy dress ball of the plumbers of the New York City area. Drop down there and see what you can see. And let us know if you hit it. Fast."

Alfred kept his voice determinedly casual. "What do you want me to look out for?"

"Well, if you don't know by this time—" the voice from the briefcase rose impatiently. "Door prizes, an award for the best costume, even a contest for Miss Pipe Wrench of 1921 or whatever year Earth is in right now. I don't think we have to worry about that last, though. It would be too damn obvious, and we haven't hit anything obvious yet."

"How about me?" Jones wanted to know.

"We'll have special instructions for you pretty soon. There may be a new angle."

They all looked interested at that, but the voice from the briefcase did not seem disposed to elucidate further.

"That will be all," it said unequivocally. "You can start leaving now."

Mr. Kelly zipped the briefcase shut, nodded at everyone, and left.

A few moments later, Mr. Cohen followed him. Then Jones yawned and said, "Well, good-bye, now." He closed the door behind him.

Jane Doe rose, but she didn't go toward the door. She came over to where Alfred Smith was standing with a punched expression in his eyes.

"Well, John?" she said softly.

Alfred Smith couldn't think of anything to say to that, except, "Well, Jane?"

"We're together again. Working on an assignment again, together. Isn't it wonderful?"

He nodded slowly, carefully. "Yes. Wonderful."

"And if we can only close it up this time, finish the whole nasty business once and for all, we'll be going back together."

"And then?"

Her eyes glistened. "You know, darling. A quiet little web somewhere, just for two. You and I alone. And piles and piles of eggs."

Alfred gulped, and, in spite of himself, turned away.

"Oh, I'm sorry, darling," she cried, taking his hand. "I've upset you. I was talking out of uniform. Well then, put it this way: a cottage small by a waterfall. And baby makes three. You and I, down the golden years together. When your hair has turned to silver. There! Is that better?"

"Lots," he managed to get out, staring at her wildly. "Lots better."

She threw her arms around him. He realized he was expected to respond, and squeezed back.

"Oh, I don't care,"she whispered into his ear. "I don't care about discipline or anything when I'm close to you.

And I'll say it, even if Command Central is listening. Darling, do you know what I'd like right now?"

Alfred sighed. He was more than half afraid of what was coming. "No, what? What would you like right now?"

"I'd like for us to be out of uniform, scuttling about and over each other in some damp, dark place. I'd like to feel your claws upon me, your antennae caressing me, *me*—instead of this clumsy emotionless disguise I'm wearing."

He thought. "It—it'll come. Be patient, darling."

She straightened up and became businesslike again. "Yes, and I'd better be going. Here's a list of all our telephone numbers, in case you want to get in touch with any of us. Remember, this operation is to be conducted strictly according to regulations. And that means no *phmpffing*, no *phmpffing* at all, except in case of the greatest emergency. For everything else, we use telephones."

"Telephones?" he found himself echoing.

"Yes." She gestured to the black instrument on its stand near the bed. "Those things."

"Oh, *those* things," he repeated, fighting the impulse to shake his head hard in a brain-clearing gesture. "Yes. Those things. But no—no, er, what did you say?"

"No *phmpffing*."

"None at all?" Surely if he continued to ask questions something would become clear. And sane!

Jane Doe looked extremely concerned. "Of course not! This is a maximum operation."

"Yes, that's right," he agreed. "A maximum operation. I'd forgotten that."

"Well, don't," she advised him earnestly. "Don't forget. That way, you'll get into trouble again. One more boner like the one you pulled in Zagreb, darling, and you're through. You'll be kicked out of the Service. And then what do you think will happen to our plans together?"

"We'll be finished, huh?" Alfred studied her. Under all that girl-flesh, he reminded himself, there was a large, black spider working at controls like a mechanic in a power crane.

"Right. I'd never marry outside the Service. We'd be finished. So do take care of yourself, darling, and give it all you've got. Stay on the ball. Fly right. Get with it. Rise and shine. Stick to the straight and narrow. Go in there and pitch. Don't let George do it. Work hard and save your money. Early to bed and early to rise. Don't be half safe."

"I'll do my best," he promised, his voice rattling.

"My little crawler," she whispered intimately and kissed him on the ear.

She closed the door behind her.

Alfred groped his way to the bed. After a while, he noticed that he was uncomfortable. He was sitting on a valise. Absent-mindedly, he shoved it to the floor.

What had he wandered into? Or, to put it more accurately, what had wandered into him?

Spies. Yes, obviously spies. But *such* spies . . .?

Spies from another planet. What were they spying on —beauty contests, conventions, plumbers' fancy dress balls? What were they looking for? What in the world— or rather the universe—*could* they be looking for?

One thing was obvious. They were up to no good. That omnipresent contempt whenever they mentioned Earth or the things of Earth.

An advance wave of invaders? Scouts preparing the way for the main body? They could be that. But why beauty contests, why fancy dress balls?

What was there of value that they could possibly learn from institutions such as these?

You'd expect to find them at nuclear research labs, at

rocket proving grounds, skulking about the Pentagon in Washington, D.C.

Alfred decided there was no point in trying to follow their thought processes. They were completely alien creatures: who knew what kind of information they might consider valuable, what might be important to them?

But they were undoubtedly spies sizing up Earth for an invasion to come.

"Filthy little spiders," he growled in a righteous access of xenophobia.

And one of them was in love with him. One of them intended to marry him. What was it she had said—piles and piles of eggs? A pretty thought! He shuddered from his neck to his knees.

But they believed he was this other Smith, John Smith. Earth still had a chance. Pure luck had given Earth a counterspy. Him.

He felt frightened, but a little proud. A *counter*spy.

The first thing to do was to check on this John Smith.

Alfred Smith reached for the telephone. "Desk!"

There was precious little information from the clerk to supplement what he had been given before. John Smith had registered here two weeks ago. He had left one afternoon and not come back. After the usual interval it was assumed he had skipped, since he owed a few days on the bill at the time. His belongings were in the hotel store room.

"No, sir, I'm sorry, sir, but hotel regulations do not permit us to let you go through his belongings. Unless you wish to claim a relationship."

"And if I did?" Alfred asked eagerly. "If I did wish to claim a relationship?"

"Then it would be necessary for you to establish proof, sir."

"I see. Well, thank you very much." He hung up.

Where was he now? This John Smith had registered

here, evidently under a previous agreement, as his room was to provide the meeting place for the entire group. Then he had walked out one day and not returned.

Since the disguises were subject to frequent change, when another Smith had registered in the same room, the spies assumed it was their man. They may not even have known of the hiatus between the two Smiths.

What had happened to John Smith? Had he defected to the United States government? To the United Nations? Hardly. There would be an F.B.I. man, a small army unit staked out in the room in that case, when John Smith's friends showed up.

No, he had just disappeared. But was he dead, killed in some freak accident while crossing a bridge—that would account for his body not being recovered—or was he only temporarily away, working on some newly discovered angle for his interplanetary organization?

And what would happen to Alfred when he returned? The young man on the bed shivered. Espionage groups, he recalled from the novels he had read, tended to a sort of hatchet-man justice. Obviously, they would not let an Earthman with knowledge of their existence and operations go on living.

Then, obviously, he had to get help.

But from where? The police? The F.B.I.? He shivered again at the picture evoked: himself, somewhat embarrassed, stammering a bit, not quite remembering all the details, telling this story to a hard-faced desk sergeant.

An interplanetary invasion, Mr. Smith? From Mars? Oh, not from Mars—from where then? Oh, you don't quite know, Mr. Smith? All you're sure of is that it's an interplanetary invasion? I see. And how did you happen to hear of this on your first day in New York? Oh, four people came up to your hotel room and told you about it? Very interesting. Very, *very* interesting. And their names were Mr. Cohen, Mr. Kelly, Mr. Jones, and Jane Doe?

And *your* name is Smith, isn't it? And all we have to do to prove your story is find the address behind one of these telephone numbers, cut open the person in whose name the phone is registered, and find a big black spider inside. . . .

"No!" Alfred groaned aloud. "Not that way—I wouldn't have a chance!"

He needed proof—tangible proof. And facts. Mostly he needed facts. Who were these spiders, what was their home planet, when were they planning to invade, what kind of weapons did they have at their disposal—stuff like that. And lots and lots of data about their organization here on Earth, especially in America.

How did you get such data? You couldn't ask—that would be the surest way to expose yourself as a bona fide human with nothing more interesting inside you than a length or so of intestine and a couple of ribs.

But they'd given him an assignment. Something about a plumber's fancy dress ball. Now, obviously an assignment like that concerned their plans, their organization. Obviously.

He grabbed for the phone.

"Desk? This is Mr. Smith in 504. Yes, Mr. Smith *again.* Listen, how do I find out where the plumbers are in New York?"

"If the plumbing in your room is out of order, sir," the smooth, patient voice explained, "the hotel will send up a—"

"No, no, no! I don't want a plumber, I want *plumbers, all* of them! The New York plumbers, how do I find them?"

He distinctly heard lips being licked at the other end as this question was digested and then, aside, a whispered comment, "Yeah, it's 504, again. We got a real beauty in that room this time. I don't envy the night man tonight, let me tell you!" Loudly and clearly, if just a shade less smoothly, the voice replied: "You will find a classified telephone directory on the desk near your bed, sir. You can look up plumbers under *P*. Most of the plumbers in Manhattan are listed there. For plumbers in Brooklyn, the Bronx, Queens, and Staten Island, I would suggest—"

"I don't want plumbers in Brooklyn or the Bronx! I don't even want plumbers in—" Alfred Smith drew a deep breath. He had to get a grip on himself! The fate of the entire planet, of the entire human race depended on his keeping his head. He forced his mind backward, inch by inch, off the plateau of hysteria it had mounted. He waited until his voice was calm.

"This is the problem," he began again, slowly and carefully. "There is a fancy dress ball of the plumbers of the New York area. It's being held somewhere in the city tonight, and I'm supposed to be there. Unfortunately, I've lost my invitation and it contained the address. Now, how do you think I could go about finding where the ball is going to be?" He congratulated himself on the swiftness of his thinking. This was really being a counterspy!

Pause. "I could make some inquiries, sir, through the usual channels, and call you back." And aside: "Now he says *he's* a plumber and he wants to go to a fancy dress ball. Can you beat that? I tell you in this business . . ." And to him: "Would that be satisfactory, sir?"

"Fine," Alfred Smith told him enthusiastically. "That would be *fine*."

He hung up. Well, he was getting the hang of this espionage business. Nothing like a sales background for practice in quick thinking and quick talking.

He didn't have to report to the office until tomorrow. That gave him this afternoon and this evening to save the human race.

Who would have thought when he was offered a job in New York with the BlakSeme Hosiery Company ("Men *Notice* BlakSemes—They're so Shockingly Stocking!")

what tremendous stakes he'd be playing for the very day of his arrival? Of course, BlakSeme knew what kind of man he was, they knew he was executive timber or they'd never have hired him right out from under PuzzleKnit, their biggest competitor. He'd made quite a name for himself, Alfred Smith was modestly willing to admit, in the Illinois territory. Highest sales increases for three years running, steadiest repeat orders for five. But to PuzzleKnit Nylons ("PuzzleKnit Attracts Their Attention and Keeps Them Guessing"), he had just been a top-notch salesman: it had taken BlakSeme, with their upper-bracket, Madison Avenue orientation, to see him as a possible district sales manager.

BlakSeme alone had seen he was big league material. But even they had not guessed how big a league it was in which he was destined to play.

The desk clerk called back. "I find, sir, that there *is* a fancy dress ball of the boss plumbers and steamfitters of the metropolitan New York area. It's at Menshevik Hall on Tenth Avenue at eight o'clock tonight. The theme of the ball is the *ancien régime* in France, and only people in pre-French Revolution costumes will be admitted. Would you like the name of a place near the hotel where you can rent the right costume for the occasion?"

"Yes," Alfred Smith babbled. "Yes, yes, yes!" Things were beginning to click! He was on the trail of the aliens' organization!

He went out immediately and hurriedly selected a Duc de Richelieu outfit. Since some small alterations were necessary; he had time to get dinner before the costume would be delivered to his hotel. He ate carefully and nutritiously: this was going to be a big night. His reading matter throughout the meal was a booklet he'd picked up in the outfitting place, a booklet giving the descriptions and background of all the costumes available for this period—sixteenth- to eighteenth-century France. Any fact might be the vital clue. . . .

Back in his room, he tore off his clothes and pulled on the rented apparel. He was a little disappointed at the result. He did not quite look like a Gray Eminence. More like a young Protestant in Cardinal's clothing. But then he found the scrap of gray beard in the box that belonged with the costume and fitted it on. It made all the difference.

Talk about your disguises! Here his body was supposed to be a disguise, a disguise which was the uniform of the Aliens' Special Agents Division, of their terrestrial spy service. And now he was disguising that supposed disguise with a real one—just as by being a supposed spy he was laying a trap for all the real secret operatives.

Alfred Smith—one lone man against the aliens! "So that," he whispered reverently, "government of humans, by humans and for humans shall not perish from the Earth."

The telephone. This time it was Jones.

"Just got word from Robinson, Smith. That special mission of mine. It looks like tonight's the night."

"Tonight, eh?" Alfred Smith felt the lace tighten around his throat.

"Yes, they're going to try to contact tonight. We still don't know just where—just that it's in New York City. I'm to be on reserve: I'll rush around to whoever finds the contact. You know, reinforce, lend a helping hand, be a staunch ally, give an assist to, help out in a pinch, stand back to back with, buddy mine, pards till hell freezes over. You'll be at the plumbers' ball, won't you? Where is it?"

Alfred shook his head violently to clear it of the fog of clichés thrown out by Jones. "Menshevik Hall. Tenth Avenue. What do I do if I—if I discover the contact?"

"You *phmpff*, guy, *phmpff* like mad. And I'll come a-running. Forget about telephones if you discover the contact. Also forget about special delivery mail, passenger pigeon, pony express rider, wireless telegraphy and couriers from His Majesty. Discovering the contact comes under the heading of 'emergency' under Operating Procedure Regulations XXXIII-XLIX, inclusive. So *phmpff* your foolish head off."

"Right! Only thing, Jones—" there was a click at the other end as Jones hung up.

Tonight, Alfred Smith thought grimly, staring into the mirror. Tonight's the night!

For *what?*

Menshevik Hall was a gray two-story building in the draftiest section of Tenth Avenue. The lower floor was a saloon through whose greasy windows a neon sign proclaimed:

THE FEBRUARY REVOLUTION WAS THE ONLY
REAL REVOLUTION BAR & GRILL
BEER—WINES—CHOICE LIQUORS
Alexei Ivanovich Anphinov, Prop.

The second floor was brightly lit. Music oozed out of its windows. There was a penciled sign on a doorway to one side of the bar:

BOSS PLUMBERS AND STEAMFITTERS OF THE
METROPOLITAN NEW YORK AREA
SEMIANNUAL FANCY DRESS BALL

You Must Be in Costume to Be Admitted Tonight

(If you haven't paid your association dues for this quarter, see Bushke Horowitz at the bar before going upstairs—Bushke's wearing a Man in the Iron Mask costume and he's drinking rum and seven-up.)

Alfred Smith climbed the creaky wooden stairs apprehensively, his eyes on the burly General Montcalm guarding the entrance at the top. To his relief, however, no invitation or ticket was demanded: his costume was sufficient validation. The red-faced general barely gave him a glance from under the plushly decorated cocked hat before waving him through.

It was crowded inside. Scores of Louis XIII's, XIV's, XV's, and XVI's were dancing sedately with Annes of Austria and Marie Antoinettes to the strains of rhumba and cha-cha. Overhead, two colored chandeliers rotated slowly, unwinding the spectrum upon the glittering, waxed floor.

Where did he begin? He glanced at the platform where the musicians sat; they alone were not in costume. Lettering on the bass drum told the world that "Ole Olsen and His Latin Five" were providing the rhythms, but that did not seem like much to go on. No one here looked like an interstellar spy.

On the other hand, neither did Jones, Cohen, Kelly nor Jane Doe. They looked almost spectacularly ordinary. That was it: you had to find these people in the unlikeliest, most prosaic places.

Pleased by the inspiration, he went into the Men's Room.

At first, he thought he had hit it exactly right. The place was crowded. Sixteen or so Musketeers stood around the washbasin, munching enormous cigars and conversing in low voices.

He insinuated himself among them and listened closely. Their talk was eclectic, ranging freely from the wholesale price of pastel-colored water closets to the problems of installing plumbing in a new housing development on Long Island that was surrounded by unsewered streets.

"I told the contractor to his face," said a somewhat sallow, undersized Musketeer, knocking his cigar ash off against the pommel of his sword, "Joe, I told him, how can you expect me to lay pipe when you don't even know the *capacity*, let alone the type—look, we won't even *talk* about the type—of the sewer system they're going to have installed out here? Joe, I said to him, you're a bright guy: I ask you, Joe, is that fair, does that make sense? You want me to maybe install plumbing that's going to be a lot weaker than the sewer system in the streets so that the first time the new customers flush the toilets everything backs up all over the bathroom floor—you want that, Joe? No, he says, I don't want that. All right, then, I say, you want me to maybe install plumbing that's a lot better than necessary, a lot stronger than the sewer system will require, and that'll add cost to the houses that doesn't have to be added—you want that, Joe? No, he says, I don't want that. So, look, Joe, I say, you're willing to admit this is a dumb proposition from top to bottom? Suppose someone asked you to build a house, Joe, and couldn't tell you whether the foundation under it is concrete or steel or sand or cinder-block. That's just exactly what you're asking me to do, Joe, that's just exactly what."

There was a rustle of approbation. A tall, weedy, mournful-looking Musketeer blew his nose and carefully replaced the handkerchief in his doublet before commenting: "That's the trouble with everybody. They think plumbers are miracle men. They got to learn that plumbers are only human."

"I don't know about that," said a stout Huguenot who had come up in the last few moments. "I take the attitude that plumbers *are* miracle men. What we got to use is our American imagination, our American know-how, our American thinking straight to the point. You show me a sewer system in a new community, like, that hasn't been installed yet, that nobody knows what it's capacity is going to be, and I'll figure out a plumbing system for the development that'll fit it no matter what. And I'll save on cost, too."

"How?" demanded the sallow, undersized Musketeer. "Tell me how."

"I'll tell you how," retorted the Huguenot. "By using my American imagination, my American know-how, my American thinking straight to the point. *That's* how."

"Pardon me," Alfred Smith broke in hurriedly as he saw the sallow, undersized Musketeer take a deep breath in preparation for a stinging rebuttal. "Do any of you gentlemen know of any prizes that will be given for the best costume, any door prizes, anything like that?"

There was a silence as they all chewed their cigars at him appraisingly. Then the Huguenot (Coligny, Alfred wondered? Condé? de Rohan?) leaned forward and tapped him on the chest. "When you got a question, sonny, the thing to do is find the right man to ask the question of. That's half the battle. Now who's the right man to ask questions about door prizes? The doorman. You go out to the doorman—he's wearing a General Montcalm—and you tell him Larry sent you. You tell him Larry said he should tell you all about door prizes, and, sonny, he'll tell you just what you want to know." He turned back to his smoldering adversary. "Now before you say anything, I know just what you're going to say. And I'll tell you why you're wrong."

Alfred squeezed his way out of the mobful of rising tempers. At the outskirts, a Cardinal's Guard who had just come up remarked broodingly to a black-hooded executioner: "That Larry. Big man. What I wouldn't give to be around when he takes a pratfall."

The executioner nodded and transferred his axe thoughtfully to the other shoulder. "One day there'll be an anonymous phone call to the Board of Health about Larry and they'll send out an inspector who can't be pieced off and that'll be that. Any guy who'll buy up junk pipe and chromium-plate it and then sell it to his friends as new stuff that he's overstocked in . . ." Over his shoulder, the rubbery blade of the axe began flapping like a flag in a breeze.

"Don't know nothing about prizes," the doorman stated, rocking his folding chair back and forth in front of the ballroom entrance. "Anything important, they don't tell me." He tilted his cocked hat forward over his eyes and stared bitterly into space, as if reflecting that with just a little more advance information from Paris the day might indeed have gone quite differently on the Plains of Abraham. "Why'n't you ask around down in the bar? All the big wheels are down in the bar."

There must, Alfred reflected, be a good many big wheels, as he apologized his way through the crowded room downstairs. The hoop-skirts and rearing, extravagant hair-do's, the knobby-kneed hose, swinging swords, and powdered wigs jam-packed *The February Revolution Was the Only Real Revolution Bar & Grill* so that the half-dozen or so regular customers in shabby suits and worn windbreakers seemed to be the ones actually in costume, poverty-stricken, resentful anachronisms from the future who had stumbled somehow into imperial Versailles and the swaggering intrigue of the Tuileries.

At the bar, Bushke Horowitz, his iron mask wide open despite the sternest decrees of King and Cardinal, accepted dues money, dispensed opinions on the future of standpipes and stall showers to the mob in heavy brocade and shot silk around him, and periodically threw a handful of largesse to the bartender, a chunky, angry-looking man with a spade beard and a white apron, along with the injunction to "set 'em up again."

There was no way to get through to him, Alfred realized. He asked several times about "prizes," was ignored, and gave up. He had to find a wheel of somewhat smaller diameter.

A tug at the sleeve of his clerical gown. He stared down at the rather thinnish Mme. DuBarry sitting in the empty booth. She gave him a smile from underneath her black vizard. "Drinkie?" she suggested. Then, seeing his blank look, she amplified: "Yousie and mesie. Just us twosie."

Alfred shook his head. "Nosie—I mean, no, thank you. I—uh—some business. Maybe later."

He started to walk away and found that his sleeve failed to accompany him. Mme. DuBarry continued to hold it between two fingers: she held it winsomely, delicately, archly, but the hold was absolutely unequivocal.

"Aw," she pouted. "Look at the whizzy-busy businessman. No time for drinkie, no time for mesie, just busy, busy, busy, all the livelong day."

Despite his irritation, Alfred shrugged. He wasn't doing himself much good any other way. He came back and sat across the table from her in the booth. Then, and only then, was his sleeve released by the dainty fingers.

The angry-looking man in the spade beard and white apron appeared at their booth. *"Nyehh?"* he grunted, meaning, quite obviously, "What'll you have?"

"I'll have Scotch on the rocks," she told Alfred. "Scotch on the rocks is absolutely the only ever drink for me."

"Two scotch on the rocks," Alfred told the bartender, who replied *"Nyehh,"* signifying "You order the stuff, I bring it. It's your funeral."

"I heard you asking about contests. I won a contest once. Does that make you like me a little better?"

"What kind of contest did you win?" Alfred asked absent-mindedly, studying her. Under that mask she was probably somewhat pretty in a rather bony, highly ordinary sort of way. There was nothing here.

"I was voted The Girl the Junior Plumbers of Cleveland Would Most Like to Wipe a Joint With. It was supposed to be The Girl Whose Joint the Junior Plumbers Would Most Like to Wipe, but some nasty people made a fuss and the judges had to change the title. It was three years ago, but I still have the award certificate. Now, does that help me at *all?*"

"I'm afraid not. But congratulations anyway on winning the title. It's not everybody who can—uh, say that."

The angry-looking man in the spade beard came back and set glasses and coasters in front of them. *"Nyehh!"* he announced, meaning, "You pay me now. That's the way we do it in this place." He took the money, glowered at it, at them, and clumped back to the becustomered bar.

"Well, what kind of contest *are* you looking for? If you tell me, I might be able to help. I know lots of little things about lots and lots of little things."

"Oh, contests, prizes, nothing particular." He glanced at the rear of the booth. There was a framed photograph on the wall of Plekhanov shaking hands with Kerensky. A much younger version of the chunky, angry-looking man in the spade beard was standing on tip-toe behind Plekhanov, straining hard to get his face into the picture. Alfred realized he was wasting time and swallowed his drink unceremoniously. "I'll have to be going."

She cooed dismay. "So soon? When we've just met? And when I like you so much?"

"What do you mean you like me so much?" he asked her irritatedly. "When, to quote you, we've just met."

"But I do like you, I *do*. You're the cream in my coffee. You're the top. You do things to me. You're what makes the world go round. I'm nuts about you. I go for you in a big way, big boy. I'm wild, simply wild over you. I'd climb the highest mountain, swim the deepest river. Body and soul. Roses are red, violets are blue. Drink to me only with thine eyes. Oh, Johnny, oh-h-h! You're in my heart and my heart's on my sleeve." She stopped and drew breath.

"Gah!" Alfred commented, his eyes almost popping. He

started to get up. 'Thanks, lady, for the pretty talk, but—"

Then he sat down again, his eyes reverting to their previous, pop-like state. The way she'd expressed herself when she'd wanted to make certain she was understood! Like Jane Doe, like Jones—

He'd established rendezvous!

"So that's how much you like me?" he queried, fighting for time, trying to think out his next step.

"Oh, yes!" she assured him. "I'm carrying the torch, all right. I idolize you. I fancy you. I dote on you. I hold dear, make much of, cherish, prize, cling to—"

"Good!" he almost yelled in the desperation of his attempt to break in on the language of love. "Good, good, good, good! Now, I'd like to go some place where we can have some privacy and discuss your feelings in more detail." He worked his face for a moment or two, composing it into an enormous leer. "My hotel room, say, or your apartment?"

Mme. DuBarry nodded enthusiastically. "My apartment. It's closest."

As she tripped out of the bar beside him, Alfred had to keep reminding himself that this was no human wench, despite the tremulous pressure of her arm around his or the wriggling caress of her hip. This was an intelligent spider operating machinery, no more, no less. But it was also his first key to the puzzle of what the aliens wanted of Earth, his entry into the larger spy organization—and, if he kept his head and enjoyed just a bit of luck, it might well be the means to the saving of his world.

A cab rolled up. They got in, and she called out an address to the driver. Then she turned to Alfred.

"Now let's kiss passionately," she said.

They kissed passionately.

"Now let's snuggle," she said.

They snuggled.

"Now let's snuggle a lot harder," she said.

They snuggled a lot harder.

"That's enough," she said. "For now."

They stopped in front of a large, old apartment house that dozed fitfully high above the street, dreaming of its past as it stared down at a flock of run-down brownstones.

Alfred paid the driver and accompanied Mme. DuBarry to the entrance. As he held the elevator door open for her, she batted her eyes at him excitedly and breathed fast in his ear a couple of times.

In the elevator, she pressed the button marked "B."

"Why the basement?" he asked. "Is your apartment in the basement?"

For answer, she pointed a tiny red cylinder at his stomach. He noticed there was a minute button on top of the cylinder. Her thumb was poised over the button.

"Never you mind what's in the basement, you lousy Vaklittian sneak. You just stand very still and do exactly what I tell you. And for your information, I know where you are and where your control cubicle is, so don't entertain any hopes of getting away with nothing more than a damaged uniform."

Alfred glanced down at the region covered by her weapon and swallowed hard. She was wrong about the location of his control cubicle, of course, but still, face it, how much living would he be able to do without a belly?

"Don't worry," he begged her. "I won't do anything foolish."

"You'd better not. And no *phmpffs* out of you either, if you know what's good for you. One solitary *phmpff* and I fill you full of holes. I ventilate you, mister. I plug you where you stand. I let daylight through you. I spray your—"

"I get the idea," Alfred broke in. "No *phmpffs*. Absolutely. I give you my word of honor."

"*Your* word of honor!" she sneered. The elevator

stopped and she backed out, gesturing him to follow. He stared at her masked face and resplendent costume, remembering that when du Barry had been dragged to the guillotine in 1793, she had screamed to the crowds about her tumbril: "Mercy! Mercy for repentance!" He was glad to recall that neither the crowds nor the Revolutionary Tribunal had taken her up on the honest offer.

Not exactly to Alfred's surprise, there was a man waiting for them in the clammy, whitewashed basement. The Huguenot. He of the American thinking straight-to-the-point.

"Any trouble?"

"No, it was easy," she told him. "I pulled him in with the Cleveland-contest-three-years-ago routine. He was smooth about it, I'll say that for him: pretended not to be interested, you know, but he must have bitten hard. I found that out a few seconds later when I told him I loved him and he asked me right off to come up to his apartment." She chuckled. "The poor, pathetic incompetent! As if any normal American human male would react like that—without so much as a remark about my beautiful eyes and how cute I am and how different I am and how about another drink, baby."

The Huguenot pulled at his lip dubiously. "And yet the uniform-disguise is a fine one," he pointed out. "That shows a high degree of competence."

"So what?" the woman shrugged. "He can design a good uniform, he can think up a splendid disguise, but what good is that if he's slip-shod about his *performance?* This one's barely learned anything about human methods and human manners. Even if I hadn't known about him before, I'd have spotted him on the basis of his love-making in the cab."

"Bad, eh?"

"*Bad?*" She rolled her eyes for maximum emphasis. "Oh, brother! I pity him if he ever pulled that clumsy counterfeit on a real human female. Bad isn't the word. A cheap fake. A second-rate ad-lib, but from hunger. No conviction, no feeling of reality, nothing!"

Alfred glared at her through the wide-open wounds of his ego. There were holes in *her* performance, he thought savagely, that would have closed any show the first night. But he decided against giving this critical appraisal aloud. After all, she had the weapon—and he had no idea how ugly a mess that little red cylinder might make.

"All right," said the Huguenot, "let's put him in with the other one."

As the red cylinder prodded into his backbone, Alfred marched up the main basement corridor, turned right at their command, turned right again, and halted before a blank wall. The Huguenot came up beside him and rubbed his hand across the surface several times. A part of the wall swung open as on hinges, and they stepped inside.

Secret panels, yet! Alfred was thinking morosely. Secret panels, a female siren, a Huguenot master-mind—all the equipment. The only thing that was missing was a reason for the whole damn business. His captors evidently had not discovered that he was a human counterspy, or they would have destroyed him out of hand. They thought he was a—what was it?—a Vaklittian. A Vaklittian sneak, no less? So there were two sets of spies—the Huguenot had said something about putting him in with the other one. But what were these two sets of spies after? Were they both grappling for pre-invasion control of Earth? That would make his mission much more complicated. To say nothing about trying to tell the police, if he ever managed to get to the police, about *two* interplanetary invasions!

And look who'd thought *he* was the counterspy in the picture. . . .

The room was large and windowless. It was almost

empty. In one corner, there was a transparent cube about eight feet on each side. A middle-aged man in a single-breasted brown business suit sat on the floor of the cube watching them curiously and a little hopelessly.

The Huguenot paused as he reached the cube. "You've searched him, of course?"

Mme. du Barry got flustered. "Well—no, not exactly. I *intended* to—but you were waiting when we got out of the elevator—I hadn't expected you for a while yet, you know—and then we got into conversation—and I just didn't—"

Her superior shook his head angrily. "And you talk about competence! Oh, well, if I have to do everything, I guess I just have to do everything!"

He ran his hands over Alfred. He took out Alfred's fountain pen and his cigarette lighter and examined them very closely. Then he replaced them and looked puzzled. "He's not carrying a weapon. Does that make sense?"

"I think so. He's not experienced enough to be trusted with anything dangerous."

The Huguenot thought about it for a while. "No. He wouldn't be running around by himself, then. He'd be under supervision."

"Maybe he is. Maybe that's the answer. In that case—"

"In that case, you both might have been followed here. Yes, that could be it. Well, we'll fool them. Contact or no contact, we'll close the operation here as of tonight. Don't go out again—in an hour or so, we'll leave the planet and take off with our prisoners for headquarters." He rubbed his hands against the cube as he had on the wall outside. An opening appeared in the transparency and widened rapidly. With the cylinder at his back, Alfred was pushed inside.

"Give him a small blast," he heard the Huguenot whisper. "Not too much— I don't want him killed before he's questioned. Just enough to stun him and keep him from talking to the other one."

There was a tiny click behind him. A rosy glow lit up the cube and the basement room. Alfred felt a bubble of gas form in his belly and rise upward slowly. After a while, he belched.

When he turned around, the opening in the transparency had closed and the Huguenot had whirled angrily on Mme. du Barry. The lady was examining her weapon with great puzzlement.

"I told you I wanted him stunned, not tickled! Is there anything I can depend on you to do right?"

"I was trying to be careful—I didn't want to kill him, like you said! I aimed right at the control cubicle and I used the medium-low Vaklittian index. I don't understand how he—how he—"

The Huguenot flapped both hands at her disgustedly. "Oh, let's get out of here and start packing! When we get back tonight, I intend to ask headquarters to assign me a new female assistant for the next Earth operation. One without so exact a knowledge of human sexual approaches, perhaps, but who can be counted on to disarm a newly captured prisoner and to tell a Vaklittian index from a hole in her cylinder!"

Mme. du Barry hung her head and followed him out of the room. The door-wall swung shut behind them.

Alfred touched the transparent wall of the cube gingerly. There was no longer any hint of the opening he had been pushed through. The stuff, while as transparent as glass, was rubbery and slightly sticky, something like newly melted plastic. But a plastic, he found out, incredibly strong. And it gave off a whitish glow which enabled him to see through it, dimly, the featureless walls of the secret basement room.

He turned and surveyed his co-prisoner, a few feet away, on the other side of the cube.

The man was looking at him suspiciously, and yet uncertainly, as if he did not quite know what to make of the situation. There was a peculiarly nondescript, uninteresting and ordinary quality to his features which made them somehow remarkably familiar.

Of course! He looked every bit as average as Jones, as Cohen, as Kelly and—in her own submerged feminine way—as Jane Doe. And so Alfred knew who the man had to be.

"John Smith?" he inquired tentatively. "I mean," he added, as he recollected one of Jones' earlier remarks, "Gar-Pitha?"

The middle-aged man rose to his feet and smiled relief. "I couldn't figure out who you were, but you had to be one of us. Unless you were a decoy they were planting here to make me talk. But if you know my real name . . . What's yours, by the way?"

Alfred shook his head coyly. "Command Central—Robinson, I mean—has me on a special mission. I'm not allowed to give my name."

John Smith nodded heavily. "Then you don't give it—and that's that. Robinson knows what he's doing. You can't go wrong by following Robinson's orders to the letter. Special mission, eh? Well, you won't complete it—now. She trapped me the same way. We're both in the soup and good."

"The soup?"

"Sure. Those filthy Lidsgallians—you heard them? They're leaving tonight and taking us with them. Once they've got us on their home planet, they'll be able to work us over at their leisure. They won't get anything out of me, and I hope, for the honor of the Academy, they won't get anything out of you, no matter *what* they do to us, but we won't be good for very much by the time they're through. Oh, those Lidsgallians know their way around a torture chamber, yessiree, Bob!"

"Torture chamber?" Alfred felt sick and knew he looked it.

The older man reached out and squeezed his shoulder. "Steady on, lad," he said. "Don't show the white feather before the natives. Keep a stiff upper lip. Bite the bullet. Fight on for old Notre Dame. Never say die. You have nothing to lose but your chains. Let's keep the old flag flying."

As Alfred said nothing, John Smith took his silence for agreement with these high principles and went on: "You can't get out of this cell—it's a spun web of pure *chrok,* practically unbreakable. But the worst of it, of course, is its insulating quality: you can't *phmpff* through *chrok* if you stand on your head. I've tried to *phmpff* for help until I almost fractured an antenna—couldn't raise a whisper. That's why they don't have to split up their force to guard us. And that's why I haven't bothered to come out of my uniform to talk to you: if we can't *phmpff* we'll make more sense to each other with the jaw attachments of our uniforms."

Grateful for this small mercy, Alfred began to look around at the enclosing walls of *chrok.* "How about using these—these jaw attachments to get help?" he suggested. "Sound seems to go through. We could try yelling together."

"And who would hear you? Humans. What could *they* do?"

Alfred spread his hands. "Oh, I don't know. Sometimes—even humans can be—"

"No, forget about it. Things are bad, but they're not *that* bad. Besides, these walls are especially thick and there are no cracks in them. If those Lidsgallians hadn't come down a couple of times a day to change the air, I'd have suffocated by now. As it was, I was in a bad way a couple of times and had to fall back on the reserve air supply in the chest—you know, the compartment right over the control cubicle? But I'll tell you this, if I ever get back to Vaklitt in one piece, there's a modification of our uniform I'll really try to talk Command Central into making. I thought of it while I was watching them search you. Do away with the air reserve in the chest, I'll tell Robinson—how often, when you come right down to it, does one of our Special Emissaries ever find himself drowning or in the middle of a poison-gas war?—and find some way an agent can take a weapon—a real, honest, claw-operated weapon, into his uniform-disguise with him. Although come to think of it, you'd need some sort of turret arrangement coming out of the human flesh to fire it, and those Lidsgallians, once they found out about it, would—"

He rambled on. Alfred, watching him, realized how hungry he'd been for companionship. And this talkative mood might be put to use. They both might be in a Lidsgallian torture chamber somewhere out in the galaxy in a couple of hours, but there was a very slender chance that they might not. And, besides, facts were always useful; he could cope with whatever lay ahead a bit more easily if he only had some coherent facts on which to base his plans. This was the time, if ever, to find out who was the greater menace to Earth, the Vaklittians or the Lidsgallians—and who was more likely to accept the proffer of friendship from a badly frightened, torture-leery human.

Only—he had to be careful how he phrased the questions. He had to be prepared to cover up any blunders quickly.

"Why do you think," he asked carelessly, "the Lidsgallians hate us so much? Oh, I know the usual answers, but I'm interested in hearing *your* opinion. You seem to have a very refreshing slant."

John Smith grunted appreciatively, thought for a moment, then shrugged. "The usual answers are the only answers in this case. It's the war. Naturally."

"Just the war? That's all, you think?"

"*Just* the war? What do you mean, *just* the war? How can an interstellar war, going on across two-thirds of the galaxy for almost three centuries, be *just* the war? Trillions upon trillions of individuals killed, dozens upon dozens of fertile planets smashed into space dust—you call that *just* the war? You youngsters must really be growing up pretty cynical these days!"

"I—I didn't mean it quite like that," Alfred said rapidly, placatingly. "Of course, the war—it's a terrible business, and all that. Awful. Positively horrible. Sickening, sickening. And our enemy, those vicious Lidsgallians—"

John Smith looked sandbagged. *"What?* The Lidsgallians aren't our enemies—they're our *allies!"*

It was Alfred's turn under the sandbag. "Our *allies?"* he repeated weakly, wondering how he was ever going to get out of this one. *"Our* allies?" he said again, trying a different intonation on for size and the bare possibility of sense.

"I don't know what the Academy's coming to any more," John Smith muttered to himself. "In my day, you got a good general education there, with just enough lab work in espionage to warrant giving you a commission in the Service if you filled all the other requirements. You came out of the Academy as a wide-awake, cultured interstellar citizen, with a good background in history, economics, art, science, and total terroristic warfare. On top of that, you had, whenever you wanted to use it, a decent and honorable trade—spying—under your belt. Of course, if you wanted to specialize, you could always go back, after graduation, for intensive study in elementary and advanced ciphers, creative disguise design, plain and fancy lying, physical and mental torture, narrow fields of scholarship like that. But that used to be strictly post-graduate work. *Now*—now, everything is specialization. They turn out dewy youngsters who can crack any code in space, but can't tell a simple espionage lie to save their heads; they graduate kids who can knock out a masterpiece of a uniform-disguise, but don't even know the difference between a Lidsgallian and a Pharseddic! Mark my words, this overspecialization will be the death of the Academy yet!"

"I agree with you," Alfred told him with ringing sincerity. He thought for a moment and decided to underline his bona fides. "Shoemaker, stick to your last. A place for everything and everything in its place. Spare the rod and spoil the child. Look to the ant, thou sluggard!" He found he was going off the track and stopped himself. "But you see, the way the Academy feels today, its graduates will go into active service and meet older, more experienced men like yourself who can give them this general political orientation right on the spot. Now, of course, in a way, I really knew all the time that the actual enemy, in the deeper sense of the word, so to speak, were the Pharseddics, but—"

"The Pharseddics? Our enemy? But the Pharseddics are the neutrals—the only neutrals! Look here, youngster, and try to get it straight in your mind for once. You absolutely can't do a first-class job of espionage on Earth unless you know the general principles and the background data from which they're derived. To begin with, the Lidsgallians were attacked by the Garoonish, right?"

Alfred assented with a positive shake of his head. "Right! Any school child knows that."

"All right, then. We had to go to war with the Garoonish, not because we had anything particular against them, or liked the Lidsgallians, but because if the Garoonish won they would then be in a position to conquer the Mairunians who were our only possible allies against the growing power of the Ishpolians."

"Naturally," Alfred murmured. "Under the circumstances, there was no alternative."

"Well, that forced the Garoonish to make common cause with the Ossfollians. The Ossfollians activated their mutual assistance pact with the Kenziash of the Rigel region, and, out of fear of the Kenziash, the Ishpolians joined forces with us and pushed the Mairunians into the Garoonish camp. Then came the Battle of the Ninth Sector in which the Ossfollians switched sides four times and which resulted in the involvement of the Menyemians, the Kazkafians, the Doksads, and even the Kenziash of the Procyon and Canopus regions. After that, of course, the war got a lot more complicated."

Alfred wet his lips. "Yes, of course. Then it got complicated." He decided, for the sake of sanity, to bring matters much closer to present time and place. "Meanwhile, here on Earth, there are the spies of—the spies of— Pardon me, but in your opinion just how many of these belligerents operate espionage networks on Earth? Regularly, I mean."

"All of them! Every single one of them! Including the Pharseddics, who have to know what's going on if they're to maintain their neutrality. Earth, as I hope you remember from your first-year course in Elementary Secrecy, is ideally situated just outside the usual battle zones but within easy access of almost all the belligerents. It's the only place left where information can be transmitted across the combat lines and deals can be made back and forth—and, as such, it's zealously respected by everyone. After all, it was on Earth that we sold out the Doksads, and where the annihilation of the Menyemians was arranged by their allies, the Mairunians and the Kazkafians. Just as now we have to watch our own oldest allies, the Lidsgallians, who have been trying to make contact with the Garoonish for the purpose of concluding a separate peace. I got the proof—I even found out the specific time nd place the contact was to be made and what the rrangements were to be—but then I ran afoul of that emale with her yacker of Cleveland contests she won hree years ago. And I got caught."

"The contact was to be made through a beauty contest of some sort, wasn't it?"

The middle-aged man looked impatient. "Naturally a beauty contest. Of course a beauty contest. How else would anyone go about contacting a folk like the Garoonish?"

"I couldn't imagine," Alfred laughed weakly. "The *Garoonish,* after all!" He sat in silence, absolutely unable to close mentally with the picture John Smith had evoked. The closest he could come to it was a memory of something he had read about Lisbon during the Second World War. But this was Lisbon squared, Lisbon cubed, Lisbon raised to some incredible exponential power. All Earth was a vast labyrinth of spy-threaded Lisbon. Spies, counterspies, counter-*counter*spies . . .

Just what, he suddenly wondered, was the correct human population of Earth? Was it a larger proportion of the total population figures than that of the disguised interstellar agents, and by how much? Or was it possibly, was it conceivably, somewhat smaller?

Life had been a lot simpler with PuzzleKnit Nylons, he decided, and that was his only real conclusion.

John Smith nudged him. "Here they come. It's off to Lidsgall for us."

They rose to their feet as the wall opened. Two men and a woman came in, dressed in street clothing. They each carried in one hand a small suitcase that looked heavy, and, in the other, the small, red cylindrical weapon.

Alfred eyed the cylinders and found himself getting tense with a dangerous idea. The weapon hadn't bothered him much before and it had supposedly been set to stun him. Well, perhaps the woman had made a mistake in her setting—and perhaps the metabolisms of Man and Vaklittian were so different that a charge that would knock out the one would merely give the other a slightly upset stomach. Then again, if Earth were so carefully maintained in her ignorance as John Smith had indicated, there might be no setting on the weapon that would damage a native terrestrial at all: in the normal course of their intrigues with and against and around each other, these people might be enjoined by their own laws and by mutual agreement from carrying weapons that could damage humans.

But if he were wrong? It still might take them quite a bit of time to tumble to the fact that the Vaklittian frequencies were having no important effect on him, and he might manage a lot of action in that time. The alternative, at any rate, was to be pulled off Earth in just a few minutes and deposited, some time in the near future, in an extraterrestrial torture chamber. Even if he were able to prove his humanity to their satisfaction, they would still have to dispose of him in some way—and the various devices of the torture chamber would be so handy. . . .

No question about it: people who go in for torture chambers do not make good hosts.

One of the men fiddled with his suitcase, and the transparent cube dissolved around Alfred and John Smith. In response to the gestures made with the weapons, they walked gingerly across the floor. They were motioned through the open wall.

Alfred found it difficult to recognize Mme. du Barry and the Huguenot without their masks and costumes. They both looked much like the new man with them, not bad, not good, just faces-in-a-crowd. Which, of course, was exactly how they wanted it.

He reached his decision as the five of them began walking through the opening in the wall. For the moment they were closely bunched together, even bumping against each other.

He grabbed the woman by the arm and swung her violently against the Huguenot, who staggered confusedly. Then, knowing that John Smith was between him and the new man in the rear, he hitched up his cassock and started to run. He turned left, and again left—and found himself in the main basement corridor. Ahead, at the far end, was a flight of stone stairs leading up to the street.

Behind him, there was the noise of struggle, then the sound of feet running in pursuit. He heard John Smith distantly yell: "Go it, laddie, go it! Over the hill! Slide, Kelly, slide! Ride em, cowboy! It's the last lap—full speed ahead! Shake a leg! Hit the road!" Then the Vaklittian's voice abruptly disappeared in a breathless grunt after the sound of a wallop.

A pinkish glow shot past him, moved back and over to light up his mid-section. He belched. The glow turned light red, deep red, dark, vicious red. He belched more frequently. He reached the stairs and was clambering up them as the glow became a throbbing, night-like purple.

Ten minutes later, he was on Sixth Avenue, getting into a cab. He had a mildly unpleasant bellyache. It rapidly subsided.

He looked behind him as they drove to his hotel. No pursuit. Good. The Lidsgallians would have no idea where he lived.

Did they look like the Vaklittians, he wondered? Spiders? Hardly, he decided. All these different racial names and these titanic interstellar animosities suggested many, many separate forms. They'd have to be small enough to fit into a normal human body, though. Snail-like creatures, possibly, and worm-like ones. Crab-like ones and squid-like ones. Perhaps even rat-like ones?

On the whole, a dreadfully unpleasant subject. He needed a good night's sleep: tomorrow would be his first day at BlakSeme's. And, then, after a bit, when he'd had a chance to think it all out, he'd decide what to do. The police, the F.B.I., or whatever. Maybe even take the whole story to one of the New York newspapers—or some top television commentator might be more sympathetic and reach a bigger audience. His story would have to be coherent and convincing, though. He'd have little proof: the Lidsgallians were probably on their way back to their home planet as of this very moment. But there was his own gang—the Vaklittians. Cohen and Kelly and Jones. And Jane Doe. He'd kid them along for a couple of days and then use them for proof. It was time Earth knew what was going on.

His own gang was waiting for him in his hotel room. Cohen and Kelly and Jones. And Jane Doe. They looked as if they'd been waiting for a long time. Jane Doe looked as if she'd been crying. Mr. Kelly was sitting on the bed with his open briefcase on his knees.

"So there you are," said Robinson's voice from the briefcase. "I hope you have an explanation, Smith. I only hope you have an explanation."

"For what?" he asked irritably. He'd been looking forward to getting out of his costume, taking a hot shower, and then bed. This late performance of "I spy" was very annoying. Repetitious, too.

"For what?" Robinson roared. "For what? Kelly, tell him for what!"

"Look here, Smith," Kelly demanded. "Did you or didn't you ask the desk clerk to find out about a plumbers' fancy dress ball?"

"I did. Of course, I did. He got all the information I needed."

There was a howl from the briefcase. *"He got all the information I needed!* Six years of general studies in espionage at the Academy, a year of post-graduate work in Intensive Secrecy, six months at the special Service school in Data-Sifting and Location-Tracing—and you have the nerve to stand there with your carapace in your claws and tell me that the only way of tracking down this fancy dress ball you could think of was to ask the desk clerk—an ordinary everyday human desk-clerk—to find out about it for you!"

Alfred noticed that the faces around him were all extremely grave. Despite his weariness and strong feelings of indifference, he made an effort to conciliate. "Well, if he was only an ordinary, everyday human, I fail to see the harm that—"

"He could have been the Garoonish Minister of War for all you knew!" the briefcase blasted. "Not that it made any difference. By the time he'd questioned his various sources and mentioned the matter to his various friends, acquaintances and business associates, every spy organization in the galaxy had been alerted. They knew what we were worrying about, what we were looking for, and where and when we hoped to find it. You accomplished one of the best jobs of interstellar communication ever. Sixty-five years of patient espionage planning gone down the drain. *Now* what have you to say for yourself?"

Alfred stood up straight and manfully pulled back his shoulders. "Just this. I'm sorry." He considered for a moment, then added: "Deeply and truly sorry."

Some kind of electrical storm seemed to go off in the briefcase. It almost rolled off Kelly's knees.

"I just can't stand this any more," Jane Doe said suddenly. "I'll wait outside." She walked past Alfred to the door, her eyes swimming in reproachfulness. "Darling, darling, how *could* you?" she whispered bitterly as she passed him.

The briefcase crackled down to some semblance of control. "I'll give you one last chance, Smith. Not that I think any conceivable defense you might have would be valid, but I hate to demote a Special Emissary, to push him forever out of the Service, without giving him every chance to be heard. So. Is there any defense you wish to have registered before sentence of demotion is passed upon you?"

Alfred considered. This was evidently a serious business in their eyes, but it was beginning to be slightly meaningless to him. There was too much of it, and it was too complicated. He was tired. *And* he was Alfred Smith, not John Smith.

He could tell them about the events of the night, about the Lidsgallians and the information he'd received from the captive Smith. It might be valuable and it might throw a weight in the scales in his favor. The trouble was that then the question of John Smith's real identity would arise—and that might become very embarrassing.

Besides, he was over the fear he'd felt earlier about these creatures: they could do little more to him than a dose of sodium bicarbonate, he'd found out. Their superweapons were to be discounted, at least on Earth. And when it came to that point, he was not at all sure that he wanted to give them helpful information. Who knew just where Earth's best interests lay?

He shook his head, feeling the fatigue in his neck muscles. "No defense. I *said* I'm sorry."

From the briefcase, Robinson sighed. "Smith, this hurts me more than it hurts you. It's the principle of the thing, you see. Punishment fit the crime. More in sorrow than in anger. You cannot make an omelet without breaking eggs. All right, Kelly. The sentence."

Kelly put the briefcase on the bed and got to his feet. Cohen and Jones came to attention. There was evidently to be a ceremony.

"By virtue of the authority vested in me as acting chief of this field group," Kelly intoned, "and pursuant to Operating Procedure Regulations XCVII, XCVIII and XCIX, I hereby demote and degrade you, Gar-Pitha of Vaklitt, from the rank of Special Emissary, Second Class, to the rank of General Emissary or such other lower rank as Command Central may find fitting and necessary in the best interests of the Service. And I further direct that your disgrace be published throughout every arm and echelon of the Service and that your name be stricken from the roster of graduates of the Academy which you have shamed. And, finally, in the name of this field group and every individual within it, I disown you now and forevermore as a colleague and an equal and a friend."

It was, Alfred decided, a kind of strong-medicine ceremony. Must be pretty affecting to someone who was really involved in it personally.

Then, from either side, Cohen and Jones moved in swiftly to complete the last, dramatic part of the ceremony. They were very formal, but very thorough.

They stripped the culprit of his uniform.

THE MASCULINIST REVOLT

I

The Coming of the Codpiece

HISTORIANS OF the period between 1990 and 2015 disagree violently on the causes of the Masculinist Revolt. Some see it as a sexual earthquake of nationwide proportions that was long overdue. Others contend that an elderly bachelor founded the Movement only to save himself from bankruptcy and saw it turn into a terrifying monster that swallowed him alive.

This P. Edward Pollyglow—fondly nicknamed "Old Pep" by his followers—was the last of a family distinguished for generations in the men's wear manufacturing line. Pollyglow's factory produced only one item, men's all-purpose jumpers, and had always operated at full capacity—up to the moment the Interchangeable Style came in. Then, abruptly, overnight it seemed, there was no longer a market for purely male apparel.

He refused to admit that he and all of his machinery had become obsolete as the result of a simple change in fashion. What if the Interchangeable Style ruled out all sexual differentiation? "Try to make us swallow that!" he cackled at first. "Just try!"

But the red ink on his ledgers proved that his countrymen, however unhappily, *were* swallowing it.

Pollyglow began to spend long hours brooding at home instead of sitting nervously in his idle office. Chiefly he brooded on the pushing-around men had taken from women all through the twentieth century. Men had once been proud creatures; they had asserted themselves; they had enjoyed a high rank in human society. What had happened?

Most of their troubles could be traced to a development that occurred shortly before World War I, he decided. "Man-tailoring," the first identifiable villain.

When used in connection with women's clothes, "man-tailoring" implied that certain tweed skirts and cloth coats featured unusually meticulous workmanship. Its vogue was followed by the imitative patterns: slacks for trousers, blouses for shirts, essentially male garments which had been frilled here and furbelowed there and given new, feminine names. The "his-and-hers" fashions came next; they were universal by 1991.

Meanwhile, women kept gaining prestige and political power. The F.E.P.C. started policing discriminatory employment practices in any way based upon sex. A Supreme Court decision (Mrs. Staub's Employment Agency for Lady Athletes *vs.* The New York State Boxing Commission) enunciated the law in Justice Emmeline Craggly's historic words: "Sex is a private, internal matter and ends at the individual's skin. From the skin outwards, in family chores, job opportunities, or even clothing, the sexes must be considered legally interchangeable in all respects save one. That one is the traditional duty of the male to support his family to the limit of his physical powers—the fixed cornerstone of all civilized existence."

Two months later, the Interchangeable Style appeared at the Paris openings.

It appeared, of course, as a version of the all-purpose jumper, a kind of short-sleeved tunic worn everywhere at that time. But the men's type and the women's type were now fused into a single Interchangeable garment.

That fusion was wrecking Pollyglow's business. Without some degree of maleness in dress, the workshop that had descended to him through a long line of manufacturing ancestors unquestionably had to go on the auctioneer's block.

He became increasingly desperate, increasingly bitter.

One night, he sat down to study the costumes of bygone eras. Which were intrinsically and flatteringly virile—so virile that no woman would dare force her way into them?

Men's styles in the late nineteenth century, for example. They were certainly masculine in that you never saw a picture of women wearing them, but what was to prevent the modern female from doing so if she chose? And they were far too heavy and clumsy for the gentle, made-to-order climates of today's world.

Back went Pollyglow, century by century, shaking his head and straining his eyes over ancient, fuzzy woodcuts. Not this, no, nor that. He was morosely examining pictures of knights in armor and trying to imagine a mailed shirt with a zipper up the back, when he leaned away wearily and noticed a fifteenth-century portrait lying among the pile of rejects at his feet.

This was the moment when Masculinism began.

Several of the other drawings had slid across the portrait, obscuring most of it. The tight-fitting hose over which Pollyglow had bitten his dry old lips negatively—these were barely visible. But between them, in emphatic, distinctive bulge, *between them*—

The codpiece!

This little bag which had once been worn on the front of the hose or breeches—how easily it could be added to a man's jumper! It was unquestionably, definitively male: any woman could wear it, of course, but on her clothing it would be merely a useless appendage, nay, worse than that, it would be an empty mockery.

He worked all night, roughing out drawings for his designers. In bed at last, and exhausted, he was still bubbling with so much enthusiasm that he forgot about sleep and hitched his aching shoulderblades up against the headboard. Visions of codpieces, millions of them, all hanging from Pollyglow Men's Jumpers, danced and swung and undulated in his head as he stared into the darkness.

But the wholesalers refused the new garment. The old Pollyglow Jumper—yes: there were still a few conservative, fuddy-duddy men around who preferred familiarity and comfort to style. But who in the world would want this unaesthetic novelty? Why it flew in the very face of the modern doctrine of interchangeable sexes!

His salesmen learned not to use that as an excuse for failure. "Separateness!" he would urge them as they slumped back into the office. "Differentness! You've got to sell them on separateness and differentness! It's our only hope—it's the hope of the world!"

Pollyglow almost forgot the moribund state of his business, suffocating for lack of sales. He wanted to save the world. He shook with the force of his revelation: he had come bearing a codpiece and no one would have it. They must—for their own good.

He borrowed heavily and embarked upon a modest advertising campaign. Ignoring the more expensive, general-circulation media, he concentrated his budget in areas of entertainment aimed exclusively at men. His ads appeared in high-rated television shows of the day, soap operas like "The Senator's Husband," and in the more popular men's magazines—*Cowboy Confession Stories* and *Scandals of World War I Flying Aces.*

The ads were essentially the same, whether they were one-pagers in color or sixty-second commercials. You saw a hefty, husky man with a go-to-hell expression on his face. He was smoking a big, black cigar and wore a brown derby cocked carelessly on the side of his head. And he was dressed in a Pollyglow Men's Jumper from the front of which there was suspended a huge codpiece in green or yellow or bright, bright red.

Originally, the text consisted of five emphatic lines:

MEN ARE DIFFERENT FROM WOMEN!
Dress differently!
Dress masculine!
Wear Pollyglow Men's Jumpers
With the Special Pollyglow Codpiece!

Early in the campaign, however, a market research specialist employed by Pollyglow's advertising agency pointed out that the word "masculine" had acquired unfortunate connotations in the last few decades. Tons of literature, sociological and psychological, on the subject of overcompensation, or too-overt maleness, had resulted in "masculine" being equated with "homosexuality" in people's minds.

These days, the specialist said, if you told someone he was masculine, you left him with the impression that you had called him a fairy. "How about saying, 'Dress masculin*ist?*' " the specialist suggested. "It kind of softens the blow."

Dubiously, Pollyglow experimented with the changed wording in a single ad. He found the new expression unsavory and flat. So he added another line in an atttempt to give "masculinist" just a little more punch. The final ad read:

MEN ARE DIFFERENT FROM WOMEN!
Dress *differently!*
Dress *masculinist!*
Wear Pollyglow Men's Jumpers
With the *Special Pollyglow Codpiece!*
(And join the masculinist club!)

That ad pulled. It pulled beyond Pollyglow's wildest expectations.

Thousands upon thousands of queries rolled in from all over the country, from abroad, even from the Soviet Union and Red China. Where can I get a Pollyglow Men's Jumper with the Special Pollyglow Codpiece? How do I join the masculinist club? What are the rules and regulations of masculinism? How much are the dues?

Wholesalers, besieged by customers yearning for a jumper with a codpiece in contrasting color, turned to Pollyglow's astonished salesmen and shrieked out huge orders. Ten gross, fifty gross, a hundred gross. And immediately—if at all possible!

P. Edward Pollyglow was back in business. He produced and produced and produced, he sold and sold and sold. He shrugged off all the queries about the masculinist club as an amusing sidelight on the advertising business. It had only been mentioned as a fashion inducement—that there was some sort of in-group which you joined upon donning a codpiece.

Two factors conspired to make him think more closely about it: the competition and Shepherd L. Mibs.

After one startled glance at Pollyglow's new clothing empire, every other manufacturer began making jumpers equipped with codpieces. They admitted that Pollyglow had single-handedly reversed a fundamental trend in the men's wear field, that the codpiece was back with a vengeance and back to stay—but why did it have to be only the Pollyglow Codpiece? Why not the Ramsbottom Codpiece or the Hercules Codpiece or the Bangaclang Codpiece?

And since many of them had larger production facilities and bigger advertising budgets, the answer to their question made Pollyglow reflect sadly on the woeful rewards of a Columbus. His one chance was to emphasize the unique nature of the Pollyglow Codpiece.

It was at this crucial period that he met Shepherd Leonidas Mibs.

Mibs—"Old Shep" he was called by those who came to

follow his philosophical leadership—was the second of the great triumvirs of Masculinism. He was a peculiar, restless man who had wandered about the country and from occupation to occupation, searching for a place in society. All-around college athlete, sometime unsuccessful prize-fighter and starving hobo, big-game hunter and coffee-shop poet, occasional short-order cook, occasional gigolo—he had been everything but a photographer's model. And that he became when his fierce, crooked face—knocked permanently out of line by the nightstick of a Pittsburgh policeman—attracted the attention of Pollyglow's advertising agency.

His picture was used in one of the ads. It was not any more conspicuously successful than the others; and he was dropped at the request of the photographer who had been annoyed by Mibs' insistence that a sword should be added to the costume of derby, codpiece, and cigar.

Mibs knew he was right. He became a pest, returning to the agency day after day and attempting to persuade anyone at all that a sword should be worn in the Pollyglow ads, a long, long sword, the bigger and heavier the better. "Sword man is here," the receptionist would flash inside, and "My God, tell him I'm not back from lunch yet," the Art Director would whisper over the intercom.

Having nothing else to do, Mibs spent long hours on the heavily upholstered couch in the outer office. He studied the ads in the Pollyglow campaign, examining each one over and over again. He scribbled pages of comments in a little black notebook. He came to be accepted and ignored as so much reception room furniture.

But Pollyglow gave him full attention. Arriving one day to discuss a new campaign with his account executive—a campaign to stress the very special qualities of the Pollyglow Codpiece, for which, under no circumstances, should a substitute ever be accepted—he began a conversation with the strange, ugly, earnest young man. "You can tell that account executive to go to hell," Pollyglow told the receptionist as they went off to a restaurant. "I've found what I've been looking for."

The sword was a good idea, he felt, a damn good idea. Put it in the ad. But he was much more interested in certain of the thoughts developed at such elaborate length in Mibs' little black notebook.

If one phrase about a masculinist club had made the ad so effective, Mibs asked, why not exploit that phrase? A great and crying need had evidently been touched. "It's like this. When the old-time saloon disappeared, men had no place to get away from women but the barber shop. Now, with the goddam Interchangeable Haircut, even that out's been taken away. All a guy's got left is the men's room, and they're working on that, I'll bet they're working on that!"

Pollyglow sipped at his glass of hot milk and nodded. "You think a masculinist club would fill a gap in their lives? An element of exclusiveness, say, like the English private club for gentlemen?"

"Hell, no! They want something exclusive, all right—something that will exclude women—but not like a private club one damn bit. Everything these days is telling them that they're nobody special, they're just people. There are men people and women people—and what's the difference anyway? They want something that does what the cod-piece does, that tells them they're not people, they're *men!* Straight down-the-line, two-fisted, let's-stand-up-and-be-counted *men!* A place where they can get away from the crap that's being thrown at them all the time: the women-maybe-are-the-superior-sex crap, the women-outlive-them-and-outown-them crap, the a-real-man-has-no-need-to-act-masculine crap—all that crap."

His eloquence was so impressive and compelling that Pollyglow had let his hot milk grow cold. He ordered a refill and another cup of coffee for Mibs. "A club," he mused, "where the only requirement for membership would be manhood."

"You still don't get it." Mibs picked up the steaming coffee and drank it down in one tremendous swallow. He leaned forward, his eyes glittering. "Not just a club—a *movement*. A movement fighting for men's rights, carrying on propaganda against the way our divorce laws are set up, publishing books that build up all the good things about being a man. A movement with newspapers and songs and slogans. Slogans like 'The Only Fatherland for a Man is Masculinity.' And, 'Male Men of the World Unite—You Have Nothing to Gain but Your Balls!' See? A movement."

"Yes, a movement!" Pollyglow babbled, seeing indeed. "A movement with an official uniform—the Pollyglow Codpiece! And perhaps different codpieces for different—for different, well—"

"For different ranks in the movement," Mibs finished. "That's a hell of a good idea! Say green for Initiate. Red for Full-Blooded Male. Blue for First-Class Man. And white, we'd keep white for the highest rank of all—*Superman*. And, listen, here's another idea."

But Pollyglow listened no longer. He sat back in his chair, a pure and pious light suffusing his gray, sunken face. "None genuine unless it's official," he whispered. "None official unless stamped Genuine Pollyglow Codpiece, copyright and pat. pending."

Masculinist annals were to describe this luncheon as the Longchamps Entente. Later that historic day, Pollyglow's lawyer drew up a contract making Shepherd L. Mibs Director of Public Relations for the Pollyglow Enterprises.

A clip-out coupon was featured in all the new ads:

WANT TO LEARN MORE
ABOUT MASCULINISM?

WANT TO JOIN THE
MASCULINIST CLUB?

Just fill out this coupon and mail it to the address below. Absolutely no charge and no obligation—just lots of free literature and information on this exciting new movement!

FOR MEN ONLY!

The coupons poured in and business boomed. Mibs became head of a large staff. The little two-page newsletter that early applicants received quickly became a twenty-page weekly, the *Masculinist News*. In turn, it spawned a monthly full-color magazine, the *Hairy Chest,* and a wildly popular television program, "The Bull Session."

In every issue of the *Masculinist News,* Pollyglow's slogan, "Men Are *Different* from Women," shared the top of the front page with Mibs' "Men Are as *Good* as Women." The upper left-hand corner displayed a cut of Pollyglow, "Our Founding Father—Old Pep," and under that ran the front-page editorial, "Straight Talk from Old Shep."

A cartoon might accompany the editorial. A truculent man wearing a rooster comb marched into cowering masses of hippy, busty women. Caption: "The Cock of the Walk." Or, more didactically, hundreds of tiny children around a man who was naked except for a huge codpiece. Across the codpiece, in execrable but highly patriotic Latin, the words *E Unus Pluribum*—and a translation for those who needed it, "Out of the one, many."

Frequently, a contemporary note was struck. A man executed for murdering his sweetheart would be depicted, a bloody axe in his hands, between drawings of Nathan Hale being hanged and Lincoln striking off the chains of slavery. There was a true tabloid's contempt for the rights or wrongs of a case. If a man was involved, the motto ran, he was automatically on the side of the angels.

"Straight Talk from Old Shep" exhorted and called to action in a style reminiscent of a football dressing room between halves. "Men are a lost sex in America," it would intone, "because men are being lost, lost and mislaid, in the country as a whole. Everything nowadays is designed to sap their confidence and lessen their stature. Who wouldn't rather be strong than limp, hard than soft? Stand up for yourselves, men of America, stand up high!"

There was a ready audience for this sort of thing, as the constantly rising circulation of the *Masculinist News* attested. From shower to washstand to wall urinal the word sped that the problems of manhood were at last being recognized, that virility might become a positive term once more. Lodges of the Masculinist Society were established in every state; most large cities soon boasted fifteen or more chapters.

Rank and file enthusiasm shaped the organization from the beginning. A Cleveland chapter originated the secret grip; Houston gave the movement its set of unprintable passwords. The Montana Lodge's Declaration of Principles became the preamble to the national Masculinist constitution: ". . . all men are created equal with women . . . that among these rights are life, liberty and the pursuit of the opposite sex . . . from each according to his sperm, to each according to her ova . . ."

The sub-group known as the Shepherd L. Mibs League first appeared in Albany. Those who took the Albany Pledge swore to marry only women who would announce during the ceremony, "I promise to love, to honor and to *obey*"—with exactly that emphasis. There were many such Masculinist sub-groups: The Cigar and Cuspidor Club, the Ancient Order of Love 'Em and Leave 'Em, The I-Owe-None-Of-It-to-the-Little-Woman Society.

Both leaders shared equally in the revenues from the

movement, and both grew rich. Mibs alone made a small fortune out of his book, *Man: The First Sex,* considered the bible of Masculinism. But Pollyglow, Pollyglow's wealth was heaped up beyond the wildest dreams of his avarice—and his avarice had been no small-time dreamer.

He was no longer in the men's wear line; he was now in the label manufacturing business. He made labels to be sewed on to the collars of men's jumpers and inside the crowns of brown derbies, cigar bands for cigars and little metal nameplates for swords. One item alone did he continue to manufacture himself. He felt an enduring and warm affection for the little fabric container bearing the legend, *Genuine Pollyglow Codpiece*: it seemed to involve him in the activities of his fellow-men everywhere, to give him a share in their successes and their failures.

But everything else was franchised.

His imprimatur came to be needed, needed and paid for, on a vast variety of articles. No manufacturer in his right business mind would dream of coming out with a new model of a sports car, a new office swivel chair or, for that matter, a new type of truss, without having *Official Equipment—Masculinist Movement of America* printed prominently on his product. The pull of fashion has always been that of the stampeding herd: many men who were not card-carrying Masculinists refused to buy anything that did not bear the magic phrase in the familiar blue isosceles triangle. Despite its regional connotations, all over the world, in Ceylon, in Ecuador, in Sydney, Australia, and Ibadan, Nigeria, men demanded that label and paid premium prices for it.

The much-neglected, often-dreamed-of men's market had come of age. And P. Edward Pollyglow was its worldwide tax collector.

He ran the business and built wealth. Mibs ran the organization and built power. It took three full years for a clash to develop.

Mibs had spent his early manhood at a banquet of failure: he had learned to munch on suppressed rage, to drink goblets of thwarted fury. The swords he now strapped back on to men's bodies were always intended for more than decorative purposes.

Swords, he wrote in the *Hairy Chest,* were as alien to women as beards and mustaches. A full beard, therefore, and a sweeping handlebar mustache, belonged to the guise of Masculinism. And if a man were bearded like the pard and sworded like a bravo, should he still talk in the subdued tones of the eunuch? Should he still walk in the hesitant fashion of a mere family-supporter? He should not! An armed male should act like an armed male, he should walk cockily, he should bellow, he should brawl, he should *swagger*.

He should also be ready to back up the swagger.

Boxing matches settled disputes at first. Then came fencing lessons and a pistol range in every Masculinist lodge. And inevitably, almost imperceptibly, the full Code Duello was revived.

The first duels were in the style of German university fraternities. Deep in the basement of their lodges, heavily masked and padded men whacked away at each other with sabers. A few scratches about the forehead which were proudly worn to work the next day, a scoring system which penalized defensive swordplay—these were discussed lightly at dinner parties, argued about in supermarkets.

Boys will be boys. Men will be men. Attendance at spectator sports began to drop sharply: didn't that indicate something healthy was at work? Wasn't it better for men to experience real conflict themselves than to identify with distant athletes who were only simulating battle?

Then the battles became a bit too real. When a point of true honor was involved, the masks and padding were dropped and a forest clearing at dawn substituted for the whitewashed lodge basement. An ear was chopped off, a face gashed, a chest run through. The winner would strut his victory through the streets; the loser, dying or badly wounded, would insist morosely that he had fallen on the radio aerial of his car.

Absolute secrecy was demanded by the Code Duello from all concerned—the combatants, seconds, officials and attending surgeons. So, despite much public outcry and hurriedly passed new laws, very few duelists were ever prosecuted. Men of all walks of life began to accept armed combat as the only intelligent way to settle an important controversy.

Interestingly enough, swords in an open field at dawn were used mostly in the East. West of the Mississippi, the two duelists would appear at opposite ends of the main street at high noon, pistols holstered to their thighs. Advance warning would have emptied the street and pointedly suggested other locales for police officials. At a signal, the two men walked stiff-legged toward each other; at another signal, they pulled out their pistols and blazed away. Living and/or dead were then bundled into a station wagon which had been kept nearby with its motor running. At the local Masculinist Lodge there would be a rousing discussion of the battle's fine points as well as medical treatment and preparations for burial.

Many variations developed. The Chicago Duel had a brief and bloody vogue in the larger cities. Two cars, each driven by a close friend of the duelist sitting in the rear, would pass in opposite directions on the highway or a busy metropolitan street. Once abreast, foe could pound at foe with a submachine gun to absolute heart's content: but firing was expected to cease as soon as the vehicles had drawn apart. Unfortunately—in the intense excitement of the moment—few antagonists remembered to do this; the mortality rate was unpleasantly high among other motorists and open-mouthed bystanders, not to mention the seconds and officials of the duel.

Possibly more frightening than the Chicago Duel were the clumps of men—bearded, sworded, cigared and codpieced—who caroused drunkenly through the streets at night, singing bawdy songs and shouting unintelligible slogans up at the darkened windows of the offices where they worked. And the mobs which descended upon the League of Women Voters, tossing membership lists and indignant members alike pell-mell into the street. Masculinism was showing an ugly edge.

Pollyglow became alarmed and demanded an end to the uproar. "Your followers are getting out of hand," he told Mibs. "Let's get back to the theoretical principles of Masculinism. Let's stick to things like the codpiece and the beard and the cigar. We don't want to turn the country against us."

There was no trouble, Mibs insisted. A couple of the boys whooping it up—it was female propaganda that magnified it into a major incident. What about the letters he'd been receiving from other women, pleased by the return of chivalry and the strutting male, enjoying men who offered them seats in public conveyances and protected them with their heart's blood.

When Pollyglow persisted, invoking the sacred name of sound business practice, Mibs let him have it. He, Shepherd L. Mibs, was the spiritual leader of Masculinism, infallible and absolute. What he said went. *Whatever* he said went. Any time he felt like it, he could select another label for official equipment.

The old man swallowed hard a few times, little lumps riding up and down the tightly stretched concave curve of his throat. He patted Mibs' powerful shoulders, croaked out a pacifying pair of phrases and toddled back to his office. From that day on, he was a wordless figurehead. He made public appearances as Founding Father; otherwise, he lived quietly in his luxurious skyscraper, The Codpiece Tower.

The ironies of history! A new figure entered the movement that same day, a humble, nondescript figure whom Mibs, in his triumph, would have dismissed contemptuously. As Trotsky dismissed Stalin.

II

Dorselblad

Masculinists had rioted in a California town and torn down the local jail. Various pickpockets, housebreakers, and habitual drunks were liberated—as well as a man who had spent eighteen years in the alimony section of the jail, Henry Dorselblad.

More than anyone else, Dorselblad was to give Masculinism its political flavor and peculiar idiom. Who that has heard it can ever forget the mighty skirl of ten thousand male voices singing—

> Oh, Hank Dorselblad is come
>   out of the West,
> Through all the wide Border his
>   codpiece is best. . . .

Hellfire Henry, Hank the Tank, Give 'Em Hell Henry, Damn 'Em All Dorselblad—this was a culture hero who caught the American imagination like no other since Billy the Kid. And, like Billy the Kid, Henry Dorselblad was physically a very undistinguished man.

Extremely short, prematurely bald, weak of chin and pot of belly, young Dorselblad had been uninteresting even as prey to most women. His middle-aged landlady, however, had bludgeoned him into matrimony when he was only twenty-two, immediately purchasing twelve thousand dollars worth of labor-saving household machinery on the installment plan. She naturally expected comfortable and diligent support thereafter.

Dorselblad fulfilled her expectations during several exhausting years by holding two full-time jobs and a part-time one on weekends. He was a skilled programer for payroll computing machines: in his day, such men had each replaced two complete staffs of bookkeepers—they were well worth their high salaries and substantial job security. The invention of the self-programing payroll computer destroyed this idyllic state.

At the age of twenty-five, Henry Dorselblad found himself technologically unemployed. He became one of the shabby, starving programers who wandered the streets of the financial district, their punching tools in their right hands, looking for a day's work in some old-fashioned, as yet unconverted firm.

He tried desperately to become a serviceman for the new self-programing computers. But twenty-five is an advanced age: personnel interviewers tended to classify him as "a senior citizen—junior grade." For a while, he eked out a bare living as a computer sweeper, clearing office floors of the tiny circular and oblong residues dropped by the card-punching machines. But even here, science and industry moved on. The punch-waste packer was invented, and he was flung into the streets again.

Her bank account shrinking at an alarming rate, Mrs. Dorselblad sued him for nonsupport. He went to jail. She obtained a divorce with alimony payments set at a reasonable level—three-fourths of its highest recorded earning power. Unable to make even a token payment as a demonstration of good faith, he was kept in jail.

Once a year, a visiting panel of women judges asked him what efforts he had made in the past twelve months to rehabilitate himself. When Dorselblad cunningly evaded the question with a speech on the difficulties of looking for a job while in prison, he was given a severe tongue-lashing and remanded to the warden for special punishment. He became bitter and sullen, a typical hardened alimony criminal.

Eighteen years passed. His wife married three more times, burying two husbands and jailing the third for nonsupport. His responsibilities in no way affected by the vicious negligence of his successors, Henry Dorselblad lived on behind bars. He learned to steep raisin-jack in a can under his cot and, more important, to enjoy drinking it. He learned to roll cigarettes made of toilet paper and tobacco from butts stomped out by the guards. And he learned to think.

He spent eighteen years brooding on his wrongs, real or imaginary, eighteen years studying the social problems from which they sprang, eighteen years reading the recognized classics in the field of relations between the sexes: Nietzsche, Hitler, the Marquis de Sade, Mohammed, James Thurber. It is to this period of close reasoning and intense theorizing that we must look if we are to understand the transformation of a shy and inarticulate nonentity into the most eloquent rabble rouser, the most astute political leader of his age.

A new Henry Dorselblad was released upon the world by the Masculinist mob. He led them, drunken rescuers and cheering prisoners alike, out of the smoking wreckage of the jail, beating time with the warden's hat as he taught them the riotous verses of a song he had composed on the spot, "The Double Standard Forever—Hurrah, Boys, Hurrah!"

One by one, the movers and shakers of his time learned to reckon with him. Rearrested in another state and awaiting extradition, Dorselblad refused to grant the governor an interview because she was a woman. A free-born male citizen, he maintained, could not accord legal or political dominance to a mere female.

The governor smiled at the paunchy little man who

shut his eyes and jumped up and down, chanting, "Kitchens and skirts! Vapors and veils! Harems and whorehouses!" But she did not smile a week later when his followers tore down this prison too and carried him out on their shoulders, nor the next year when she was defeated for re-election—both disasters to the accompaniment of the self-same chant.

Nor did Shepherd L. Mibs smile much after Henry Dorselblad's guest appearance on "The Bull Session." Once it became apparent that he was political dynamite, that no state and no governor would dare move against him, he had to be tapped for the Masculinist program. And almost every viewer in the United States and Canada saw Shepherd Mibs, the moderator of the program and the National President of Masculinism, forced into a secondary, stammering position, completely eclipsed by Hellfire Henry.

Throughout the country, next day, people quoted Henry Dorselblad's indictment of modern society: "Women needed the law's special protection when they were legally inferiors of men. Now they have equality *and* special protection. They can't have both!"

Columnists and editorial writers discussed his pithy dictum: "Behind every successful woman there stands an unsuccessful man!"

Everyone argued the biopsychological laws he had propounded: "A man who enjoys no power during the day cannot be powerful at night. An impotent man in politics is an impotent man in bed. If women want lusty husbands, they must first turn to them as heroic leaders."

Actually, Dorselblad was simply rephrasing passages from Mibs' editorials which he had read and reread in his prison cell. But he rephrased them with the conviction of a Savonarola, the fire and fanaticism of a true prophet. And, from the beginning, it was observed, he had almost the same impact on women as on men.

Women flocked to hear him speak, to listen to his condemnations of their sex. They swooned as he mocked their faults, they wept as he cursed their impudence, they screamed *yeas* as he demanded that they give up their rights and return to their correct position as "Ladies—not Lords—of Creation."

Women flocked; men massed. Dorselblad's personality tripled the membership of the Movement. His word, his whims, were law.

He added an item to Masculinist costume, a long, curling eagle's feather stuck in the brim of the derby. All over the world, eagles were hunted down relentlessly and plucked bare for the new American market. He added a belligerent third principle to those enunciated by Mibs and Pollyglow, "No legal disabilities without corresponding legal advantages." Men refused to be breadwinners or soldiers unless they were recognized as the absolute monarchs of the home. Wife-beating cases and paternity suits clogged the courts as the Masculinist Society pledged its resources to any man fighting the great fight for what came to be called the Privilege of the Penis.

Dorselblad conquered everywhere. When he assumed a special office as the Leader of Masculinism—far above all Founders and Presidents—Mibs argued and fought, but finally conceded. When he designed a special codpiece for himself alone—the Polka-Dotted Codpiece of the Leading Man—Mibs scowled for a while, then nodded weakly. When he put his finger on Masculinism's most important target—the repeal of the Nineteenth Amendment—Mibs immediately wrote editorials damning that irresponsible piece of legislation and demanding the return of elections held in saloons and decisions made in smoke-filled cubicles.

At the first National Convention of Masculinism in Madison, Wisconsin, Old Shep shared a docile anonymity with Old Pep, in a corner of the platform. He yelled and stamped with the rest when Hank the Tank thundered: "This is a *man's* civilization. *Men* built it, and—if they don't get their rights back—*men* can tear it down!" He chuckled with the others at the well-worn barbs that Dorselblad threw: "I didn't raise my boy to be a housewife" and "Give me the name of one woman, just one woman, who ever—" He was in the forefront of the mob that marched three times around the hall behind Hellfire Henry, roaring out the Song of Repeal:

Cram! Cram! Cram! the ballot
  boxes—
Jam! Jam! Jam! the voting
  booths. . .

It was a stirring spectacle: two thousand delegates from every state in the union, their derbies bouncing rhythmically on their heads, their eagle feathers waving in majestic unison, swords jangling, codpieces dangling, and great, greasy clouds of cigar smoke rolling upwards to announce the advent of the male millennium. Bearded, mustachioed men cheered themselves hoarse and pounded each other's backs; they stamped so enthusiastically on the floor that not until the voting began was it discovered that the Iowa delegation had smashed themselves completely through and down into the basement below.

But nothing could destroy the good humor of that crowd. The more seriously injured were packed off to hospitals, those with only broken legs or smashed collar bones were joshed uproariously and hauled back to the convention floor for the balloting. A series of resolutions was read off, the delegates bellowing their agreement and unanimity.

Resolved: that the Nineteenth Amendment to the Constitution of the United States, granting universal female suffrage, is unnatural biologically, politically, and morally, and the chief cause of our national troubles. . . .

Resolved: that all proper pressure be brought to bear on the legislators of this nation, both holding and seeking office. . . .

Resolved: that this convention go on record as demanding. . . .

Resolved: that we hereby. . . .

There were mid-term congressional elections that year.

A Masculinist plan of battle was drawn up for every state. Coordinating committees were formed to work closely with youth, minority and religious groups. Each member was assigned a specific job: volunteers from Madison Avenue spent their evenings grinding out propagandistic news releases; Pennsylvanian coal miners and Nebraskan wheat farmers devoted their Saturdays to haranguing the inmates of old-age homes.

Henry Dorselblad drove them all relentlessly, demanding more effort from everyone, making deals with both Republicans and Democrats, reform elements and big city bosses, veterans' organizations and pacifist groups. "Let's win the first time out—before the opposition wakes up!" he screamed to his followers.

Scrabbling like mad at their beloved fence, the politicians tried to avoid taking a definite position on either side. Women were more numerous and more faithful voters than men, they pointed out: if it came to a clear contest, women had to win. Masculinist pressure on the ballot box was considerable, but it wasn't the only pressure.

Then the voice of Hank the Tank was heard in the land, asking women—in the name of their own happiness—to see to it that the long, long winter of feminism was definitely past. Many women in his audiences fainted dead away from the sheer flattery of having Henry Dorselblad ask them for a favor. A ladies' auxiliary to the Masculinist Movement was organized—The Companions of the Codpiece. It grew rapidly. Female candidates for office were so ferociously heckled by members of their own sex that they demanded special police protection before addressing a street-corner rally. "You should be ironing your husband's shirts!" the lady masculinists shouted. "Go home! Your supper's burning!"

One week before election, Dorselblad unleashed the Direct Action squads. Groups of men, wearing codpieces and derbies, descended upon public buildings all over the country and chained themselves to lampposts outside. While officers of the law chopped away at their self-imposed bonds with hacksaws and acetylene torches, the Masculinists loudly intoned a new liturgy: "Women! Give us your vote—and we will give you back your men! We need your vote to win—you need to have us win! Women! Give us your vote on Election Day!"

Where, their opponents inquired cruelly, was the vaunted pride and arrogance of Masculinism in such an appeal? Were the Lords of Creation actually begging the weaker sex for a boon? Oh, for shame!

But Dorselblad's followers ignored these jeers. Women must themselves return the vote they had falsely acquired. Then they would be happy, their men would be happy, and the world would be right again. If they didn't do this of their own free will, well, men were the stronger sex. There were alternatives. . . .

On this ominous note, the election was held.

Fully one-fourth of the new Congress was elected on a Masculinist platform. Another, larger group of fellow travelers and occasional sympathizers still wondered which way the wind was really blowing.

But the Masculinists had also acquired control of three-quarters of the state legislatures. They thus had the power to ratify a constitutional amendment that would destroy female suffrage in America—once the repeal bill passed Congress and was submitted to the states.

The eyes of the nation swung to its capitol. Every leader of any significance in the movement hurried there to augment the Masculinist lobby. Their opponents came in great numbers too, armed with typewriter and mimeograph against the gynecocratic Ragnarok.

A strange hodge-podge of groups, these anti-Masculinists. Alumna associations from women's colleges fought for precedence at formal functions with Daughters of 1776; editors of liberal weeklies snubbed conservatively inclined leaders of labor unions who in turn jostled ascetic young men in clerical collars. Heavy-set, glaring-eyed lady writers spat upon slim and stylish lady millionairesses who had hurried back from Europe for the crisis. Respectable matrons from Richmond, Virginia, bridled at the scientific jocosities of birth controllers from San Francisco. They argued bitterly with each other, followed entirely divergent plans of action and generally delighted their cod-pieced, derbied, cigar-smoking adversaries. But their very variety and heterogeneity gave many a legislator pause: they looked too much like a cross-section of the population.

The bill to submit repeal of the Nineteenth Amendment to the states wandered through an interminable Congressional labyrinth of maneuver and rewording and committee action. Mobs and counter-mobs demonstrated everywhere. Newspapers committed themselves firmly to one side or the other, depending on their ownership and, occasionally, their readership. Almost alone in the country, *The New York Times* kept its head, observing that the problem was very difficult and asking that the decision—whatever it eventually was—be the right one—whatever that might be.

Passing the Senate by a tiny margin, the bill was sent to the House of Representatives. That day, Masculinist and anti-Masculinist alike begged and battled for a gallery pass. Hellfire Henry and his followers were admitted only after they had checked their swords. Their opponents were forcibly deprived of a huge sign smuggled to the gallery in four sections. "Congressman!" the sign shouted. "Your grandmother was a suffragette!"

Over the protests of many legislators seeking anonymity on this issue, a roll-call vote was decided upon. Down the list of states it went, eliciting so many groans and cheers from the onlookers that the Speaker finally had to lay aside his damaged gavel. Neck and neck the two sides went, the Masculinists always holding a slim lead, but never one large enough. Finally the feverish talliers in the gallery saw that a deadlock was inevitable. The bill lacked one vote of the two-thirds majority necessary.

It was then that Elvis P. Borax, a junior Representative from Florida who had asked to be passed originally, got to his feet and stated that he had decided how to cast his vote.

The tension was fantastic as everyone waited for Congressman Borax to cast the deciding vote. Women crammed handkerchiefs into their mouths; strong men whimpered softly. Even the guards stood away from their posts and stared at the man who was deciding the fate of the country.

Three men rose in the balcony: Hellfire Henry, Old Shep and white-haired Old Pep. Standing side by side, they forebodingly held aloft right hands clenched around the hilts of invisible swords. The young Congressman studied their immobile forms with a white face.

"I vote nay," he breathed at last. "I vote against the bill."

Pandemonium. Swirling, yelling crowds everywhere. The House guards, even with their reinforcements from the Senate, had a hard, bruising time clearing the galleries. A dozen people were trampled, one of them an elderly chief of the Chippewa Indians who had come to Washington to settle a claim against the government and had taken a seat in the gallery only because it was raining outside.

Congressman Borax described his reactions in a televised interview. "I felt as if I were looking down into my open grave. I had to vote that way, though. Mother asked me to."

"Weren't you frightened?" the interviewer asked.

"I was very frightened," he admitted. "But I was also very brave."

A calculated political risk had paid off. From that day on, he led the counter-revolution.

III

The Counter-Revolution

The anti-Masculinists had acquired both a battlecry and a commander-in-chief.

As the Masculinist tide rose, thirty-seven states liberalizing their divorce laws in the husband's favor, dozens of disparate opposition groups rallied to the standard that had been raised by the young Congressman from Florida. Here alone they could ignore charges of "creeping feminism." Here alone they could face down epithets like "codpiece-pricker" and "skirt-waver," as well as the ultimate, most painful thrust—"mother-lover."

Two years later, they were just strong enough to capture the Presidential nomination of one of the major parties. For the first time in decades, a man—Elvis P. Borax—was nominated for the office of chief executive.

After consulting the opinion polls and his party's leading strategists, not to mention his own instincts and inclinations, he decided to run on a platform of pure, undiluted Mother.

He had never married, he explained, because Mother needed him. She was eighty-three and a widow; what was more important than her happiness? Let the country at large live by the maxim which, like the Bible, had never failed: Mother Knew Best.

Star-studded photographs of the frail old lady appeared all over the land. When Dorselblad made a sneering reference to her, Borax replied with a song of his own composition that quickly soared to the top of the Hit Parade. That record is a marvelous political document, alive through and through with our most glorious traditions. In his earnest, delicately whining tenor, Borax sang:

> Rule, Maternal! My mother
>   rules my heart!
>
> Mother never, never, never was
>   a tart!

And there was the eloquence of the famous "Cross of Swords" speech which Borax delivered again and again, at whistle stops, at church picnics, at county fairs, at state rallies.

"You shall not press down upon the loins of mankind this codpiece of elastic!" he would thunder. "You shall not crucify womankind upon a cross of swords!"

"And do you know why you shall not?" he would demand, his right hand throbbing above his head like a tambourine. The audience, open-mouthed, glistening-eyed, would sit perfectly still and wait eagerly. *"Do you know?"*

"Because," would come a soft, slow whisper at last over the public address system, "because it will make *Mother* unhappy."

It was indeed a bitter campaign, fought for keeps. The Dorselbladites were out to redefine the franchise for all time—Borax called for a law to label Masculinism as a criminal conspiracy. Mom's Home-Made Apple Pie clashed head-on with the Sword, the Codpiece and the Cigar.

The other party, dominated by Masculinists, had selected a perfect counter-candidate. A former Under-Secretary of the Army and currently America's chief delegate to the thirteen-year-old Peace and Disarmament Conference in Paris: the unforgettable Mrs. Strunt.

Clarissima Strunt's three sturdy sons accompanied her on every speaking engagement, baseball bats aslant on their shoulders. She also had a mysterious husband who was busy with "a man's work." In photographs which were occasionally fed to the newspapers, he stood straight and still, a shotgun cradled in his arm, while a good hound dog flushed game out of faraway bushes. His face was never clearly recognizable, but there was something in the way he held his head that emphatically suggested an attitude of no nonsense from anybody—especially women.

Hellfire Henry and Kitchen-Loving Clarissima worked beautifully together. After Dorselblad had pranced up and down a platform with a belligerently waving codpiece, after he had exhorted, demanded and anathematized, Clarissima Strunt would come forward. Replying to his gallant bow with a low curtsy, she would smooth out the red-and-white-checked apron she always wore and talk gently of the pleasures of being a woman in a truly male world.

When she placed a mother's hand on the button at the top of her youngest son's baseball cap and fondly whispered, "Oh, no, I didn't raise my boy to be a sissy!"—when she threw her head back and proudly asserted, "I get more pleasure out of one day's washing and scrubbing than out of ten years' legislating and politicking!"—when she stretched plump arms out to the audience and begged, "Please give me your vote! I want to be the *last* woman

President!"—when she put it that way, which red-blooded registered voter could find it in his heart to refuse?

Every day, more and more Masculinist codpieces could be counted on subways and sidewalks, as well as the bustle-and-apron uniforms of the ladies auxiliary.

Despite many misgivings, the country's intellectual leaders had taken up Borax' mom-spangled banner as the only alternative to what they regarded as sexual fascism. They were popularly known as the Suffragette Eggheads. About this time, they began to observe sorrowfully that the election was resolving an ancient American myth—and it looked like the myth made flesh would prevail.

For Borax campaigned as a Dutiful Son and waved his mother's photograph up and down the United States. But Clarissima Strunt was Motherhood Incarnate; and she was telling the voters to lay it on the line for Masculinism.

What kind of President would Strunt have made? How would this soft-voiced and strong-minded woman have dealt with Dorselblad once they were both in power? There were those who suggested that she was simply an astute politician riding the right horse; there were others who based a romance between the checked apron and the spotted codpiece upon Mrs. Strunt's undeniable physical resemblance to the notorious Nettie-Ann Dorselblad. Today, these are all idle speculations.

All we know for certain is that the Masculinists were three-to-two favorites in every bookmaking parlor and stockbroker's office. That a leading news magazine came out with a cover showing a huge codpiece and entitled *Man of the Year*. That Henry Dorselblad began receiving semi-official visits from U. N. officials and members of the diplomatic corps. That cigar, derby, and sword sales boomed, and P. Edward Pollyglow bought a small European nation which, after evicting the inhabitants, he turned into an eighteen-hole golf course.

Congressman Borax, facing certain defeat, began to get

hysterical. Gone was the crinkly smile, gone the glow from that sweet, smooth-shaven face. He began to make reckless charges. He charged corruption. He charged malfeasance, he charged treason, murder, blackmail, piracy, simony, forgery, kidnaping, barratry, attempted rape, mental cruelty, indecent exposure, and subornation of perjury.

And one night, during a televised debate, he went too far.

Shepherd Leonidas Mibs had endured displacement as Leader of the Movement far too long for a man of his temperament. He was the position at the rear of the platform, at the bottom of the front page, as an alternative speaker to Hellfire Henry. He burned with rebellion.

He tried to form a new secessionist group, Masculinists Anonymous. Members would be vowed to strict celibacy and have nothing to do with women beyond the indirect requirements of artificial insemination. Under the absolute rule of Mibs as Grand Master, they would concentrate on the nationwide secret sabotage of Mother's Day, the planting of time bombs in marriage license bureaus, and sudden, night-time raids on sexually non-segregated organizations such as the P.T.A.

This dream might have radically altered future Masculinist history. Unfortunately, one of Mibs' trusted lieutenants sold out to Dorselblad in return for the cigar-stand concession at all national conventions. Old Shep emerged white of lip from an interview with Hank the Tank. He passed the word, and Masculinists Anonymous was dissolved.

But he continued to mutter, to wait. And during the next-to-last television debate—when Congressman Borax rose in desperate rebuttal to Clarissima Strunt—Shepherd Mibs at last came into his own.

The videotape recording of the historic debate was destroyed in the mad Election Day riots two weeks later. It is therefore impossible at this late date to reconstruct precisely what Borax replied to Mrs. Strunt's accusation that he was the tool of "the Wall Street women and Park Avenue parlor feminists."

All accounts agree that he began by shouting, "And *your* friends, Clarissima Strunt, *your* friends are led by—"

But what did he say next?

Did he say, as Mibs claimed, "—an ex-bankrupt, an ex-convict, and an ex-homosexual"?

Did he say, as several newspapers reported, "—an ex-bankrupt, an ex-convict, and an ex-heterosexual"?

Or did he say, as Borax himself insisted to his dying day, nothing more than "—an ex-bankrupt, an ex-convict, and an ex-homo bestial"?

Whatever the precise wording, the first part of the charge indubitably referred to P. Edward Pollyglow and the second to Henry Dorselblad. That left the third epithet—and Shepherd L. Mibs.

Newspapers from coast to coast carried the headline:

MIBS CLAIMS MORTAL
INSULT
CHALLENGES BORAX
TO DUEL

For a while, that is, for three or four editions, there was a sort of stunned silence. America held its breath. Then:

DORSELBLAD
DISPLEASED
URGES MIBS CALL IT
OFF

And:

OLD PEP PLEADING
WITH OLD SHEP—
"DON'T DIRTY YOUR HANDS WITH HIM"

But:

MIBS IMMOVABLE
DEMANDS A DEATH

As well as:

CLARISSIMA STRUNT
SAYS:
"THIS IS A MAN'S AFFAIR"

Meanwhile, from the other side, there was an uncertain, tentative approach to the problem:

BORAX BARS DUEL—
PROMISE TO MOTHER

This did not sit well with the new, duel-going public. There was another approach:

CANDIDATE FOR
CHIEF EXECUTIVE
CAN'T BREAK LAW,
CLERGYMEN CRY

Since this too had little effect on the situation:

CONGRESSMAN OFFERS
TO APOLOGIZE:
"DIDN'T SAY IT BUT WILL RETRACT"

Unfortunately:

SHEP CRIES
"FOR SHAME!
BORAX MUST BATTLE ME—

OR BEAR COWARD'S
BRAND"

The candidate and his advisors, realizing there was no way out:

MIBS-BORAX DUEL SET
FOR MONDAY
HEAVYWEIGHT CHAMP
TO OFFICIATE

Pray for Me, Borax Begs Mom:
Your Dear Boy, Alive or Dead

Nobel Prize Winner Gets Nod
As Bout's Attending Sawbones

Borax and ten or twelve cigar-munching counselors locked themselves in a hotel room and considered the matter from all possible angles. By this time, of course, he and his staff only smoked cigars under conditions of the greatest privacy. In public, they ate mints.

They had been given the choice of weapons, and a hard choice it was. The Chicago Duel was dismissed as being essentially undignified and tending to blur the Presidential image. Borax' assistant campaign manager, a brilliant Jewish Negro from the Spanish-speaking section of Los Angeles, suggested a format derived from the candidate's fame as a forward-passing quarterback in college. He wanted foxholes dug some twenty-five yards apart and hand grenades lobbed back and forth until one or the other of the disputants had been satisfactorily exploded.

But everyone in that hotel room was aware that he sat under the august gaze of History, and History demanded the traditional alternatives—swords or pistols. They had to face the fact that Borax was skillful with neither, while his opponent had won tournaments with both. Pistols were finally chosen as adding the factors of great distance and uncertain atmospheric conditions to their side.

Pistols, then. And only one shot apiece for the maximum chance of survival. But the site?

Mibs had urged Weehawken Heights in New Jersey because of its historical associations. Grandstands, he pointed out, could easily be erected along the Palisades and substantial prices charged for admission. After advertising and promotion costs had been met, the purse could be used by both major parties to defray their campaign expenses.

Such considerations weighed heavily with Borax' advisors. But the negative side of the historical association weighed even more heavily: it was in Weehawken that the young Alexander Hamilton had been cut down in the very flower of his political promise. Some secluded spot, possibly hallowed by a victory of the raw and inexperienced army of George Washington, would put the omens definitely on their side. The party treasurer, a New England real estate agent in private life, was assigned to the problem.

That left the strategy.

All night long, they debated a variety of ruses, from bribing or intimidating the duel's presiding officials to having Borax fire a moment before the signal—the ethics of the act, it was pointed out, would be completely confused by subsequent charges and countercharges in the newspapers. They adjourned without having agreed on anything more hopeful than that Borax should train intensively under the pistol champion of the United States in the two days remaining and do his level best to achieve some degree of proficiency.

By the morning of the duel, the young candidate had become quite morose. He had been out on the pistol range continuously for almost forty-eight hours. He complained of a severe earache and announced bitterly that he had only the slightest improvement in his aim to show for it. All the way to the dueling grounds while his formally clad advisers wrangled and disputed, suggesting this method and that approach, he sat in silence, his head bowed unhappily upon his chest.

He must have been in a state of complete panic. Only so can we account for his decision to use a strategy which had not been first approved by his entire entourage—an unprecedented and most serious political irregularity.

Borax was no scholar, but he was moderately well-read in American history. He had even written a series of articles for a Florida newspaper under the generic title of *When the Eagle Screamed,* dealing with such great moments in the nation's past as Robert E. Lee's refusal to lead the Union armies, and the defeat of free silver and low tariffs by William McKinley. As the black limousine sped to the far-distant field of honor, he reviewed this compendium of wisdom and patriotic activity in search of an answer to his problem. He found it at last in the life-story of Andrew Jackson.

Years before his elevation to high national office, the seventh President of the United States had been in a position similar to that in which Elvis P. Borax now found himself. Having been maneuvered into just such a duel with just such an opponent, and recognizing his own extreme nervousness, Jackson decided to let his enemy have the first shot. When, to everyone's surprise, the man missed and it was Jackson's turn to fire, he took his own sweet time about it. He leveled his pistol at his pale, perspiring antagonist, aiming carefully and exactly over the space of several dozen seconds. Then he fired and killed the man.

That was the ticket, Borax decided. Like Jackson, he'd let Mibs shoot first. Like Jackson, he would then slowly and inexorably—

Unfortunately for both history and Borax, the first shot was the only one fired. Mibs didn't miss, although he complained later—perfectionist that he was—that defective sights on the antique dueling pistol had caused him to come in a good five inches below target.

The bullet went through the right cheek of the Congressman's rigid, averted face and came out the left. It imbedded itself in a sugar maple some fifteen feet away, from which it was later extracted and presented to the Smithsonian Institute. The tree, which became known as the Dueling Sugar Maple, was a major attraction for years and the center of a vast picnic grounds and motel complex. In the first decade of the next century, however, it was uprooted to make way for a through highway that connected Schenectady, New York, with the new international airport at Bangor, Maine. Replanted with much ceremony in Washington, D.C., it succumbed in a few short months to heat prostration.

Borax was hurried to the field hospital nearby, set up for just such an emergency. As the doctors worked on him, his chief campaign manager, a politician far-famed for calmness and acumen under stress, came out of the tent and ordered an armed guard posted before it.

Since the bulletins released in the next few days about Borax' condition were reassuring but cryptic, people did not know what to think. Only one thing was definite: he would live.

Many rumors circulated. They were subjected to careful analysis by outstanding Washington, Hollywood and Broadway columnists. Had Mibs really used a dum-dum bullet? Had it been tipped with a rare South American poison? Had the candidate's mother actually traveled all the way to New York from her gracious home in Florida's Okeechobee Swamp and hurled herself upon Old Shep in the editorial offices of the *Hairy Chest,* fingernails scratching and gouging, dental plates biting and tearing? Had there been a secret midnight ceremony in which ten regional leaders of Masculinism had formed a hollow square around Shepherd L. Mibs and watched Henry Dorselblad break Mibs' sword and cigar across his knee, stamp Mibs' derby flat, and solemnly tear Mibs' codpiece from his loins?

Everyone knew that the young congressman's body had been so painstakingly measured and photographed before the duel that prosthesis for the three or four molars destroyed by the bullet was a relatively simple matter. But was prosthesis possible for a tongue? And could plastic surgery ever restore those round, sunny cheeks or that heartwarming adolescent grin?

According to a now firm tradition, the last television debate of the campaign had to be held the night before Election Day. Mrs. Strunt gallantly offered to call it off. The Borax headquarters rejected her offer: tradition must not be set aside; the show must go on.

That night, every single television set in the United States was in operation, including even the old black-and-white collectors' items. Children were called from their beds, nurses from their hospital rounds, military sentries from their outlying posts.

Clarissima Strunt spoke first. She summarized the issues of the campaign in a friendly, ingratiating manner and put the case for Masculinism before the electorate in her best homespun style.

Then the cameras swung to Congressman Borax. He did not say a word, staring at the audience sadly out of eloquent, misty eyes. He pointed at the half-inch circular hole in his right cheek. Slowly, he turned the other cheek. There was a similar hole there. He shook his head and picked up a large photograph of his mother in a rich silver frame. One tremendous tear rolled down and splashed upon the picture.

That was all.

One did not have to be a professional pollster or politician to predict the result. Mrs. Strunt conceded by noon of Election Day. In every state, Masculinism and its protagonists were swept from office overwhelmingly defeated. Streets were littered with discarded derbies and abandoned bustles. It was suicide to be seen smoking a cigar.

Like Aaron Burr before him, Shepherd L. Mibs fled to England. He published his memoirs, married an earl's daughter, and had five children by her. His oldest son, a biologist, became moderately famous as the discoverer of a cure for athlete's foot in frogs—a disease that once threatened to wipe out the entire French frozen-frogs-legs industry.

Pollyglow carefully stayed out of the public eye until the day of his death. He was buried, as his will requested, in a giant codpiece. His funeral was the occasion for long, illustrated newspaper articles reviewing the rise and fall of the movement he had founded.

And Henry Dorselblad disappeared before a veritable avalanche of infuriated women which screamed down upon Masculinist headquarters. His body was not found in the debris, thus giving rise to many legends. Some said that he was impaled on the points of countless umbrellas wielded by outraged American motherhood. Some said that he escaped in the disguise of a scrubwoman and would return one day to lead resurgent hordes of derby and cigar. To this date, however, he has not.

Elvis P. Borax, as everyone knows, served two terms as the most silent President since Calvin Coolidge and retired to go into the wholesale flower business in Miami.

It was almost as if Masculinism had never been. If we discount the beery groups of men who, at the end of a party, nostalgically sing the old songs and call out the old heroic rallying cries to each other, we have today very few mementoes of the great convulsion.

One of them is the codpiece.

The codpiece has survived as a part of modern male costume. In motion, it has a rhythmic wave that reminds many women of a sternly shaken forefinger, warning them that men, at the last, can only be pushed so far and no farther. For men, the codpiece is still a flag, now a flag of truce perhaps, but it flutters in a war that goes on and on.

ABOUT WILLIAM TENN

Theodore Sturgeon, writing in *If* magazine, had the following to say:

> It would be too wide a generalization to say that *every* sf satire, every sf comedy and every attempt at witty and biting criticism found in the field is a poor and usually cheap imitation of what this man has been doing since the '40s. [But] his incredibly involved and complex mind can at times produce constructive comment so pointed and astute that the fortunate recipient is permanently improved by it. Admittedly the price may be to create two whole categories for our species: humanity, and William Tenn. For each of which you must create your ethos and your laws. I've done that. And to me it's worth it.

William Tenn is the pen name of London-born Philip Klass. He began writing in 1945 after being discharged from the Army, and his first story was published a year later. His stories and articles have been widely anthologized, a number of them in best-of-the-year collections. Currently he teaches writing in the Department of English at The Pennsylvania State University.

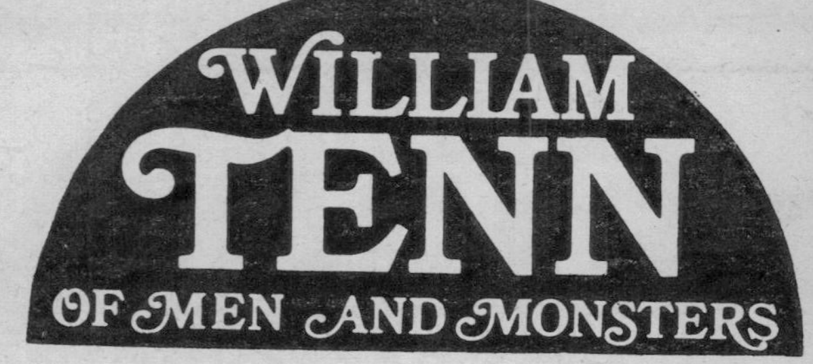

In science-fiction circles, the work of William Tenn is noted, oddly enough, for its scarcity (among other things, we hasten to add). Perhaps this has been because each succeeding story was hailed with such rare delight that the legend of scarcity became self-reinforcing. In fact, over the years, Mr. Tenn has been reasonably prolific; consequently we are able to bring you a group of five volumes containing the best of his published works—a remarkable and happy occasion all by itself.

But in addition, and in delighted triumph, Ballantine Books presents this sixth volume, completely original, and so far the only full-length science-fiction work by William Tenn. In OF MEN AND MONSTERS, he manages to weave a fine sense of the dramatic into an overall theme which exemplifies Tenn at his ironic best—a clear-eyed tribute to the audacity, shrewdness, stupidity, courage, and ultimate ineradicability of the human pest.

U6131 $.75

To order by mail, send price of book plus 5¢ for postage and handling to Dept. CS, Ballantine Books, Inc., 101 Fifth Avenue, New York, N.Y. 10003.